To all I love without condition
To all I love without omission

Never doubt

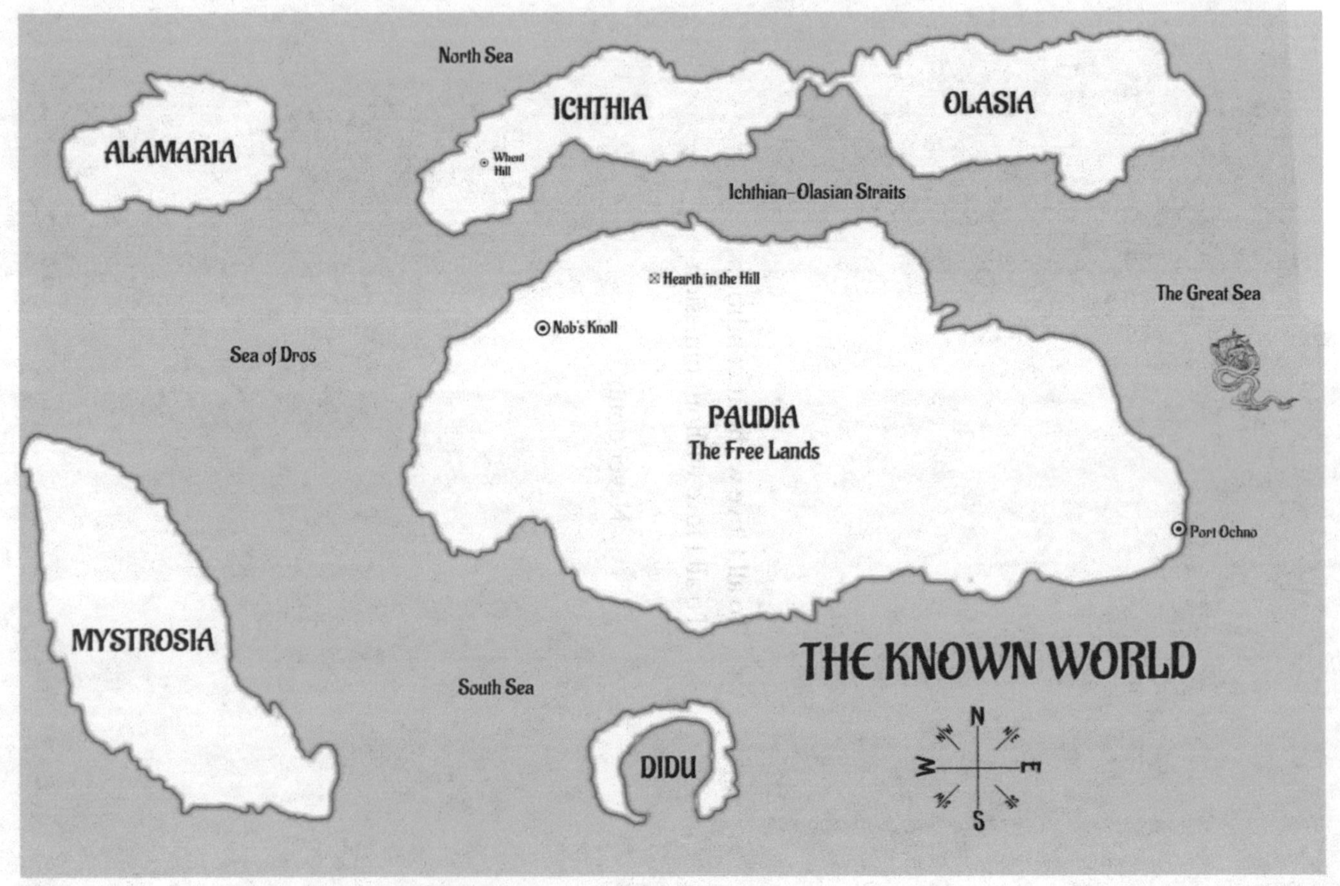

THE KNOWN WORLD
ALAMARIA
North Sea
ICHTHIA
Wheat Hill
OLASIA
Ichthian–Olasian Straits
Hearth in the Hill
Nob's Knoll
The Great Sea
Sea of Dros
PAUDIA
The Free Lands
Port Ochno
MYSTROSIA
South Sea
DIDU
N
E
S
W

THE CHRONICLES OF RANDALL | BOOK ONE

THE CAVE OF THE SIX ARROWS

LEN BOSWELL

Black Rose Writing | Texas

ISBN: 978-1-68433-745-3
PUBLISHED BY BLACK ROSE WRITING
www.blackrosewriting.com

Printed in the United States of America
Suggested Retail Price (SRP) $19.95

The Cave of the Six Arrows is printed in Calluna

*As a planet-friendly publisher, Black Rose Writing does its best to eliminate unnecessary waste to reduce paper usage and energy costs, while never compromising the reading experience. As a result, the final word count vs. page count may not meet common expectations.

The Cave of the Six Arrows

Part 1

"With love and care the spider web weaves its spider."
(African proverb)

"Wise men have interpreted dreams, and the gods have laughed."
—H. P. Lovecraft

Part I

"It begins with thunder, as so many tales do, a mighty storm to set the stage for a tale of lords and knaves, heroes and fools. Yes, as always, there will be blood and suffering and death. It is about life, after all. And yes, there will be quests both noble and ignoble. It is a tale I would tell you, stranger, if you would tarry here by the fire to hear it, perhaps share my mutton—if you've the teeth for it—because the story involves your kinsman, long dead, a man much taller than you, and wider, but with the same gray cloak and green diamond sigil you seem to wear so proudly, and as fully dead as you are alive. Ah, I see I have piqued your interest. Let us begin, then, at your kinsman's end and work our way back to you and this foul night. It all begins, as I said, with thunder, a warrior named Calax Halfhand, and a young girl still finding her shape, a runaway more powerful than she realizes."

The sky rumbled, raven clouds roiling, whipping rain near sideways. He had to tug hard on the reins to keep the horse steady as they crested the rock-strewn hill, everything so gray that, if not for the bright yellow shaft of the arrow, he would certainly have passed by the body of the man in gray, thinking him nothing more than another boulder.

Calax Halfhand had seen dead men before, and he much preferred them to the wide-eyed screaming wounded that he'd had to dispatch over the years, sending them to their peace and their gods and the carrion eaters with his broadsword. He dismounted, tied his steed to a scrub pine, and approached the body, tugging out the strange arrow before turning the body over to see the man's face.

The man's eyes, gray as his cloak, stared up at Calax blankly, the rain pooling in them, making them seem to twitch with life. But he was dead, all right, a man two score at least, his beard grizzled, his face a lacework of scars, though none recent. He was tall, maybe two hands taller than Calax, and built like an ox, heavy in the chest. He was right-handed certainly, his forearm huge from repeated swings of a broadsword or mace. His hair, black as wood char, was shorn close, with a diamond pattern shaved to the skin above each ear. Green dye of some sort had been applied there to match the sigil on his cloak, one unknown to Calax. He smelled of woodsmoke and sweat, a sign that he'd been traveling for some distance. Days, certainly, perhaps weeks.

The man was unarmed save for a small dagger sticking from his scuffed boot. Calax pulled it out and hefted it—light, much lighter than his own. The grip was carved bone, common enough, but the blade had a green cast to it, as if its maker had somehow combined iron with emeralds. Calax slid the dagger into his own boot and turned his attention to the cracked leather pouch hanging around the man's neck, opening it and emptying its contents on the man's chest: a few coins from an unknown kingdom, a piece of weir's root for sour stomach, a flint, some moss from a witch's oak, and a small scroll tied with gut.

Calax opened the scroll and read a single sentence written in the common tongue: *You will know him by his hand, or the half of it, and the name Calax Halfhand. You must bring him to me.*

Calax blinked, hard. *What?*

He read the scroll again, but the words persisted. Someone wanted to see him, or perhaps kill him. Why else would he send a warrior? And why was this strange warrior killed? Was it because of Calax?

He looked around to see if anyone else was nearby, perhaps lying in wait for him, but all he saw was the steady rain in the failing light. He put everything back into the pouch and tucked it under his belt.

His stead stamped its hoof into the gray mud and snorted.

"All right, Gash," said Calax. "Let's find us some shelter for the night."

He stood, grabbed the reins, and led Gash toward an outcropping that seemed tall enough and deep enough to get them both out of the rain. Gash began shaking almost immediately, spraying Calax.

"Oh, come on, wasn't the rain enough?"

Gash snorted and looked away.

"That's better. Now let me see if there's anything here that will burn. I don't know about you, but I could use a good fire right about now."

He pulled off Gash's saddle and tied him loosely to a sapling that was clearly struggling to grow in the shadow of the outcropping.

"Well, let's see now. Ah, there you are."

He gathered some moss and orange rock lichens and fluffed them into a ball beneath a handful of twigs. Three strikes of the flint was all he needed to get the fire going. There wasn't much dry wood beneath the outcropping, so the fire would be small and short-lived, but it would be enough to warm him and dry him off a bit before he fell asleep.

He looked down at his left hand, or what served as a hand. It was really nothing more than a piece of wood, artfully carved to match his right hand and hidden beneath a glove. The wood extended upward, becoming his wooden forearm. Rawhide straps held the fake forearm fast to his real hand, a withered, malformed hand with just three fingers, seemingly bursting from his elbow. The fingers were not without skills however. They could manipulate the articulated hand, tugging on gut strands to open and close the fingers with every nuance of a natural hand. And three fingers were enough to hold a dagger if the need arose. The birth defect had been a challenge for him as a child, but had given him a name now feared by all who knew it: Calax Halfhand, warrior. Calax Halfhand, berserker.

If he had not been in battle armor, most people would have taken him for an ordinary man, a tradesman perhaps, or a baker. Nothing about him suggested his prowess on the battlefield. He was not overly tall and though he was strong, he was nothing like the muscular brutes he often fought in battle. His hair was a thatch of brown, as was his unkempt beard. A nob of a nose was set squarely between eyes that matched the sky. For all his fighting, he had but one velvety scar, which ran from his ear to his chin, the work of a well-aimed sword, seen a second too late.

Calax started to unstrap the arm extension, but then thought better of it. Better to let the rawhide dry naturally. Taking it off now would just complicate things in the morning. Besides, he was exhausted.

He fed the fire as long as he could, then settled down near Gash, his back resting against the wall of the outcropping. It was dark enough now that he could no longer see the gray body that lay just a few yards away in the rain. On the morrow, he would have to deal with that, and find the warrior's horse. And then he'd have to figure out who this man was and what his failed errand was all about.

Sleep came quickly, and with it dreams.

2

Calax had two kinds of dreams. When he was at war, sleeping with his comrades on the hard ground, all he dreamed about was war and the preparations for war. He would dream of sharpening his ax and his sword. He would dream of the smell of blood and gore, and the sight of dismembered bodies. He would dream of charging into battle astride Gash, his war horse's nostrils flaring, snorting steam. He would dream of battle and its carnage, the faces of his screaming victims startling him awake.

But when he was away from war, as he was now, he had a dream that came at him night after night, and was always the same.

He was a young boy again, in the dreaded room of his guardian, Salibar, who stood over him now in the dream. He was a tall man and as thick as a tree, with forearms knotted with the muscle that comes from swinging a broadsword in many battles. His eyes were black as a pit, his hair the color of scrub wheat. An old scar, silky and smooth, divided his cheek in half. As always, he wore his brown leather breastplate, which also bore the scars of war. In memory, he always smelled of onions.

"Are you ready?" said Salibar.

"Yes, master."

"Put on the blindfold, then, and be quick about it."

Calax began to put on the blindfold, a long scrap of red wool.

"No," said Salibar. "With your left hand, your little fork."

Calax dipped his head down, so he could reach the blindfold with his left hand, and managed to tug the blindfold in place. Salibar disappeared from view, which was fine with Calax. He didn't like the looks of the man, anyway.

Salibar would not have been anyone's choice for a guardian of a young boy, let alone a young boy with Calax's deformity. But guardian he was, and he ruled his ward without mercy.

"Very good," said Salibar, "the more you use those fingers, the better you'll be at everything. What have I always said?"

Calax knew the answer all too well. "Use the tools you have, not the tools you wished you had."

Salibar grunted. "Indeed. Now, stay where you are, then react to the sounds as you've been taught."

Calax nodded and took a deep breath. He tried his best to hear Salibar's footsteps, but for all his bulk the man was quieter than a stalking cat.

Minutes passed without a sound, and then there was a loud thump coming from a far corner. Calax dropped to the floor, rolled to his left and began running.

A strong arm grabbed him around the waist, stopping him cold. Salibar was shouting at him, poking him in the chest with each word. "Wrong, wrong, wrong!"

Calax startled awake to see a young girl poking him in the chest with a stick.

Calax batted at the stick, then ripped it from her hands. "What the—"

She took a step back. "Sorry, but you were screaming in your sleep."

Calax rubbed at his chest. The lass had a powerful poke for her size. She couldn't have been more than fifteen years old, and it was clear from her torn and dirty dress that she was a peasant girl. But what was she doing out here?

"What? Who are you?"

She brushed back a shock of red hair from her face, and took a step closer to him, but cautiously. "They calls me Tool or Pisspot or Little Bitch most days, but my name be Rhynt."

Calax rubbed his eyes and tried to take her in. She was quite the imp, small-boned and lithe, no more than five feet tall, with freckled skin and deep green eyes. And beautiful in her way. Put her in the proper gown, not this rag dress she was wearing, and she could easily pass for a princess.

Of course, she didn't smell like a princess, and he could tell by her limp and the way her foot turned out, that she was as deformed as he was.

She caught him looking at her foot. "Born this way, but it don't slow me down none. I bet I can outrun a brute like you."

"Oh, so now I'm a brute?"

She shook her head. "Maybe. I don't know. All I knows is that you have a fine horse and by the looks of your saddle there, I'd say you're a sellsword or some such returning from that war everyone's so happy about at its ending."

Calax grunted at her. "How would you know about the war?"

She put her hands on her hips. "I ain't stupid. I hear things."

"Hear things where?"

She glanced over her shoulder. "Back there, at Nob's Knoll. A tavern."

"You work there?"

Rhynt frowned. "More like *slave* there."

"And they let their slaves roam free to poke sleeping men in their sleep?"

She smiled at him. "Not exactly." She turned and pointed at a horse she had tied to a tree. "I was fetching water from the stream, and then saw him, and thought to make my escape."

Calax knew without looking that the horse belonged to the warrior lying in the mud just steps away. He nodded in the body's direction. "That would be his."

Rhynt looked in the direction of the body, then startled. "Oh, my, I never seen it. Dead is he?"

"Completely, and I've never seen his likes before."

Rhynt walked over to the body and bent over it. "I recognize the sigil. Several such men have come through Nob's Knoll the past few days. Strange bunch. Quiet like."

"Quiet?"

"You know, the ones that sit apart and talk in whispers to one another."

"At the tavern?"

"Yes."

"I don't suppose you heard what they were whispering about."

Rhynt beamed at him. "Why, a'course I did. They pay me no mind. It's like I'm not even there."

Calax leaned toward her. "Well?"

"Oh, well, they're looking for someone."

Calax frowned.

"Oh, no, not you, sir," she said. "They're looking for a man with half a hand." She pointed down at him. "Clearly, not you."

Calax flexed the fingers in his false hand. "No, of course not." He took a deep breath and stood, stretching out the kinks from his awkward sleeping position. He pointed at the arrow, which lay beside him on the ground. "And that arrow there. Have you ever seen men carrying arrows like that?"

She looked down at the arrow. "No, but maybe my master, d'Abo Pourcrey, has."

Calax's eyes widened. "The Red Monk? I thought he was dead."

Rhynt nodded. "The very one, and very much alive, and as mean as he is magical."

Calax scratched at his beard. He'd have to shave that when he had a chance. "They say he is the last of the d'Abo monks."

"That may be, but you'll have to ask him yourself. He doesn't share much with me, his pisspot."

Calax wanted to do just that. "Could you take me to him?"

Rhynt was incredulous. "What, and miss my chance to escape?"

"No, no, you can still escape. We'll leave the horses tied up here, and while I'm talking to your master, you can slip out of the tavern and make good your escape."

Rhynt cocked her head, considering the offer. "Very well, but I have a condition."

"What?"

"I'll slip out of the tavern when I see you've got his attention, but I'll wait for you back here with the horses."

"Are you sure? Once I leave the tavern, he'll be after you, I'm sure. Why not take advantage of a head start?"

She held her arms out. "Look at me. A little runt of a girl. I need protection. So, I'll do what you say, but only if you let me ride along with you afterwards. A girl alone on a fine horse won't last long in this world."

Calax smiled back at her. "Agreed, but only long enough to get you to a safe place."

"A safe place? Is there really such a thing?"

Calax looked down at the body. Maybe there wasn't.

3

Calax struggled to keep up with Rhynt as she made her way down the hillside, through the brambles and thickets, to the rutted, red clay road. She may have had a bad foot, but she was fast. He'd have to give her that.

She pointed at a bend in the road. "Just around here and we're there."

She started walking again, but Calax grabbed her by the shoulder. "Are you sure about this? You could just take that horse and go."

Rhynt nodded. "Very sure. Now come, let's go."

They continued on around the bend, sticking to the side of the road to avoid being sucked down in the mud that still lingered from last night's storm.

Nob's Knoll Tavern came into view, looking more like a rundown stable than a place of food and drink. A half dozen horses were tethered to a rail out front, and it didn't take Calax long to figure out that at least two of them were warhorses, no doubt owned by sellswords or berserkers returning from battle. Or maybe men of the yellow arrow. He lifted his sword up and down in its scabbard to make sure it could easily be drawn.

Rhynt couldn't help noticing. "Here, you're not going to start a fight, are you?"

"No, but better to know I'm ready if need be."

"Okay, then. Let me run ahead, so he doesn't think we're together."

Calax nodded. "All right."

"You can't miss d'Abo Pourcrey, what with his red cape and hood."

"Right, go on then."

He paused to watch her race to the back of the tavern, and then he walked to the front door, pushing it open slowly. The smell of roast boar and potatoes that greeted him was like a slap in the face, making him drool.

How long had it been since he'd had more to eat than dried mutton and tree lichens?

In the brief moment while the door was open, he had the upper hand on all the men who were squinting at him, trying to figure out who the stranger was silhouetted by the bright sunlight. Two men in battle dress sat at the closest table, playing cards. To the right of them sat a tradesman of some sort, counting out coins for the tavern keeper, who eyed Calax suspiciously. Beyond them, two men in gray cloaks sat at a table, whispering. Calax could just make out their diamond sigils. He'd have to be wary of them. In a far corner, he could see a man dressed all in green and playing a somber tune on a lute. Finally, he saw d'Abo Pourcrey sitting in a chair in front of the fire, warming his hands, which seemed thin and claw-like in the flickering light of the fire. He and his red cloak seemed to shimmer in the light of the fire, as if they were illusions, mere tricks of the light.

The tavern keeper growled at him. "Shut the damn door, you idiot."

Calax slammed the door behind him. Now everyone in the tavern had the advantage on him. Some looked away quickly, not wanting to meet his eyes. Others checked their swords and twisted in their chairs, ready to attack or defend themselves if needs be. The two men in the gray cloaks peered at him intently; then, satisfied that he was in full possession of two hands, turned back to their whispering. The man in green, obviously a minstrel or bard, stopped his playing and cocked his head to one side to get the measure of the man. Did he have a song for him, one that would tease a coin or two out of the warrior's pocket?

"Tables are full up," said the tavern keeper. "But there's an extra chair by the fire. "Will you be having the boar?"

"And potatoes," said Calax. "And eggs on top if you've got them."

The tavern keeper shrugged. "Aye, cooked or raw?"

Calax couldn't abide cooked eggs. It just seemed unnatural. The best way to eat an egg was to poke a little hole in the pointy end, and suck the liquid out. The second best way to eat an egg was to crack the shell open and plop the egg down on top of whatever else you were eating. It made even the toughest meat go down easy.

"Raw, on top."

The tavern keeper frowned. "What, you think there's something wrong with my boar?"

"No, I—"

"Don't need no help. Goes down good. No extra slippery needed."

Calax couldn't help laughing. "No, no, good sir. I just prefer my eggs raw. Nothing against your boar. I'm sure it's wonderful."

The tavern keeper started to say something, then just nodded, gave him a little grunt, and headed for the kitchen, which was really only a small fire in the far corner of the tavern. A small woman sat there, stirring potatoes in a pot. From the look of her, a woman fully beaten and defeated, he guessed she was the tavern keeper's wife.

Calax spotted the empty chair by the fire, and the man he wanted to talk to, sitting right next to it. The Red Monk was a small man with a long white beard that he stroked and tugged at again and again as if he were thinking of some great plan. He was so frail looking it seemed a wonder he was still alive.

The d'Abo religion had been banned throughout the known kingdoms. Disciples and monks of the order had all been hunted down and killed. And yet the Red Monk lived on, which could only have been a testament to his power. D'Abo Pourcrey was a monk, yes, but a wizard foremost. Calax had heard stories worthy of wonder and a minstrel's song. The monk could disappear like a vapor, bring storms with his staff, and slow or stop the very progress of time itself. And all this in a man who looked like he'd have trouble lifting a feather.

As Calax began to make his way to the empty chair, the minstrel strummed his lute hard, a single chord to announce a new song. His voice was low and deep.

> *They comes and they goes to the Battle of Whent*
> *And they falls to the ground in a right torrent*
> *Blood and bones and gore be sent*
> *By the sword of the hero of the Battle of Whent*
>
> *He had a full hand and a half you see*
> *And his sword would swing and the men would flee*
> *No man could stand in his path you see*
> *So he soon put an end to the enemy*

Calax paused and gave the minstrel a questioning look. Did the man know who he was? How could he? The minstrel just nodded back at him with a smile and continued his song, which seemed to have endless verses, all as poorly crafted as the first.

Calax turned back and saw Rhynt standing beside d'Abo Pourcrey, who had her by the ear.

"Hold, sir," he said, walking quickly to her aid. "What's she done to deserve such a twist?"

D'Abo Pourcrey let loose her ear and turned to face Calax. "And who might you be to get between a man and his pisspot?"

Calax thought to announce himself, but thought better of it, even though the mere mention of his name was usually enough for even the bravest warriors to back off. "Just a lone traveler seeking a meal and a sit down. The mud has pulled at me all morning."

D'Abo Pourcrey looked him up and down. As frail as the monk was, his steel blue eyes suggested otherwise; they seemed to be probing Calax with an intelligence and power that gave Calax pause.

The monk sneered. "A traveler? No, you're a sellsword returning from battle. A warrior of the first rank, if I'm not mistaken. I smelled it the instant you threw open the door."

"Smell?"

"Of war, young man. The scent of death. It follows you even now."

Calax took a deep breath and looked around the room. Everyone was staring at them, including the two men in gray. He turned back to the monk. "You are very perceptive, sir, but who I am has little to do with the way you're mistreating this little girl."

"Mistreat, *mistreat?* Why, what *should* I do when the little pisspot takes half an hour to fetch a single pail of water?"

Rhynt interrupted. "The creek be far, master. I did my best."

D'Abo Pourcrey raised a hand as if to strike her, but then thought better of it. "Ah, one excuse after another. And yet you come back with no water at all."

"I tripped master, I tripped."

D'Abo Pourcrey turned to Calax. "You see what I have to put up with? The insolence. The talking back."

Calax shook his head. "I see but a young girl, a mere waif with a bad foot, trying to do her best."

D'Abo Pourcrey sighed. "Very well, then. Perhaps I will give her another opportunity to prove me wrong."

"That would be wise, sir," said Calax.

"Also, I see by the way you walked directly toward me that you seek me out for some reason. You want to talk, about something you've found. Something unknown to you but perhaps well within my ken. Am I right?"

Calax nodded.

"Very well, then. We shall talk." He turned to Rhynt. "Go fetch another pail of water, and be careful about it this time."

Rhynt bowed. "Yes, master." She moved away quickly, heading for the back door of the tavern. When she reached the door, she turned and winked at Calax.

Calax, who had turned away from the monk to follow her progress, winked back. He turned back to the monk, who was smiling slyly.

"Well, then," said the monk. "Let us talk. Time is the enemy of old men. Let us not waste it."

4

Calax poked at the fire with a stick, trying to rouse it back to full flame.

Rhynt shook her head. "Stop, you're just making it worse."

Frustrated, Calax threw the stick in the fire, but even then the little stick wouldn't ignite. It sizzled briefly, emitting a puff of white smoke, and then settled back to being a wet stick on a poor fire.

"Here," said Rhynt. "Let me try."

"Try what?"

"Just step back, and I'll show you."

Calax moved away from the fire and watched as Rhynt raised both arms toward the fire, closed her eyes, and mumbled words under her breath. The fire leaped to life, roaring with the intensity of a forge.

"What the—"

Rhynt beamed at him. "D'Abo taught me that."

Calax gave her a puzzled, appraising look. "And why would he train his pisspot?"

Rhynt shrugged. "He's a very arrogant, boastful man. Letting me in on one of his little tricks was just his way of proclaiming his brilliance. Surely, you understand that after talking with him."

Calax cocked his head. She had a point. The man was almost insufferably arrogant. "Aye, I do."

Rhynt looked down at the fire, which had settled down to a good cooking fire. "Here, where's your cook pot? I've some terra flowers, fresh picked this morning. We can have us some tea."

Calax pointed at his warhorse. "Hanging from the back of Gash's saddle."

"Gash? Why do you call him that?"

"It's what he does, in battle. Gashes through the lines. He's fearless."

Rhynt eyed the horse. "He's *huge*. Is it safe to approach him?"

"Yes, he's like a puppy when he's not in battle."

Rhynt limped over to the horse and fetched the pot. "There's a stream just down the hill. I'll be back in a minute."

Calax grunted and watched her go. He wasn't sure if he'd made the right decision in befriending her, but she made a right fine fire starter.

Gash stamped his foot to get Calax's attention.

"Okay, boy, let's get that saddle off you. We have a hard ride tomorrow, so you'll need a good rest."

He tugged the saddle off and dropped it to the ground. "Here now, there's plenty of grass, so have your fill."

Rhynt came up behind him. "Do you always talk to him?"

Calax turned and smiled at her. "Usually no one else to talk to, so yes. He doesn't talk back, of course, but he's a fine listener."

Rhynt motioned him toward the fire. "Come on, let's get this pot on the fire. Terra tea won't fill your stomach, but it will make you feel like you've had a feast."

Calax followed her to the fire and sat down beside her. She pulled the terra blossoms out of her pocket, dumped them into the pot, gave them a good swirl, and then set the pot in the middle of the fire. "Shouldn't be long."

"Good, I could use the feeling of a feast. Things happened so fast back there, I never had my boar and potatoes."

Rhynt eyed him silently.

"What?" said Calax.

"Your conversation with my master. How did that go?"

Calax thought about their talk, and sighed. "He's a strange man. Talks in riddles."

Rhynt chuckled. "Oh, he does that for sure."

"I asked about the men in gray, but all he said was to avoid them."

"Then you must," said Rhynt. "He knows danger. And he knows what I know, too."

Calax gave her a puzzled look. "What *you* know?"

"That you are Calax Halfhand."

Calax smiled at her. "What? You think I am that warrior? But look, I have two fine hands." He opened and closed the fingers of both gloved hands in front of her face. "See?"

Rhynt shook her head, reached down for her foot, and tugged it off with a hard twist. "I dare say, your left hand comes off just as easily."

Calax sighed and rolled his eyes. "Damn."

Rhynt waggled her eyebrows at him. "Indeed."

"Well, then," said Calax, tugging off the wooden hand. "I could use a good scratch, anyway."

He rolled up his sleeve, revealing his malformed, three-fingered little hand.

"Whoa," said Rhynt.

Calax smirked at her, and began scratching. "You can look away, you know."

"Oh, no, I was admiring it. See here, look at my little foot." She pulled up her skirt, revealing a tiny, shrunken foot with but two toes.

"Whoa right back at you," said Calax. "We're a right fine pair."

Rhynt laughed. "We are indeed."

Calax smiled at her, then grew somber. "How is it you're still alive? Most babes like you are put to death at birth."

Rhynt shrugged. "So I've heard, but I really have no idea. What about you?"

Calax shook his head. "Likewise. No idea why I wasn't put down."

"No matter," said Rhynt, giving her toes a good scratch. "Here, we best put our helpful appendages back on. Who knows who might be lurking about?"

"Aye." Calax gave his hand one last scratch and then attached the wooden hand again, flexing his fingers to make sure all was working properly.

Rhynt wondered at it. "That's an amazing piece of work."

"It is that, though the man who made it is now long dead."

Rhynt sighed. "Too bad. I could use something better than this thing I call a foot." She reached for it and clicked it back in place with a hard twist. "It's near worthless."

"Still, it does the job."

"Aye." She looked down at the fire, then back at Calax. "So, what did d'Abo tell you?"

Calax puffed out his cheeks. "That's a long story."

Rhynt crossed her legs and leaned toward him. "I'm all ears."

Calax nodded and began his story. After settling down in the chair opposite the monk, Calax had gotten right to the point, asking who the men in gray were. D'Abo Pourcrey had merely shrugged, telling Calax that all he knew of the men is the direction from whence they came. And when Calax had lifted the yellow arrow from beneath his cloak, the monk's eyes had grown wide. But so had the eyes of the men in gray. All hell broke loose. Swords were drawn, and the fighting began.

Rhynt interrupted, a look of concern on her face. "And the monk?"

Calax remembered it clearly. One second the monk was there, and the next he had vanished. "Fine as far as I know. He used some magic to disappear."

Rhynt nodded. "Yes, he can do that." She motioned him to continue. "Go on."

The fight was quick. He had dispatched the men in gray with two strokes of his sword, and the two warriors with two more. The tradesman and the minstrel had fled, leaving only the tavern keeper and his wife huddled together in a corner.

"It was strange. Though their weapons were fine, they seemed to lack the skills of swordsmen. After it was over, I searched the pouches of the men in gray, and each carried the same note carried by the other man we left back there in the mud."

Rhynt looked puzzled. "What note?"

Calax fumbled in his pocket and dropped the three notes in front of her.

Rhynt picked up one and opened it. "Well, they clearly want you—for *something*—but there's nothing that says they're going to kill you. Just bring you to *him*, whoever him is."

"Well, the look in their eyes said otherwise. They came at me in a fury, swords drawn."

Rhynt dropped the note back into the pile. "Curious. You know, you should have spared one, to get down to the bottom of things."

She was right. "Aye, perhaps next time. Sometimes, the blood rises in me to the point I can't control myself. I'm a berserker, after all."

She squinted at him. She wasn't quite sure what a berserker was, or did. "Yes, next time."

Calax reached into his boot and pulled out three bone-handled daggers, all made of the same greenish metal. "You want curious, take a look at these."

Rhynt hefted one, and whistled in appreciation. "So light and sharp. And this metal. I've never seen the like."

"Nor I."

"May I have one, for protection?"

Calax picked up a second dagger and tossed it her way. "Take two. I've no sword to offer you, but you could do damage with two of these."

Rhynt smiled, holding each up to the light and swinging them in the air.

Calax wondered at her skill. "You've had training."

Rhynt nodded. "Some, but nothing like your skills."

She poked the fire with a stick and whispered words to it, the flames jumping once more, sending out a wave of heat that forced them both back from the fire. Rhynt stood and extended the stick into the fire, snagging the pot of terra tea.

"Ready as it will ever be and fully a'bubble."

"Here, let me get the cups," said Calax, moving away from the fire and withdrawing two cups from his saddlebags.

Rhynt poured the tea and they sat back down near the fire. "So," she began. "You're on the run, or rather, we're on the run. But where to?"

Calax took a sip of tea and then pointed east. "That way."

Rhynt followed his finger. "What, into the woods? Is that it?"

"Your master was very specific. He didn't know where they came from, but he said they came out of the east."

Rhynt frowned. "But if that's true, shouldn't we be headed west?"

Calax took another sip of tea. She was right, it seemed to restore his energy. "I mean to find the man who sent those grays our way."

Rhynt raised her eyebrows. "Really? It seems a fool's errand to me."

Calax chuckled. "Then say hello to this fool. No, we go east. Or at least I do. You're free to go in any direction you please."

Rhynt shook her head. "No, I'm with you." She hefted the daggers again. "And I'm very happy to have two fine daggers in the bargain." She stuck them in the ground in front of her and picked up her cup to take a sip of tea.

Calax laughed, then shouted to the sky. "Make way for Rhynt of the Green Dagger."

Rhynt convulsed in laughter, spraying tea on Calax and the fire.

Not far away, hidden behind a tree, someone was trying hard to stifle his own laugh. He would wait till morning.

5

In the dream, Salibar had him by the shoulders, moving him toward the center of the room.

"Always choose the center if you have a choice."

Young Calax frowned. "But wouldn't a corner be a better choice? No one could sneak up on me from behind."

Salibar groaned in frustration. "Think about it. A corner seems safe, yes, but it is also a sure trap. No, stick to the middle."

Calax nodded. "Yes, master."

"Now, young lad, look once around the room, then close your eyes."

"What? Why?"

Salibar jabbed a finger into Calax's chest. "Just do it."

Calax scanned the room. The wall to the left was floor to ceiling with bookshelves, but there were no books. In front of him was a large cooking hearth. To his right a grand table with benches long enough to accommodate fifty knights. Above it, a single chandelier of teardrop crystals. And above that, the only window in the room. He turned and looked behind him. A large expanse of wall and nothing more.

He closed his eyes.

"Good," said Salibar. "When I strike my staff to the floor, imagine I am here to kill you, then think of where I am in the room and respond."

"Respond?"

"Yes, respond. You need to save yourself. Find a weapon, lad."

Calax opened his eyes. "But why?"

Salibar growled at him. "Because I said so, is why. Now close your eyes and wait for the sound."

Calax closed his eyes and waited. Minutes went by, and then a sharp sound coming from the wall to the left. He raced to the right, hoping to hide under the table, but he miscalculated the distance, tripping over the benches and slamming his head into the table.

Salibar was on him in a second, poking him in the back with his staff. "And now you're dead."

Calax opened his eyes, his head throbbing with pain. "Why are we playing this stupid game?"

Salibar grabbed him by the shoulders and began shaking him. "Because it's not a game. Not a game at all. Your life will depend on it one day."

Calax broke from Salibar's grip and raced for the door, but the door was locked.

"There's no escape, lad. You either learn this, or you die. When the time comes, there will be no choice."

Calax turned to face him, and began screaming. "Why? Why are we doing this? Why are we doing this?"

Then Rhynt was pushing at his chest, trying to rouse him. "Wake up, Calax. Wake up."

Calax opened his eyes, then quickly closed them, shielding them from the bright morning light.

"That was quite a dream you were having. You right scared the horses."

Calax was instantly on his feet, sword in hand. "Gash don't scare. There's someone about."

Rhynt spun around. "What? Where?"

And then they came, the men in gray. Four of them, with swords drawn, racing toward them.

Calax screamed at Rhynt. "Behind me!"

But Rhynt was already racing toward the fire, where her daggers awaited, still stuck in the ground where she had left them. She dove for them, picked them cleanly from the earth, and rolled back up, launching one of the daggers at the nearest man in gray, who took the dagger in the eye and dropped.

Another man raced toward her, his arm already swinging, a look of anger on his face. Then suddenly Calax was between her and the man, his sword quicker, swifter, the man's head lifted from his body in a gush of blood, the head rolling away, the man's eyes still wide from surprise.

Two to go, thought Calax, *I'll spare one this time*. But when he spun around to face them, they were already dead on the ground, yellow arrows protruding from their chests.

He turned back to Rhynt, who was bent over, throwing up. "Are you all right?"

She nodded, dagger still at the ready. "So far."

"Your first kill?"

"Yes," she said, taking a deep breath to steady herself.

"It is always so. And the feeling will pass." He scanned the treeline. "Did you see the archer?"

"No, but the arrows came from over there." She pointed to the tree where the horses stood.

Calax dropped his sword to his side, and shouted. "Come out, sir, whoever you are."

Silence.

"Sir, I would thank you for your help. Come out."

Nothing.

Rhynt shrugged. "I guess he's gone."

Calax scanned the treeline once more, then wiped his sword across the back of the nearest body and put his sword back in its scabbard. "We owe him our lives, whoever he is."

He turned to the bodies. "Check their pouches. Let's see if there's anything more to learn."

"Aye," said Rhynt. She began collecting pouches, tossing each to Calax as she went.

He opened pouch after pouch, and each contained the same note, scribed in the same hand: *You will know him by his hand, or the half of it, and the name Calax Halfhand. You must bring him to me.*

"All the same," he said.

"No surprise there," said Rhynt. In addition to the pouches, she had collected all the men's daggers, which she struggled to hold onto.

"Six daggers now, is it?" said Calax. "Any more and you can make a fine living as a seller of daggers."

Rhynt laughed. "Yes, and look, they're all identical. What magician of the forge could do such work with such precision?"

Calax shook his head. "I know of one, and his forge is not far. A day's ride north. If there's anything to learn from them, he'll be the person who knows."

"But we need to go east."

Calax looked at the bodies. "Maybe that's what they're expecting us to do. Let's see if we can throw them off the track. We'll go north, and then turn east after we've had a talk with my friend about those daggers."

Rhynt scanned the treeline again. "Do you think he'll follow?"

"Perhaps, but I think that can only be a good thing."

Rhynt wasn't so sure. "Whoever sent those men must have given them reason of a reward. Perhaps our yellow archer is just eliminating his competition."

Calax cocked his head. She was wise for her age. "Then we'll have to keep close watch."

He pointed at the bodies. "Get their swords as well. They seem to be of the same strange metal."

Rhynt nodded, dropped the daggers at her feet, and began scooping up the swords.

Calax went to his saddle bag, drew out a large leather bag, and tossed it in Rhynt's direction. "Put them in that, along with the daggers."

"Right," said Rhynt.

Calax scanned the treeline again, hoping to see some sign of the yellow archer, but there was nothing and no one.

"Got 'em," said Rhynt, holding up the bag with some effort.

Calax grabbed the bag from her and pointed at Gash and the other horse. "Come on, let's saddle up and get out of here."

They headed north, keeping away from the roads, stopping only to rest and water the horses. Forest gave way to rolling hills, which gave way to a vast plain of short grasses and red clay that seemed to stretch to the horizon.

"Are we there yet?" said Rhynt, breaking a long silence between them.

Calax chuckled. "No, still a ways. This plain stretches to more rolling hills and then to a forest and my friend's forge. We should be there by nightfall, or at worst by tomorrow morning. Not sure the horses can make it in one go, so we may have to stop for the night."

"Who is this man?"

"A short question, a long answer. His name is Zyrx, and the first thing you should know about him is that he is a blacksmith and master forger. If you need a fine sword, Zyrx is your man."

"And I suppose there's a second thing to know?" said Rhynt.

"Aye, and a third and a fourth and beyond counting. But the second thing is that he is a dwarf and very sensitive about his height. He's killed men for even slightly looking askance at him or offering up a jape or joke about his size."

"I'll remember that."

"Good."

They grew silent for a time. Calax scanned the horizon, then turned in his saddle to see if they were being followed.

He turned back to Rhynt. "I have a question for you."

"Yes?"

"Back there, with the gray men, the way you tumbled to get the dagger, the way you threw it."

Rhynt gave him a puzzled look. "What?"

"It showed some skill, some training. Where did you learn that?"

Rhynt turned away from him and sighed.

Calax frowned. "What? Have I touched a nerve?"

Rhynt turned back to him and nodded. "Indeed you have."

Calax cocked his head. "It's best we have no secrets, Rhynt."

Rhynt took a deep breath, then puffed it out, hard. "Before I was with my master, d'Abo Pourcrey, I was a runaway from a terrible man. What fighting skills I have I got from him. He sought to make little me an invincible warrior, or so he said, which is the last thing I wanted to be."

Calax nodded. "I have a similar story. I ran away from just such a man when I was thirteen."

Rhynt smiled at him. "Truly?"

"Yes, and I was well rid of him."

"Still," said Rhynt. "He clearly taught you how to be a formidable warrior."

Calax shook his head. "No, I learned most of what I know from another man, a warrior named Phalyn, who took me under his wing. He helped get me my hand and was the first to call me Halfhand."

"You speak of him with sadness in your voice."

Calax nodded. "Yes, he died in the Battle of Whent Hill, when I was but one and twenty."

Rhynt's eyes grew wide. "You were there?"

Calax closed his eyes, trying to fight back the memory. The blood, the gore, the ebb and flow of battle as men and horses struggled to last just one minute more.

"I was and am lucky to have survived it."

"Were there really a thousand killed?"

"And a thousand more and yet a thousand more. And five times that who came home with scars and without limbs."

Rhynt whistled softly. "I'd heard it was bad, but never those numbers."

"I thought it would have been the end to war, that battle. So many killed and wounded, and for what? An exchange of insults between kings? War is madness."

Rhynt frowned. "But you continue to fight."

"Aye, for money. It's all I know how to do, and I'm good at it."

"I don't think I could do that."

"Nor should you." Calax suddenly laughed. "You should be a fire starter."

7

They rode on, the flat plain turning back to rolling hills, a grand forest ahead, the leaves of the trees golden in the late afternoon sun.

"How's your horse?" said Calax.

Rhynt returned his question with a wry laugh. "That's not the question. The question is, how's my arse?"

Calax chuckled. "And how is it?"

"I'm not sure. It went numb a few miles back."

"Shall we stop?"

Rhynt grunted. "How much farther?"

"I'd say an hour at most. Should arrive at dusk, and if memory serves, that's when Zyrx sits down to dinner."

Rhynt sighed longingly. "Ah, dinner. Yes, let's keep going."

They continued on, up a hill, down a hill, and into the forest. As soon as they entered, they were in near darkness, even though sunset was still an hour away.

"Wow," said Rhynt.

"Indeed," said Calax. "The third thing you should know about Zyrx is that he prefers to live in darkness. This forest is dark even at midday."

"We'd best press on, then, before the whole world turns black on us."

Calax looked up at the canopy of trees, where sunlight twinkled like stars in the heavens. "We'll make it. Not far now. See the creek ahead? We'll follow it to his house, if you can call it that."

"Is that a fourth thing?"

"Yes, it's more like a cave, or at least like a house buried in the side of a hill."

Calax and Gash were the first to splash into the creek. "Stay to the left side, where it's shallow."

Rhynt followed without a word, the only sound the splashing of the horse's hooves in the cool water.

And then came a wild roar, and another, and another, the horses whinnying and balking.

"Easy, Gash, easy," said Calax coaxing the horse forward. He turned back to Rhynt. "Stay close and follow me."

"What is that?" said Rhynt, alarmed.

"It's just a fifth thing, and a sixth, and a seventh."

"What?"

"Hill tigers. Zyrx has three. Don't worry, they're more roar than bite. They're just announcing our arrival."

"We're here?"

"We should see his fire just around the bend."

"Is that the eighth thing?"

Calax laughed. "No, it's just a plain ordinary fire, and from the smell, I'd say we're having rabbit for dinner."

8

Rhynt had stopped counting the things to remember about their host, Zyrx. He had greeted them both as if they were old friends and ushered them into what he called his "hearth in the hill," a small, low-ceilinged dwelling made of logs and mud and dug deep into the hillside. Everything about the place was small, from its chairs to its tables to its bowls and spoons.

The menu did indeed feature rabbit, roasted to a delectable pink and so delicate in flavor that Rhynt could not help but ask for seconds, and thirds, even as she kept a wary eye on the three hill tigers circling the table, begging for scraps.

She had heard of hill tigers, but never imagined they would be so big. She had seen a dire wolf once, and wondered at its size. But these tigers were bigger still, taller at the shoulder and longer head to tail. Their stripes, which were amber in color, with tinges of black along the edges, ran the length of their bodies and seemed to roll like waves when they moved.

As for Zyrx, he was indeed a dwarf, but carried himself like the tallest warrior. Like Rhynt, he had a shock of red hair, kept short no doubt because of his occupation. Long hair and forges did not go hand in hand. His beard was also cropped short, probably for the same reason. Swinging a hammer all day had knotted his muscles to the point that his body seemed to be bursting from its clothing, a white tunic topped by a brown leather apron scorched and scarred by hot metal. His face was ruddy, the result of heat, but his eyes were an icy gray, and seemed to fix a person in place.

Just as they did now. "What are you looking at?" said Zyrx, annoyed.

Rhynt started from her reverie. "Oh, sorry, didn't mean to stare."

"See that you don't, and don't worry about the tigers. I see they bother you, but have no fears. They're my brothers and sisters, or maybe nephews and nieces, I forget."

"What?"

Calax laughed. "What our fine host is trying to say is that he suckled at the teat of a tiger when he was but a babe."

"I'm not sure I like the way you put that, Calax Halfhand, but the gist of it is correct. My parents abandoned me in this very forest soon after I was born. So, yes, I was raised by hill tigers, and much preferred it to being their meal." He motioned toward Rhynt's leg. "I see you have a deformity of your own. How did you manage to survive?"

Rhynt shook her head. "I have no idea."

Zyrx cocked his head. "Really? Well, then, I guess we've exhausted this line of inquiry." He grunted and turned to Calax. "Your story is amazing. Men in gray? Green daggers? Come, I must see those blades."

Calax reached down for the sack he had brought in with them and dumped its contents on the table.

Zyrx's eyes grew wide. "I don't believe it. I thought these were a myth." He picked up a dagger and held it to the light of a nearby candle. "What craftsmanship."

Rhynt spoke up. "And look, they're all identical."

Zyrx lined up the daggers and studied them, inspecting them one by one. "It is as she says. Identical. Impossibly identical."

"You mentioned a myth," said Calax. "What can you tell us?"

Zyrx picked up one of the swords. "So light. Unbelievably light."

Calax pressed him again. "The myth, Zyrx."

Zyrx set the sword down. "I heard a tale from a man who passed through here several years ago. He had come from a land he called Enturia, which he said was where knives such as these are made."

Calax frowned. "Enturia? I've seen many maps, but never one with a country by that name."

"Indeed," said Zyrx, "but the man claimed it was east of here, a three days ride to begin, and then a sea voyage of another two days."

Rhynt interrupted, beaming. "A sea voyage? I've never been to sea. It will be wonderful!"

Calax held up a hand. "I said I'd get you to a safe place, not put you in further danger."

"But I want to go," said Rhynt. "I can be of help. You've seen my skills with a dagger."

Calax rolled his eyes. "Yes, you have skills, but not enough to face even those men in gray."

Rhynt was incredulous. "What? *What?* You saw me take one down with a single throw."

Calax shook his head. "Which exposed you to the sword of another gray man, who would have sliced you in half if it wasn't for me."

Rhynt crossed her arms, furious. "No, that's not right. I want to go."

Calax started to object again, then stopped with a sigh. "All right, let me think on it. For now, I'd like to learn more about this greenish metal." He turned to Zyrx. "Can you tell us what it is?"

Zyrx threw up his hands. "I've never seen its like, and see here, you aren't proposing to dump this little girl on me, are you?"

"Dump is not the right word. What I'm proposing is that she earn her keep helping out at the forge."

"Help? Look at this waif. I doubt that she could even lift a hammer, and I'm sure she will right wilt from the blast from my forge."

"Hey," said Rhynt, "I may be a girl, but I'm strong and I have *powers.*"

Zyrx cocked his head. "Powers? *Powers?*"

"Indeed," said Rhynt, puffing out her chest. "I can start fires, for one."

Zyrx raised his head toward the ceiling and guffawed. "Oh, little girl. I need no help with fires. I am lord and master of fires, child."

"Whoa, whoa, whoa," said Calax. "The girl is right. She has powers beyond your ken, taught to her by the Red Monk."

Zyrx's eyes grew wide. "The Red Monk? I thought he was dead."

"Unfortunately, not," said Rhynt. "And I think what Calax was getting at is that I can make your fires *hotter, faster.*" She paused. "Not that I want to."

Zyrx laughed. "Ha! Now that I'd like to see." He stood and motioned them to follow. "Come, let's go to my forge, and we'll see what's what."

They started to follow, but Zyrx stopped and pointed at the table. "Bring the weapons along, and let's see how they behave in the fire."

Calax and Rhynt trailed after him, along with his hill tigers, who sniffed at Rhynt as they bounded along beside her.

Rhynt took a deep breath and let it out slowly. Perhaps they wouldn't eat her.

9

Rhynt said her secret words, and the little fire that Zyrx had banked for the night leaped into life with a roar and a burst of flame that forced them all backwards.

"Yikes," said Zyrx. "The girl be a witch indeed."

"I told you," said Calax, patting her on the back with almost fatherly pride.

Rhynt shrugged his hand away. "Like I said, I have powers, powers that would come in handy on land or sea, at home or in battle."

Calax sighed. "I *said* I would think about it."

Zyrx laughed. "Are you sure you're not father and daughter? Please stop bickering, we have work to do." He pointed at Rhynt. "Hand me a sword."

She complied and watched as he swung it deftly in the air. "It's light, yes, but is it strong?"

He moved to his vise and tightened it around the blade. "Calax, strike it hard with your sword—near the middle."

Calax drew his sword and brought it down hard on the edge of the strange green blade. His sword immediately snapped in two. Calax looked at the snapped end in horror. "By the gods!"

Zyrx whistled. "That's a fine blade you have, Calax. I know, because I made it. But it's no match for this metal, whatever it is."

Calax was still in shock. "My sword, my sword."

Zyrx put a hand on his arm to calm him. "There, there, my son, it is not the end of the world."

"No, just the end of a sword that has seen me through many a battle."

"But not the battle ahead, my son, as you can plainly see. It is no match for the green blade."

Calax sighed heavily, then nodded, dropping the sword to the ground. "Then I'll be using one of theirs when I face them. Rhynt, go fetch me another of their swords."

"Aye, sir."

She started to go, but Zyrx grabbed her by the arm. "Stay." He turned to Calax. "Don't be so sure. Their swords have magic in them, true. But perhaps I can forge something even better."

"Better?"

"Here," he said, extending his arm toward Rhynt. "Let's heat one of these daggers up and see just how it behaves."

Rhynt handed him a dagger. Zyrx cleaned it with a brush and then grasped it with a pair of long tongs before resting it in the center of the fire.

"This will take a minute, so listen to my proposition," he said.

Calax looked puzzled. "Proposition?"

Zyrx waggled his head. "A deal, if you will."

"Go on," said Rhynt.

"Calax, here, needs a new sword. Oh, I know he could just take one of the gray men's swords, but that won't do. As strong as they are, they're the wrong length and heft for my friend Calax."

Calax nodded. "That is true."

"So," said Zyrx, continuing, "I propose that the two of you stay here for a week. Rest up, enjoy the forest and my hospitality whilst I endeavor to make Calax a fine new sword, one that is better and stronger than the gray men's swords."

Calax smiled. "And you think you can do that?"

Zyrx looked down at the now molten metal and laughed. "Now that I see it in the flames, yes. I can take their metal, layer it with mine, fold the two metals upon themselves again and again, perhaps twenty times, and create a sword like no other."

Rhynt's eyes grew wide. "Could you make me one as well?"

Zyrx stroked his beard and looked at Calax, who nodded.

"Very well, but I will need to measure you and test the limits of your strength."

Rhynt clapped her hands. "Yes!"

Zyrx nodded and smiled at her and Calax in turn. "These will be swords worthy of names, so give that some thought."

Rhynt beamed. "A name? Oh, I will, and it will be a grand name worthy of your fine craftsmanship."

Zyrx laughed. "Ha! The girl knows how to wheedle through praise."

Calax rolled his eyes. "I told you she had powers."

Rhynt shook her head. "Stop, you're making fun of me."

Zyrx chuckled. "Not at all, child. In fact, as part of this bargain, I'll have a surprise for you at the end of the week. Something unexpected."

Rhynt hopped up and down. "Tell me!"

Zyrx shook his head and turned back to the molten metal. "No, I'll tell you at the end of the week. It will be a test of your patience, an important trait for a warrior. Now, the two of you need to leave me be for a time. I've work to do. You'll find soft beds within. I suggest you make the most of them. Morning is not far away."

The word bed was all Rhynt needed to hear. She was exhausted. "Oh, that sounds good to me."

Calax nodded. "And me."

"Go then, and don't worry about the hill tigers. They won't eat you in the night." He smiled at them, then frowned. "Or at least I hope not."

The days went by, each day much like the next. Calax would awaken in a sweat, Rhynt hovering over him, her face replacing the face of his old master, Salibar, who had screamed at him all night as Calax failed and failed again in that dreaded room. Each would then put on their wooden appendages and stretch to get rid of their aches from the too-soft beds.

Breakfast would already be set out for them, as if by some fairy in the night. As they sated their hunger on hard rolls, marinated mushrooms, and apple ale, the repeated pings of Zyrx's hammer would fill their ears, along with the little man's shouted curses.

After breakfast they would go their own ways. Calax would borrow Zyrx's bow and head into the dim light of the forest. Sometimes he would come back quickly, dragging a weir deer or some creature unknown to Rhynt. Other times, he would be gone all day, not returning until well after sunset, but always dragging something else to be skinned, butchered, and set upon a spit over Zyrx's hearth fire.

Rhynt would spend her days near the house in the hill, never straying too far from its door, and always followed by Zyrx's three hill tigers, who seemed to be bonding with her more and more each day. By the third night, when they all gathered for the evening meal, the tigers would position themselves at Rhynt's feet, preferring her over their master, who noticed the change in them with a grunt.

"Look at that, would you," said Zyrx. "They're like kittens around her."

Rhynt smiled at him. "We have grown to like each other's company, is all. And you've been busy."

Zyrx nodded. "Yes, I have, but you're the first person to get anything more than a wary eye from them."

Calax chuckled. "It's true. Why, every time I return from the forest, the three of them crowd around her, as if to protect her from some very beast."

Rhynt beamed. "I call them Mela, Mila, and Spook."

Zyrx slapped his hand on the table with a laugh. "I love it. She's named them. And let me guess, Spook is the shy one, right?"

Rhynt nodded.

Calax shook his head in wonder. "I dare say, they'll be happy to see me go and her stay."

Rhynt frowned and started to protest, but Zyrx jumped in before she had a chance to speak.

"Speaking of which," he said. "I'll need an extra day. Joining these metals has been more of a challenge than I first thought."

Calax gave him a look of concern. "Really?"

Zyrx threw up his hands. "In my first attempt, the metals would just not join whatsoever. It was as if they were fighting each other. I had to think on that a long while."

"And?" said Calax.

"And then I remembered an old trick of my master. All I needed to do was dust each metal with mushroom spores before I attempted to join them."

Rhynt giggled. "Mushroom spores?"

"Yes," said Zyrx. "You know, from those mushrooms that look like big thumbs."

"Eww."

Calax smiled at Zyrx. "So it worked?"

Zyrx shrugged. "Some. I could combine them and fold them and hammer them out fine, but the quench made them brittle."

Rhynt looked puzzled. "The quench?"

"Aye, lass. When you have the shape just right, you need to quench your blade. You know, dip it in water to harden the metal and make it strong."

"I see. So it didn't work. Is there a solution?"

Zyrx nodded. "Aye, again I had to reach back to my master's lessons and remember something I'd never needed before."

"And that was?" said Calax.

"Creek mud, believe it or not. Part dirt, part sand, part salamander slime, part frog poop, and part magic. It worked like a charm. The quench went perfectly."

"So you are back on schedule," said Calax.

"Well, minus a lost day for all this testing and remembering and testing again and again."

Rhynt cocked her head. "And my surprise? Will I still have my surprise?"

Zyrx gave her a sly smile. "We'll see, girl, we'll see."

II

After one week and a day, almost to the minute, Zyrx gathered them at the feast table to reveal his two new swords, but only after they had enjoyed his mushroom and weir deer stew. Rhynt had already decided that if she were forced to stay with Zyrx, she would grow round as a tree nut.

Throughout the meal, Rhynt and Calax had continued to glance at the two sword-shaped lumps under the weir skin, one large, one small, wondering just how good or bad the new swords might be.

Finally, Zyrx was ready to reveal them. "Before I show you my handiwork, a word or two about their making."

He looked at both of them in turn, and each nodded. "Good, now, as I said at the beginning, I melded the green blade with my most favored metal, and at first it didn't work."

Calax, frustrated, broke in. "Oh, just get on with it, man."

Zyrx gave him a sour look. "Patience, warrior. Now, eventually I sorted everything out, but not before I realized the addition of a third metal might make these swords unbreakable."

Calax raised his brow. "Really?"

"Indeed," said Zyrx. "It is a new metal, actually a combination of metals, and I call it merilium. Although it's a light metal, when bound with other metals, it greatly increases strength and edge retention." He pointed at the blades under the weir skin. "These swords will hold their edge even if you slam them against a rock all day."

"Well, I like that," said Calax.

"I also coiled the metal of the handles to create the look of intertwined ropes. It's not just decorative. The texture gives you a firm grip that will hold fast under any blow."

Zyrx stopped talking and then just looked at them.

"What?" said Rhynt.

Zyrx grabbed the edge of the weir skin and whipped it off the swords. Rhynt's eyes went wide, and Calax actually gasped.

"My word," said Calax, picking up the larger sword and hefting it in his hand. "If it does everything you say it can, it is a very miracle. It feels like part of my arm."

Zyrx smiled. "It's all about balance. It seems I judged it rightly for a man of your imposing strength."

"Indeed, you have." Calax stood and swung the sword in a wide arc. "Incredible."

Zyrx looked at Rhynt, who had been staring in wonder. "Go on, girl, pick it up, test it out."

Rhynt picked it up, and it was as Calax said. It seemed to be a natural extension of her arm, and it sang a high note as it passed through the air.

"Sir, I'm speechless."

Zyrx beamed. "I'm so glad you like them. Now, of course, there are scabbards for them. I left them back at the forge. We'll go get them in a minute, but there's at least one more order of business before we have our claxberry pie."

Now it was Rhynt's turn to beam. "The surprise?"

Zyrx feigned confusion. "Surprise? What surprise?"

Rhynt looked crestfallen. "You know, you said there would be a surprise for me."

Zyrx threw his head back and laughed. "Yes, yes, just teasing a bit."

He reached under the table and pulled out two sacks. "Here," he said, "one for each of you."

Rhynt jumped at her sack and peeked inside. "Oh, what wonder is this?"

"Go on, girl, take it out," said Zyrx.

She pulled out the metal object, a fully articulated metal foot attached to a lifelike but gleaming lower leg, with a weir skin cushion at its end, along with binding straps.

"It may take some getting used to," said Zyrx, "but even the toes bend the way toes bend, so your walk will appear natural. You can say goodbye to that limp of yours. In fact, I think with practice you'll be able to run like the wind."

Rhynt rushed around the table and gave Zyrx a big hug. "Oh sir, oh sir," was all she could manage through her tears of joy.

"Think nothing of it, girl. Go, try it on." He turned to Calax. "Are you not interested in your own surprise, warrior?"

Calax was shaking his head. "I know you are a fine craftsman, Zyrx, but I doubt anything you could make could surpass the artistry of my hand."

"Well, then," said Zyrx, "this truly will be a surprise for you. Come on, pull it out."

Calax pulled the metal hand and partial arm out of the bag. "Why, it looks just like my wooden hand."

"Yes, yes, but it's metal. Much stronger, and if you would but try it on, I think you'll find its articulations and movements far surpass what can be done with mere wood."

"We'll just see, then," said Calax. He rolled up his sleeve and tugged the arm off, strapping the new arm in its place, and flexing the metal fingers. "It is magnificent. How did you do this?"

Zyrx beamed. "I have skills, you see, but it's the merilium that makes the difference."

Calax continued to flex his new fingers in front of his face, trying his best to find a flaw, some movement they were incapable of, but there was none. "Incredible, and if anything, it is lighter than wood."

Zyrx smiled. "Again, that would be the merilium. Light, but very strong. You can take a mighty blow now and still not lose your hand."

Zyrx started to say more, but Rhynt was now running around the room, her new foot in place. "Look at me, Calax, I can run."

"Yes, yes," said Zyrx, "now stop for a moment, if you will."

Rhynt pulled up and sat back down at the table. Zyrx motioned Calax to sit back down as well. "Now, there's one more surprise." He looked Calax in the eye. "And not a pleasant one where you're concerned, Calax."

"Oh?"

Zyrx turned to Rhynt. "She won't be able to stay after all."

Rhynt was delighted. "Yes!"

Calax started to object but Zyrx held up a hand. "I received a bird, with an urgent message. It seems my services are needed elsewhere."

Calax shook his head. "Elsewhere? Well, can't you take her with you? She'd be safer with you than with me."

"No, I wouldn't," said Rhynt, interrupting. "And now that I have such a fine sword and a wonderful new foot, I can hold my own against any man."

Calax snorted. "As if."

"At any rate," said Zyrx, "she can't come with me, and that's final."

Calax took a deep breath and let it out slowly. "Could she stay here then while you're away? She knows the place now, and the hill tigers seem to like her well enough to protect her from harm."

Rhynt leaned across the table. "Say no, Zyrx."

Zyrx nodded. "Yes, the answer to that is also no. She would have no protection here because the hill tigers are coming with me."

Calax relented. "Very well." He turned to Rhynt. "You'd best get a good night's sleep. We leave at first light."

Zyrx held up a hand. "One last thing. No, two."

Calax sneered at him. "What, another surprise?"

"Yes and no."

"Out with it, then."

Zyrx pulled the yellow arrow out from under the table.

"Hey," said Calax. "How did you come by my arrow?"

Zyrx snorted. "You both sleep fitfully but soundly. I could have made off with everything you own, and you'd both still be fighting demons in your sleep."

Calax nodded. "So what about the arrow?"

"I thought it no harm to test it against my own arrows."

"And?"

"And it is far superior."

Calax leaned toward Zyrx, who had his full attention now. "In what way?"

"In every way, from tip to shaft to fletch to notch, it's just better. On the same pull, it goes nearly twice as far as my arrows and hits with an incomparable force."

Calax frowned. "Great, but how does that help me?"

"Ah," said Zyrx, rubbing his hands together. "That which can be built can be *copied*."

"Yes?"

"And improved upon."

Rhynt jumped in. "Let me guess. Your merilium?"

"Smart girl," said Zyrx, pulling another arrow from under the table.

Even Calax had to smile. "The only difference I see is the color of the arrow."

Zyrx nodded vigorously. "In appearance, yes. I stained this one with the sap of the coury tree, which gives it its deep green luster. But the important difference, as our smart girl has already pointed out, is that its merilium tip hits harder and penetrates deeper than the tip of the yellow arrow."

Calax looked puzzled. "That's all well and good, Zyrx, but how does this one little arrow help me?"

Zyrx chuckled and turned to Rhynt. "Your warrior friend could use some of your brains."

Rhynt giggled as Zyrx turned back to Calax. "Because, when you go to your beds this night, you will each find a quiver with twenty such arrows, along with bows of merilium made just for you."

Calax's eyes went wide. "Well, now, that's different."

Zyrx turned to Rhynt. "And you, young lady, shall also find a tunic and trousers befitting a warrior, as well as a breast plate of merilium."

Calax began laughing.

"What?" said Zyrx. "What's so funny?"

"Nothing. It's just that your merilium can be used for so many things. I just wondered if it could be drunk like a tonic."

Zyrx started to laugh, then had a thought. "Hmm."

12

In Rhynt's dream they are running, girl and hill tigers alike over a vast, empty plain, red dust whirling up from them as they run with a speed and grace imagined but never seen, toward a forest that grows taller and greener with every stride, the enemy's boastful shouts growing louder, more distinct, the white puffs of their collected breaths blooming and trailing around them as the sky grows dim from a thousand yellow arrows rising, arcing, and descending with a singular sibilant hiss that forces a single word from the girl's mouth: "Charge!"

Rhynt woke with a start, the only sounds in the room the heavy breathing and mumbled words coming from the warrior sleeping in the far too small bed against the far wall and the soft purrs of the hill tigers curled up near her bed. *What a dream!* Still, she wondered what it would be like, a battle, and how she would behave. Would she really charge? She sighed and closed her eyes. That would be a thought for the light of day, such as it was in this dark forest world. For now, she would try her best to dream of a fine roast rabbit.

In Calax's dream, Salibar loomed over him, stick in hand, putting him to the test once more. Calax knew every wrong answer would mean a painful strike from his master.

"So, let's go over it again," said Salibar. "You are forced into a corner. What do you do?"

"Push back?"

The stick came down hard on his good hand. "No, you die. You die. Never let yourself be forced into a corner."

Calax nodded sheepishly and looked down at the floor.

"Now," said Salibar, "if given a choice, which wall do you race for?"

Calax knew this and smiled. "The wall with the hearth."

Salibar seemed pleased but pressed further. "And why do you choose the hearth?"

Calax smiled again. "Because there will be weapons, the iron tools for tending the fire."

"And which of these tools will you choose?"

Calax thought about it. Not the shovel. Not the tongs. "The long pointy thing with the hook?"

Salibar frowned and began tapping his stick on his palm. "Is that a question?"

"No, no sir. I definitely want the pointy thing."

Salibar nodded, pleased. "And what about the wall of bookshelves? Any advantage in running there?"

Calax knew this one, too. "Not the best choice, but the shelves can be climbed to avoid an opponent or gain advantage."

"Good," said Salibar. "And what about the wall with the table and benches?"

"The benches and tables can be climbed or used as obstacles to prevent an opponent's approach."

"And?"

And? Was there more to the answer? And then it came to him. "Yes, the chandelier. I can get higher."

Salibar began tapping his stick. "Are you sure you can jump that high?"

"Yes."

"Good, and when you reach it, do you just hang there?"

"No, my opponent could strike at my legs. I have to climb atop it."

"Yes, and then what? Do you swing for the window?"

"No, the window is too far away."

"What then?"

Calax beamed. "I stay there."

Salibar raised his stick and began lashing out at Calax, striking him repeatedly on the head. "No, no, no!"

Calax woke, arms flailing, trying to avoid the blows that wouldn't come. The room was dark, but he could hear the steady purrs of the hill tigers and the soft snore of his new companion in arms. He wondered whether she would perform well when the time came. Or would she be like him as a boy, stuck atop a chandelier, not knowing the answer. The answer? He thought about it a little more, and then it came to him. "Ah, yes, that's what I'd do."

He knew it was useless trying to get back to sleep, so he sat up and began dressing. He would let her sleep until he had coaxed the hearth fire back to life. And tea. He'd make some tea.

13

Rhynt woke to the sound of clattering dishes and muffled voices coming from the low-ceilinged greatroom, where she knew Calax and Zyrx were eating breakfast and no doubt talking about the coming adventure.

Her new clothing and armor were laid out for her on the floor near her bed, so after affixing her new lower leg and foot, she set to trying them on. The tunic was just right, but the trousers, a garment alien to her, were more of a struggle. Eventually, though, she managed to tug them on and lace them tight at the waist. The trousers were cold and stiff at first, but the more she moved, the suppler and warmer they became. It was as if they had a life of their own and were trying their best to conform to her body. She knew if she asked, Zyrx would no doubt credit their suppleness to his magical metal, merilium.

The breastplate was a work of art, and like her tunic and trousers, the same color green. She would have no trouble blending with the forest, but when they emerged from the trees, well, that would be a different matter. She held the breastplate up to the light. The outside of each small cup for her breasts was engraved with the head of a hill tiger, and just below, on the area that would protect her stomach was an image of three hill tigers running at speed with a young girl that could only be her. *My dream? How could he know?*

She slipped the breastplate over her head and adjusted the drawstrings on each side until the breastplate was tight but not too tight. After a near futile search, she finally found her boots under her bed, where they had no doubt been pushed by one of the hill tigers during the night. She tugged them on, placing a dagger in each boot. Then she attached the belt and scabbard around her waist and made sure the sword could be freed with ease. She pulled it out and waved it about. "I will call you *Snit*, after the sound you make at the end of each arc."

Satisfied, she picked up her new bow and the quiver of arrows, and walked into the greatroom.

Calax and Zyrx were hunched over a small map laid upon the table, talking in earnest, but when they caught sight of Rhynt, they both laughed.

"What's so funny?" said Rhynt.

Calax held his arms out to show her his own new clothing. "You see, we're twins."

Rhynt looked at Zyrx. "I think you mean triplets."

Zyrx chuckled. "Yes, yes, I figured so long as I was making two sets, I may as well make three. It's been a time since I had new clothes." He held up his arms. "What do you think?"

Rhynt smiled at him. "You cut a fine figure, sir."

"Indeed, I do," said Zyrx, turning back to Calax and the map and motioning Rhynt to come see.

The map was made of weir deer skin that had been shaved and rubbed smooth. Lines and dots of many colors went this way and that, with little squiggles indicating streams and sharp pointy things marking the location of mountains. A large expanse of blue no doubt indicated a vast sea, and beyond it an island with a tall castle, which was marked *Enturia*.

"Now," said Zyrx, "As you see, there are many paths to the sea, but they all lead to but one single port. That's where you'll have to be most careful. Once there, you need to make your way to the docks and find the ugliest boat and the ugliest man you're ever likely to see, and they're both named Marthe."

Rhynt pointed at the map and a road that seemed to go straight from the edge of the forest to the port town. "It looks like we could save a full day by taking this road."

Zyrx frowned. "If you were going to a feast, yes, but you would not last a day on that road. No, I have told Calax the safest way, and I don't want to waste another minute explaining it to you. Now, your horses await, so be off with you."

Rhynt took a step back. "Go? I haven't had breakfast."

Zyrx picked up a small satchel from the table and tossed it to her. "Bread, a pear, and a gourd of tea. You can eat along the way. Now, off with you. Shoo."

Rhynt reluctantly threw the satchel over her shoulder and walked to the door, where her new friends, the hill tigers, were pacing back and forth. She gave each a pat on the head and a stroke of the back. "I'll miss you, but have no fear, I'll return one day to spend more time with you."

Calax followed, giving the tigers a wide berth. They hadn't exactly warmed to him, so he wasn't sure what they would do if he had even come close to them. At the door, he turned to say goodbye to Zyrx.

"Be safe, my friend, and may your journey be fruitful."

"Yes," said Rhynt. "And thank you."

Zyrx nodded and winked. "And may you find what you seek."

Calax tapped Rhynt on the arm. "Come, it's time."

They walked outside, where the horses waited, each with new armor of the same green.

Rhynt whistled. "The man is a magician."

"Ha!" said Calax. "That he is."

They climbed into their saddles and headed toward the forest, each turning back to wave at Zyrx, who stood just outside the door, watching them go.

A voice behind him beckoned him back inside. He made one final wave and went in.

D'Abo Pourcrey, the Red Monk, awaited him at the table. "You have done well, Zyrx."

Zyrx frowned. "I fear I have sent them to their deaths."

The Red Monk shrugged. "To their *fate*, which could be good or bad or something in-between."

Zyrx shook his head. "I don't know. Calax can handle himself, but I'm not sure about the girl."

The Red Monk chuckled. "Oh, don't you worry about her. She has all the skills she needs, and in the end, will know what she must do."

Zyrx was puzzled. "Know what she must do? And what would that be?"

The Red Monk smiled and looked at the steaming kettle on the hearth. "Is there going to be breakfast, or not? I have a pigeon to send, and would like to do it on a full stomach."

Zyrx rolled his eyes and reached for the ladle.

14

The journey through the forest had been slow and easy, at least to Rhynt's mind. Calax seemed in no hurry, even with the roars of Zyrx's hill tigers in their ears the whole way. Or perhaps he was in no hurry *because* of the hill tigers. Once they left the woods, the hill tigers would no doubt retreat back to the hearth in the hill, leaving them unprotected and out in the open.

And so it was. When they emerged from the forest, the roars went silent. Rhynt turned in her saddle and peered back into the darkness, wondering whether she would ever see them again.

"I'll miss them," she said, turning back to Calax, who was riding just ahead of her.

"Aye, lass, they seem to like you."

Rhynt smiled. "They do, don't they?"

Calax said nothing for some moments, then slowed Gash and pulled up beside her. "Perhaps you should return to the hearth on the hill now."

"No, I would follow you."

"There will be danger, and I'm not sure I can protect you from all harm."

Rhynt scowled at him. "Where you go, I go."

Calax shook his head and laughed. "You are a wonder."

"Oh, in what way, sir?"

"Your determination."

Rhynt nodded. "Aye, but no more than your own. Why do you race toward danger? Shouldn't you be fleeing gray men and yellow arrows?"

Calax shrugged. "I'm a sellsword. My whole life has been about danger."

"Yes, but you were paid for it. That's not the case this time. You just came from a war. Shouldn't you just be resting in a safe place until you're called again?"

"That was the plan, but that note from the gray man's pouch changed all of that. I would know the man who started all of this and have him at the tip of my sword."

Rhynt shook her head. "Whoever he is, he has men, many men. The tip of your sword could face a hundred pointed at you."

"And yet I would still know the why of it. Why is he searching for me? Why are the gray men trying to kill me?"

"All good questions," said Rhynt, nodding.

Calax pulled the map out from under his breastplate and gave it a quick glance. "We'll need to stay along the treeline until we come to a bridge." He looked up at the sun. "We should get there before evening."

Rhynt grimaced. "It cannot come too soon. These saddles are made for hardened arses."

Calax laughed and urged Gash forward. "Then let's get to it."

Gash went from a walk to a trot to a gallop in an instant, leaving Rhynt and her horse behind.

She shouted after them. "Wait for me!"

She kicked her legs back onto the horse, causing him to rear and then race away toward Calax, who had already disappeared over a hill.

That man!

15

The day stretched on, hills yielding to plains, yet the forest was always there to their left as they rode, each trapped in their own thoughts, each dealing with pains of the saddle, each trying to coax their tired horses a little farther. By nightfall, the trees began to thin, and they could hear the roar of a mighty river up ahead.

"Can't be far now," said Calax.

"I don't see any bridge," said Rhynt. "Where is it?"

Calax stood in his stirrups and peered into the darkness. "By the gods!"

"What?"

"Over there, along the ridge. A campfire."

Rhynt squinted as she scanned the ridge. "Ah, I see it."

Calax pulled up and dropped down from Gash. "Come, we'll have to walk from here."

Rhynt balked. "What? To where?"

"To the fire."

"But there could be gray men there."

"We have no choice. They block the way to the bridge."

"Can't we just go around or take another route?"

"No, enough talk. Get down from your horse."

Rhynt persisted. "No, let me have a look at the people around the fire."

Calax snorted. "Oh, fine, girl. And how do you propose to do that?"

"I know things. Here, hold my reins whilst I see."

Calax grabbed the reins of her horse and watched as she crossed her arms over her chest and seemed to fall asleep sitting up.

"Two people sit at the fire," she began. "A man and a woman, both warriors but with different sigils and dress. They are not grays."

"How do you do this?" said Calax.

"Quiet. The man is as wide as he is tall, with a thick black beard striped with blue dye."

Calax's eyes widen. "Does he have both eyes?"

Rhynt shook her head. "Just one, icy blue, with a brown leather patch over the other."

"I know such a man. We fought together at the Battle of Whent Hill. By any chance is his nose covered in warts?"

Rhynt nodded. "Aye, it is, and it's twisted to the left a bit."

"Ha! He got that from a battle-axe. He be none other than Blusk, a sellsword of some repute, and a friend."

"The woman seems to be angry with him. She keeps pointing in all directions."

"Tell me about her."

"Okay. She's taller than the man by a head, and lithe as a hill tiger. She has dark skin, almost black, and her hair is like dark honey, longer than mine and curled up and fastened to the top of her head with a strand of animal teeth of some kind."

"Hog's tusks," said Calax. "And there can only be one such woman. That is Phendour, also a sellsword, and a true hero of the Battle of Whent Hill. The things she did. By the gods, it will be good to speak with her once more."

"So we go to the fire?"

"Yes, but cautiously. Get down from your horse. We'll need to walk in. Say nothing to startle them. Phendour is a fine archer, and could take us down in the blink of an eye."

Rhynt slid down from her horse as quietly as she could and began following Calax toward the fire. She should have been scared, but her only thought was food and a warm fire.

16

Phendour pulled her dagger out and waved it in front of Blusk's face, which made the warrior jump back.

"Hold, Phendour! This be an argument, not a battle."

Phendour stuck the dagger into the ground. "Then stop pointing that sword of a fat finger in my face, you lummox."

"See here, I was just trying to make a point, that a fire is a bad idea in these parts. Who knows what it will attract?"

She scowled at him. "Well, I don't give a dead fool's arse about it. I'm hungry, and I'll have my piece of this river rat *now.*"

She started to reach for the rat, which had turned a pleasing brown on the spit, but a sound behind her made her flinch. Someone was out there in the darkness. She rolled away from the fire, grabbed her bow, and began to nock an arrow, but then suddenly stopped.

Someone was singing, the words becoming clearer by the second.

"There was an old sellsword from Calibedax . . ."

She knew immediately who the voice belonged to, and answered with the next line of the song. "Who had a wife like a battle-axe."

And now Blusk was on his feet, laughing. "And whenever he tried to swing his sword . . ."

Calax finished it as he walked up to them. "She'd cut him down with a cold, sharp word."

The three of them met at the fire, with whoops and hugs all around. And then they all turned and looked at Rhynt, who was standing off twenty feet or so, holding the reins of the horses.

Phendour squinted at her. "And who be this little green warrior?" She turned back to Calax. "Don't tell me you've taken this sprout to wife."

Calax laughed. "No, Phendour, if ever I take a wife, it surely shall be you."

Phendour threw back her head and laughed. "As if you could handle one such as me."

Blusk interrupted them. "Well, who she be?"

Rhynt tugged at the horses and moved closer to the fire. "They calls me Rhynt."

Blusk chuckled. "*Runt* is it?"

Before he could get out another word, Rhynt had rolled toward Blusk, rising with a dagger to his throat. "The name is *Rhynt.*"

Blusk nodded quickly. "Rhynt it is then. Put up your dagger, lass, I meant no offense."

She dropped the dagger to her side. "As I said, my name is Rhynt and like Calax here, I am on a quest."

Phendour was trying her best not to laugh. "Child, child, what *quest* might that be that brings you to our fire this night?"

Rhynt looked down at the spitted meat. "Is that rat?"

Phendour nodded. "Yes, and a noble quest it is. Here, lass, sit by the fire and have your fill while I set another to cooking."

Rhynt dropped down and pulled the spitted rat from the fire. The meat was juicy and pink, and maybe too hot, but she popped a piece into her mouth anyway.

"How is it?" said Phendour.

Rhynt already had a second and a third piece in her mouth, enough to prevent her from speaking, so she just nodded and continued with her private feast.

Phendour put a second spitted rat on the fire, and turned back to Calax and Blusk. "Now, what *really* brings you to our fire?"

Calax began his tale of the gray men and yellow arrows, Phendour and Blusk exchanging strange glances, seeming to grow more and more alarmed with each word.

"We have seen both," said Blusk.

"Yes," said Phendour. "We came upon a group of them. Three on horse and one in a cart, wounded by just such an arrow."

Calax shook his head in wonder. "The yellow arrows seem to follow the gray men."

"And the gray men seem to be following you," said Blusk. "They asked about you."

Phendour laughed and slapped her leg. "But they think Halfhand means you have half a hand, and not—not—what you have."

She looked down at his new hand. "Speaking of which, what in the realm of wonders is this?"

Calax tugged off the glove to reveal the shimmering black hand and its finely articulated fingers, which he proceeded to demonstrate were as nuanced in their movements as any real fingers would be.

"Wow," said Blusk. "I doubt that anyone would suspect that wasn't real—when gloved, of course."

Phendour reached out and touched Calax's metal hand. "Who made this? I thought your wooden hand a marvel, but this, this is magical."

"I have a friend, a blacksmith and armorer of some repute. Perhaps you have heard of him. Zyrx is his name."

Blusk was drop-jawed. "What? The mythical dwarf in the wood?"

Calax chuckled. "He is no myth, but he is magical. He crafted the hand, as well as swords and armor for me and the girl. Oh, and her foot. You would not know it to look at her, but she is as crippled as I am."

Phendour turned and looked back at Rhynt, who was picking the bones of the first rat while eyeing the second one as it browned and sizzled on the spit. "You would never know it, the way she moved against Blusk."

"Aye," said Blusk. "She was as fluid in her movements as any sellsword."

"At any rate," said Phendour, "with this fine new clothing and armor, I doubt anyone would even stop you upon the road."

Calax shook his head. "I'm not so sure. They seemed to spot me well enough at a tavern a ways back." He looked over at Rhynt. "That's when I had the pleasure—or *burden*—of picking up that little girl's company."

"Who is she, anyway?" said Phendour.

Calax sighed. "She is, or rather was, a servant to d'Abo Pourcrey, the Red Monk."

Blusk whistled softly through his teeth. "I thought he was dead."

"Far from it," said Calax. "I was talking with him at the tavern when we were jumped by gray men."

"Who you dispatched," said Blusk.

"Aye."

"And the monk?" said Phendour.

"Disappeared. Vanished. There one second and gone the next."

"Leaving you with the girl," said Phendour.

"Exactly." He looked over at Rhynt, who was pulling meat from the second rat. "Hey, girl, leave some for us."

Phendour leaped to her feet and strode to the fire, pulling the spitted rat away from Rhynt. "There's *three* of us who've had none, deary."

"Oh," said Rhynt. "Sorry."

Phendour shook her head, scolded Rhynt with an annoyed grunt, and then turned back to Calax and Blusk, holding out the spit so each of them could pull off pieces of the succulent meat.

Calax looked from one to the other. "So, what brings you two to this fire in the middle of nowhere? The last we talked, you were going to take a break."

Blusk swallowed a hunk of meat and wiped his mouth. "We were, but then someone made us a fine offer for our services."

"Aye," said Phendour. "We were stopped along the road by a man posing as a beggar. Called us by name and offered us a job providing security for a prince in a land called Enturia."

Calax's eyebrows shot up. "Enturia. That is where we're going, to find the man who wants me dead. Tell me more about this prince."

"His name is d'Bedo Brendyl," said Blusk, "but he refers to himself as the Green Monk, though it is probably more important that he is the son of King Braque."

"And we were given gold," said Phendour.

Blusk beamed. "Twenty pieces each for the road, and another twenty a month once we arrive in Enturia."

"And all we have to do is protect the prince," said Phendour.

Calax chewed at another piece of rat. "From what?"

Blusk shrugged. "I don't know."

"But for so much gold," said Phendour, "what does it matter?"

Calax nodded. "A prince, a king, and a man who seeks my death."

"Yes," said Phendour. "It appears we're on the same path for different reasons."

Blusk shrugged. "Still, it will be good to have your company along the way. And perhaps the prince can throw you some coin as well."

Calax smiled. "I would not turn away from coin, but first I must deal with the man who would kill me."

"Aye," said Phendour, "but speaking of first things, the first thing we need to do is get some rest. There's a long road ahead of us tomorrow."

"Right," said Blusk, and we'll need our strength to deal with the troll."

Calax's eyes went wide. "What?"

"Oh," said Phendour. "I guess we should have mentioned this earlier, but the bridge we must cross is guarded by a troll."

Calax sighed. "Oh, great."

17

In the dream, Calax was fighting his way up Whent Hill, the sounds of men's screams and the clank and clash of steel on steel ringing in his ears. Faces appeared before him and were then gone as he swung his sword into and through them, lopping off arms, noses, and heads as he climbed steadily toward the top, where the Ichthians were making their last stand.

After three days of hard fighting to get through the Isthmus of Dray, a narrow stretch of land joining Icthia with Olasia, he and the Olasians who'd hired him had made their way onto the wider lands and through the marshes, leaving thousands of dead in the muck, men joined together forever in death, their sigils now of no importance, even to the carrion birds wheeling above them, biding their time.

Only one obstacle remained in his path, a fearsome troll with arms and legs the size of full-grown men. The beast was easily twelve feet tall, and the mace he swung was as tall and heavy as Calax himself.

He knew there was only one way to kill him. They'd have to get him off his feet. Come up behind him somehow and throw a rope around his legs, so a score of men could trip him. Then they could slice off his club arm, climb atop him, and deal the death blow.

Calax looked to his right, where he could see Blusk dispatching another Icthian warrior. "Blusk, the rope!"

Blusk didn't hear him, so he screamed again. "Blusk, to me!"

Blusk shook him awake. "What in the gods are you screaming about? Quiet now, you'll wake the troll."

Calax sat up and looked around. "A dream."

"More like a nightmare, if you ask me," said Phendour, coming up beside them. "Whent Hill again, was it?"

"Aye," said Calax.

Phendour nodded. "I have them as well. It was a terrible time."

"Me, too," said Blusk. "Was it the troll you were fighting? You said something about a rope."

Calax nodded. "Yes, and speaking of which, do we have one?"

"Aye," said Phendour, we laid it out last night at one end of the bridge. Covered it with dirt. All we need to do is get the troll from under the bridge and then we just tug at the rope and he'll go down right quick, I suspect."

"Good," said Calax. He looked around. "Where's Rhynt?"

"She's gathering firewood. Thought it best that we eat before we take on the troll."

Calax nodded. "Let's just hope it's not our last meal."

Phendour laughed ruefully. "Indeed."

"So," said Calax, "where is this bridge we must cross?"

Blusk motioned him to stand. "Come, have a look. It's just down the hill."

Calax stood and followed Blusk and Phendour to the crest of the hill. And then they all just stopped, stunned. Rhynt was standing at one end of the bridge, the troll hovering over her, a club that looked like it had once been the stump of a tree held high over its head, ready to strike. Rhynt was motioning the troll forward, cocking a finger again and again to beckon him closer. The troll grew closer and leaned over to hear what she was saying.

Calax turned to Phendour and Blusk. "Quickly, to horse!"

They all turned as one and raced for their swords and their horses. Blusk started to put a saddle on his horse, but Calax stopped him. "No time. Ride!"

The jumped on their horses and rode bareback to the crest of the hill and down, screaming to get the attention of the troll.

But the troll was gone. Rhynt was standing at the bridge, watching them charge down the hill, wondering what all the commotion was about. When they arrived and jumped off their horses, all she could think to say was, "Where are you going? I thought we were going to have breakfast."

Calax rushed up to her. "Are you all right? Where's the troll?"

Rhynt cocked her head. "You mean Bebo?"

"Bebo?" said Calax.

"Aye," said Rhynt, "that's his name, and he's a friendly sort if you ask me. Here, why do you have your swords? You weren't planning on killing him, were you?"

Blusk sheathed his sword and came up to her. "Aye, we were, and it's an odd thing that you're still alive."

"Yes," said Phendour. "Why aren't you dead?"

Rhynt looked at them like they were crazy. "Dead? That's just silly."

"I'm having trouble understanding what just happened, Rhynt," said Calax. "What did you say to the troll?"

"Oh, I asked him if he'd like to hear a joke."

Calax was incredulous. "You what? Why on earth would you do that?"

Rhynt cocked her head. "But don't you know? Trolls love jokes, particularly jokes they've never heard before."

"What?" said Phendour. "Who told you that, child?"

Rhynt shrugged. "My master, d'Abo Pourcrey, the Red Monk. He knows things, and he taught me some. Not all, mind. Calax rescued me before he could finish his training of me."

"Wait, wait," said Calax. "Back to the joke. What was it and where is the troll now?"

"Oh, I can't tell you the joke. It's only meant for the ears of trolls. It would make no sense to you, because it makes no sense to me. And I swore never to reveal it to any man or woman."

"Um, okay," said Calax, "but where's the troll?"

"Oh, him. Well, the thing about new jokes is that trolls love to share them. It's kind of a contest for them, telling the best jokes. So Bebo has gone off to tell his friends the joke. He was quite happy when he left."

Calax, Phendour, and Blusk looked at each other and then stared back at her.

"So," she said. "Are we having breakfast, or what?"

18

Rhynt wasn't sure why Phendour and Blusk, and even Calax, were giving her strange looks. It could have been how she handled the troll—she couldn't believe they were going to kill him just to cross the bridge—but she suspected it was the fire. Phendour and Blusk had leaped back, startled, when she had said her words over the newly collected wood and it had burst into flames.

Whichever it was, the strange looks continued through breakfast and well into the morning as they rode across the bridge and headed back into a forest that Zyrx's map said was called Blackling. Rhynt had expected a dark forest much like the one Zyrx lived in, where the light could barely penetrate the canopy. But this collection of trees was so widely spaced that the underbrush had grown to the height of men. The challenge here was not darkness, but the constant need to cut their way through the vines and sticker bushes that clawed at the sides of the horses.

After several hours of slow progress, they made their way into a sunny meadow with flowers of every color and a shallow creek cutting the meadow in twain.

Calax raised his arm to bring them all to a stop. "Let's rest here," he said. "There's food for the horses and water for all."

They climbed down from their horses and let the reins drop to the ground, a signal the horses knew freed them to nibble on the grass and blossoms and drink from the creek.

"Shall I start a fire," said Rhynt. "I have a hunger."

Calax shook his head. "No, we're too much in the open here. The smoke would give us away to anyone following."

Rhynt sighed with disappointment. "But we'd hear them coming for miles. No man or beast can get through those brambles without a lot of noise and cries of pain."

Calax laughed. "You may be right, but we'll have to make do on dried meat and hard bread."

"I don't like hard bread. It bends my teeth."

"Soak it in the creek," said Phendour. "Calax is right. And for my money, we'd right make it quick here."

"Aye," said Blusk. "I always get a bad feeling in open spaces."

"Oh, you people," said Rhynt in a huff. She strode off to her horse, retrieved a large hunk of hard bread, and went to soak it in the creek.

Calax turned to the others. "We'd best do the same. From the position of the sun, I'd say we are still hours away from our goal this day."

"And that would be?" said Phendour.

Calax pulled the map out from behind his breastplate. "There's an old hunter's lodge hard upon a mountainside. Mostly fallen down, no roof to speak of, but the stone walls will provide some protection."

"All right," said Phendour. "But first I'm going to soak my feet in that creek and have a chat with our little friend."

Calax shrugged. "Suit yourself, but we leave as soon as we've eaten. Don't get caught with your boots off."

"I hear you," said Phendour, striding away to fetch food and join Rhynt at the creek.

Calax turned to Blusk. "Let's eat and fill our gourds."

Blusk nodded. "Right, right, I'll make it quick. The flowers are beautiful, but I don't like this place."

"Nor I," said Calax, scanning the meadow and the encircling forest. "Remember that feeling we would get just before a battle?"

"Aye," said Blusk with a shiver. "I called it the *Hush*. A calmness would set in and you became fully aware of yourself."

Calax nodded. "I could feel the blood rushing through me. Oh, and the silence. So deep there should have been another word for it. Even the horses seemed to know."

Blusk scanned the treeline. "I tell you, I feel it now, so for my money, I'd rather be on my horse and gone from here."

Calax looked over at Phendour and Rhynt. Both of them had their boots off and were splashing their feet, or at least three of them, in the cool waters of the creek.

He turned back to Blusk. "Give them a minute, and then, aye, let's get out of here."

Blusk started to say something, but an arrow black as night suddenly burst from his shoulder, and he fell to his knees with a groan. "I'm shot!"

Calax drew his sword and hunched down, waiting for more arrows or a charge by men on horse or foot. Then Phendour and Rhynt were by his side, barefoot, with swords drawn, all of them surrounding their fallen companion.

"Where are they?" said Phendour.

"I don't know," said Calax.

Rhynt dropped her sword to the ground, closed her eyes, crossed her arms over her chest, and began whispering words to herself.

"What are you doing?" said Phendour.

Calax answered. "Don't bother her. She's far-seeing."

Phendour's eyes went wide. "What?"

"She can see at great distances."

Phendour stood there, mouth open. And then Rhynt suddenly dropped her arms to her side and opened her eyes. "Odd. There is nothing and no one within a mile of us."

"That's good news," said Blusk, "but he seems to have left his calling card in me."

Phendour quickly kneeled down beside him. "Let me have a look at that."

"I don't think it's too bad," said Blusk, "but the impact dropped me to my knees. Whoever he is, he draws a powerful bow."

Rhynt looked down at Blusk's shoulder. "The arrow has missed the bone, and there's not too much damage to the muscle. Once we get it out, a little maiden's hair and mud will see you right."

Blusk looked up at her. "How could you know that?"

Rhynt shrugged. "I can see far, and I can see inside things, even people. It will be as I have said. You need not worry."

Phendour, Blusk, and Calax exchanged glances. Finally, Calax threw up his arms. "She has skills."

Rhynt beamed and started walking back to the creek. "I'll fetch our boots, Phendour. We're safe for now, but we best be on our way."

"Aye," said Calax. "Let's attend to Blusk, fill our gourds, and be on our way." He turned to Blusk. "I'll get some mud."

Blusk groaned. "Fine, but could someone please get this damned arrow out of me."

Before he had time to say another word, Phendour grabbed the arrow and yanked it out.

Blusk screamed "By the gods!"

"You're welcome," said Phendour, handing the arrow to Calax. "I'll fetch some maiden's hair from our friend Rhynt, and we'll see to it, Blusk."

Blusk took a deep breath and puffed it out. "A few inches down, and I'd be dead. Did he mean to kill me, or was this just a warning?"

"I don't know, but I'm thankful you're still with us." He looked down at the arrow. "Yellow arrows, black arrows, what does it all mean?"

19

They arrived at the ramshackle hunter's lodge just before dusk, giving them time to set the place in some order before nightfall. Overturned furniture, weathered to near white, littered the dirt floor, along with pots, pans, and the moldy skins and bones of unknown animals. There was no roof at all, giving the remaining windows no apparent worth. Still, its walls, which were taller by a head than Rhynt, provided some protection from the winds and whatever dangers lurked in the gathering darkness.

The first order of business was to set right a bed for Blusk, who had grumbled and groaned the whole way from the meadow. Rhynt got him settled in, covering him with some of the better looking skins.

"Don't say it," she said to Blusk. "I see you sniffing. Yes, they smell to the heavens, but they will keep you warm this night."

"Aye, lass, reminds me of my first wife."

Rhynt laughed. "Well, there's no wife for you tonight. Here, I'll go fetch some firewood and some herbs. A nice fire and a healing tea is just what you need."

"Wait," said Blusk, giving her an appraising look. "What be ye?"

"What do you mean?"

"These skills of yours. Be you a wizard or a witch?"

Rhynt shook her head and smiled. "Neither. I am nothing more than a runaway pisspot. My master was—*is*—a master in the arts of the d'Abo religion."

"The last of them, I hear."

"Yes, and these skills of mine, such as they are, were taught me by the monk. Not for my benefit, mind, but for his. His sight is failing, so he taught me to see far for him. And he taught me some remedies, again for his benefit."

"What else can you do?"

"Oh, this and that. Starting fires is easy for me. And as for that, I'd best be collecting kindling and wood before we lose the light."

Blusk cocked his head. "So I don't suppose you could just lay hands on my wound and heal it right here and now?"

Rhynt gave him an odd look, one that Blusk took to be evasive. "Come now, child, can you or can't you?"

She shook her head. "I didn't get that far in the lessons, and half magic is bad magic. Best keep to rest and a nice herb tea. Your wound will be less troublesome by morning."

"You can see that, can you?"

She nodded, turned, and left him there in his bed. The wind was picking up and she had things to do before the sun set completely.

She stepped outside the walls of the lodge, calmed herself, and began far-seeing. Not a human in sight, only birds, rabbits, weir deer, and squirrels. She would have loved to have seen three hill tigers racing towards her, but she knew they were miles and miles away on a quest with Zyrx.

She thought of the hearth in the hill and wondered whether she should have stayed behind, as Calax had wanted. The thought made her shake her head. No, she had things to do, and wood and herbs to collect.

She set about her business as the winds howled.

20

The night had been near sleepless for all of them, despite their decision to take turns on the watch. The howling of the winds and the cracking of branches kept everyone in a state of alertness and readiness, except for Blusk, whose snore alone could have kept them all awake. Rhynt's herbal tea had at least kept him still during the night, giving his shoulder time to heal.

At first light, Rhynt gathered more wood and set about building a breakfast fire within the walls of the lodge. Phendour grabbed her bow and quickly returned with a squirrel and two fine rabbits, which she skinned and dressed for the spit. The warmth of the fire and the smell of sizzling meat soon brought them all together around the fire, including Blusk, who greeted them with a big smile.

"What a night. I slept like a wee baby."

Calax rolled his eyes. "I guess, then, you didn't hear the wind and the cracking trees and your damnable snoring."

Blusk looked confused. "What?"

Phendour laughed. "I think Calax is trying to tell you that you and you alone slept with the gods last night. The rest of us had hardly a wink."

Blusk looked at them one by one. "I see. You do look a bit bedraggled."

"Indeed," said Rhynt. "How's the shoulder?"

Blusk slowly rotated his arm, and winced. "A bit better, but still hurting, I'm afraid."

Rhynt nodded. "Good. Have some meat and tea, and then I'll attend to your shoulder. The mud must be removed now to let the flies in."

Blusk's eyes went wide. "You don't mean . . ."

Rhynt gave him a quick nod. "I do. Maggots is just what you need now. They'll eat what's dead and clean the rest."

Blusk gave a little shiver. "By the gods, girl, do I have to?"

Rhynt chuckled. "If you hope to ever fight again, yes."

Blusk shuddered. "As you wish." He turned to Calax. "So, what's the plan?"

Calax pulled out the map and laid it on the ground so all could see. "We're here, and way over here are the docks where we're to meet this ugly boatman, Marthe."

Blusk was shaking his head. "So about two finger lengths to go?"

Calax laughed. "Aye, but at two days' ride to the finger, that's four days of riding, camping, and staying safe."

"Probably longer," said Phendour. "See here, that squiggle on the map is a mountain, is it not?"

"Aye," said Calax, "but this little circle here suggests a tunnel through it."

Rhynt put a finger on the map. "And what's this symbol here mean?"

"Ah," said Calax, "if I remember Zyrx's words correctly, that is a deep canyon, and just beyond that a waterfall. We must get by each, for there's no way around them."

Phendour puffed out her cheeks and sighed. "I don't much like the idea of a canyon. A few gray men with bows could pick us off with ease."

"I can far-see," said Rhynt. "If anyone approaches, we can deal with them."

Phendour smiled and tousled Rhynt's hair. "I'm beginning to like this one."

Rhynt beamed back at her. "And I you."

Calax laughed. "Enough of map reading. Let's eat our fill and be on our way. The day goes quickly, and we have miles to cover this day."

Eight hands, seven real, began tearing at the pitted meat.

21

The miles came and went, the four of them riding by the twos, with Calax and Phendour in front and Rhynt and Blusk trailing. They road quietly at first, Calax using the interval between Blusk's groans to set the pace. The smaller the interval, the slower the pace. But then Phendour dropped back and motioned Blusk forward, so she could ride along with Rhynt.

"We're about to come upon another bridge, Rhynt. Maybe a troll. Do you see anything?"

Rhynt concentrated. She could see the bridge, but there was only a squirrel running across it. No signs of a troll. "Nothing, we're good."

Phendour shouted out to Calax. "No troll."

Calax shouted back. "We'll get to our camp all the sooner then."

Phendour turned to Rhynt. "Thanks, I'll get back then."

She started to urge her horse forward, but Rhynt motioned her to stay. "Hold a minute. I would talk with you."

Phendour slowed her horse and settled in beside Rhynt. "All right, what?"

"Could you tell me more about Calax?"

Phendour gave her a questioning look. "I don't understand. He's a sellsword, same as me."

"No," said Rhynt. "I mean, how do you know him? What's he like? What motivates him to do what he does?"

Phendour shook her head. "Why?"

"I would know him better. Like you, I follow him into danger. I would know more of him, if you've a mind to tell me."

Phendour sighed. "There's not much to tell. I've known him about five years now. We've fought in many of the same battles, sometimes on opposite sides."

Rhynt's eyes grew wide. "Opposite sides? You mean you fought one another?"

"Not exactly. We sellswords tend to fight alongside one force or another, and more often than not sellswords focus on the local combatants, not their fellow sellswords."

Rhynt shook her head. "But what if you came face to face with him in a battle?"

Phendour chuckled. "I would probably be dead meat. That man is pretty much a berserker. He'll cut down anything and anyone in his path when blood's in his eyes."

Rhynt's mouth dropped open. "So that's what berserker means?"

"Yes, so I've always given him wide berth, even when we're fighting for the same side. It hasn't been difficult. My skill is the bow and his is the sword, so we are rarely positioned close to one another."

"I see," said Rhynt, shaking her head. "And what of the man between battles?"

Phendour gave her a wry smile. "My, you really do want to know him better. Well, I can't be of much help there. We sellswords tend to go our own ways after the dust settles, and as you've probably found out already, he is not a man to string words together, let alone emotions."

"Aye," Rhynt said with a heavy sigh. "He is a puzzlement."

Phendour laughed out loud. "Ha, he is indeed."

"Okay, okay, I guess I'll have to learn the rest by myself."

They rode silently for a few minutes, and then Phendour turned to her. "May I ask you a question?"

"Yes, of course."

"How did you come to be with Calax in the first place? I know about the incident at the tavern, but how did you come to be there with the Red Monk?"

Rhynt sighed. "Well, that's a long story."

"Come on, out with it. Start at the beginning."

Rhynt grew silent for a moment and then began. "I don't know who my parents are or were. I was raised by a guardian, an evil man with strange ideas about the world and my life in it."

"Who was he?"

"Just a man, and a year ago, I managed to escape his grasp."

"Interesting, so how did you end up with the monk."

Rhynt laughed. "He found me along the side of the road, hungry and much the worse for wear. I thought him kind at first. He fed me, clothed me, and offered his protection."

"And then?"

Rhynt shook her head. "And then he turned me into a servant, what he called his faithful pisspot."

"Out of the pot, into the fire."

Rhynt chuckled. "Exactly."

"So, Calax came along?"

"Yes, we made a bargain. He wanted information from the monk, and I wanted my freedom."

Phendour shook her head. "So now you're out of the pot, out of the fire, and headed into the unknown with companions you know little to nothing about."

Rhynt nodded. "Aye, that's pretty much it."

"Some advice then. Calax is not the fatherly type. Be friendly, but be wary."

"And don't get too close to him in a fight."

Phendour laughed. "Aye, child, you got that right."

22

They approached the bridge cautiously. As reliable as Rhynt's far-seeing had been, Calax wanted to check it out with his own eyes before proceeding across it. Trolls were not to be dallied with, even given their apparent sense of humor.

Finally, Rhynt spoke. "Let's go across. There's no trolls about."

Calax puffed out a breath. "Aye, so it seems. Let's pick up the pace then."

Calax coaxed Gash forward, the others following in short order. Once they were over the bridge, Rhynt suddenly pulled up and looked back, alarmed.

Calax pulled up. "What?"

"Riders," said Rhynt. "Moving fast. We need to hide, now!"

"To the trees," said Calax, kicking at Gash's haunches, sending him into a full gallop. The others followed, not stopping until they were safely in the darkness of the treeline.

Calax motioned them to dismount. "Here, behind the thicket."

They all dismounted and led their horses behind a tall thicket of grumbo, plants so thorny and dense that nothing could get through them, even light.

Calax turned to Rhynt. "Tell us what you see."

Rhynt sat down on the ground and closed her eyes. "Six riders, all dressed in black, riding fast. Warriors, certainly. They are just about to go over the bridge. Listen."

"Aye," said Blusk. "I hear them plain."

The sound of the galloping horses rose and fell as they raced across the bridge, passed the thicket, and continued on down the road.

"All right," said Calax. "Let's go."

"No, wait," said Rhynt. "More are coming. Oh, my."

"What?" said Calax.

"They come by the hundreds, the thousands. A sea of black, marching this way."

"Can you see any flags or sigils?" said Phendour.

"Yes, the flags are black, with a white patch of some sort at the center. Wait, not a patch, but a crow. A white crow."

Phendour shuddered. "I know them. Mystrosians. I sold my sword to them once. They are as greedy as they are merciless. My guess is they have designs on Enturia."

Calax looked puzzled. "But why do they march across Paudia? Wouldn't it make more sense to approach Enturia by sea?"

Phendour nodded. "It would, but perhaps they want to lock down the east Paudian docks to assure safe passage for their fleet."

"Yes, that would make sense." He turned to Rhynt. "Do you really see *thousands?*"

Rhynt nodded. "Yes, the land is black with them."

"So many," said Calax. "And with a fleet of perhaps thousands more."

Blusk whistled softly through his teeth. "Looks like bad times lay ahead for Enturia. Phendour, perhaps that's why they've hired us on."

Phendour nodded. "Yes, that makes sense." She thought about it a little more. "But we are just two. No, we were hired to provide security for something, not to do battle with an army."

Rhynt shook her head. "So what do we do? Go ahead or turn around?"

Calax looked at each of them. "We go ahead."

"But the army," said Rhynt.

"The advance riders will reach the docks long before we do, but an army is a slow-moving snail. We'll be in Enturia long before they make it to the docks."

Phendour wasn't so sure. "Will we? We can't use this road anymore. There will be more riders to come. It just isn't safe."

"Aye," said Blusk. "We're as good as stopped."

Calax pulled out the map. "There's another way. See here, we're in the Forest of Synt. Zyrx told me to avoid it, but I don't see that we have a choice, and it will save us at least a day in the bargain."

"Why did he say to avoid it?" said Phendour.

"He didn't give a reason. Just said not to."

Phendour turned to Rhynt. "Can you see anything in the forest?"

Rhynt closed her eyes and scanned the forest. "Animals, many animals. Maybe it was the great bears he feared. There are a lot of them."

Calax shook his head. "Great bears look fiercer than they are. As long as we do not startle them, we should be fine. Anything else?"

Rhynt suddenly gasped. "Yes, a tower, impossibly tall, made of wood."

"Wait a minute," said Phendour. "I've heard of that. There's a song the minstrels play, The Tower of Synt."

"A song?" said Rhynt.

"Aye," said Phendour. "Let me see now, it goes something like this: *Beware the tower in the forest of Synt, and the beastie there with teeth of flint. Give it wide berth by day or night or . . .* something, something, I forget."

"Oh, great," said Blusk. "A fine time to be forgetful."

Phendour threw up her arms. "Let me think on it. I'm sure it will come to me."

"Whatever," said Calax. "We'd best be going. Rhynt, how far is the tower?"

Rhynt closed her eyes and looked again. The tower had moved. "Wait, that's not possible, is it?"

"What?" said Calax.

Rhynt opened her eyes and pointed into the woods. "It's about three miles that way, and it's *moving.*"

23

Calax had three choices: they could proceed down the road according to the original plan laid out by Zyrx; they could backtrack with hopes of evading the Mystrosian army, and then proceed on an alternate path to the sea; or they could go deeper into the Forest of Synt and the unknown dangers of a tower that seemed to move on its own by means of magic. After consulting the map again and again, searching for a viable fourth option, Calax dropped the map to his side and sighed.

"We must go deeper into this forest."

Phendour shook her head. "Or we could give up this quest. I warn you, Calax, at some point we must face that army, and unless Enturia has an army twice its size, this will not end well, even for the Enturian who seeks your death."

"Aye," said Blusk. "And what about the wee girl here. We put her at risk with every step toward your goal."

Rhynt bristled. "Me, a *wee girl.* I should have left that wound of yours to fester. No, I say we go into these woods, avoid the tower as best we can, and make our way to the boatman Marthe, and then on to Enturia."

Calax nodded again and again as she spoke. "I do not think of you as a wee girl, and I doubt I would consider taking another step without you and your many skills." He turned to the others. "You may do as you wish, but Rhynt and I are proceeding through these woods. With her as our eyes, I think we'll be fine."

Phendour shook her head. "My father told me to never follow fools." She let out a long sigh, then smiled. "But then again, I never liked my father. I'm in."

Blusk rolled his eyes. "Very well, count me in as well."

Calax smiled. "Thank you, my friends. Now, Rhynt, lead the way."

Rhynt grabbed the reins of her horse and began walking through the underbrush, trying her best to avoid the thorns of the thickets. "This way. We'll have to walk the horses a mile before the forest opens up enough to ride."

"Okay," said Calax. "Stay clear of that tower."

"I'll do my best. Come, we need to proceed quickly."

The others grabbed the reins of their horses and began following Rhynt. Just as she said, the underbrush soon gave way to clear, flat land that permitted them to ride among the trees at speed.

They galloped at first, to put some distance between themselves and the tower, but Rhynt soon signaled them all to slow to a walk. "The tower is well away from us and proceeding in the opposite direction. Calax, is there somewhere up ahead where we might rest for the night?"

Calax pulled out his map and glanced up at the sun, which was approaching the high point for the day. "There is a river about four hours ride from here. We can camp there, then follow it to the sea."

Rhynt turned to Blusk. "How's the shoulder? Can you do that?"

Blusk laughed and whirled his arm around. "Your magic has done its work. I am fit to go, you wee wizard."

Rhynt smiled. "Okay, then, let's go."

They rode on, not realizing that behind them, deep in the woods, the tower had turned.

24

Four hours seemed like four days as they made their way through the forest and out onto the rock-strewn rolling hills that led to the river. Its roaring waters could be heard miles before they came upon it. Calax had hoped for an easy passage across it, but there was no way the horses could make it through those rapids.

They unsaddled the horses and set about making camp. Rhynt, as always, was tasked with finding firewood and starting a fire, while the others selected the best place to bed down, away from the soaking mist thrown up by the river. Firewood was scarce and wet, so it was well near dusk before Rhynt managed to get the cook fire going. Everyone was eager to roast the fish that Phendour had managed to catch with a special arrow she'd fitted with a long gut string for retrieving the arrow with each miss, as well as with each catch.

The fish were like none they had ever seen before, short and fat and striped with yellow and green bands, with large green eyes that seemed to almost pop out as they gasped for their final breaths. Phendour managed to spear eight of them on a single spit, and sat back with a sigh.

"I think I could eat them raw at this point," she said, stretching her arms out and yawning. "A long day."

"Aye," said Blusk. "I ate raw fish once, after a battle in the pouring rain. It wasn't half bad."

Rhynt grimaced. "Ick, how could you?"

Blusk laughed. "Sometimes, lass, you just have to make do. It's called survival."

Calax scanned the area in all directions. "Do you think we need to set a watch?"

Phendour turned to Rhynt. "Do you see anything?"

Rhynt closed her eyes and concentrated. "A large bear and her cubs, fishing about a mile downstream. Some goats and weir deer. A few mice."

"But no warriors?" said Calax.

"No."

Blusk chuckled. "What about our walking tower?"

Rhynt shook her head and opened her eyes. "Nothing for miles. It's probably wandering around in the forest."

"Hard to imagine," said Phendour. "I half wish we could have come upon it. You know, to see what makes it move."

"You have to be careful about wishes," said Calax. "Now, while we wait for the fish, let's have another look at the map and figure out how we get across this damned river."

He pulled the map out once more and began tracing various routes with his finger, grunting with each scenario. "I wasn't expecting this river to be so fierce. It's just a line on the map."

"Any bridges?" said Phendour.

"No, but if the map is correct, it narrows and races through a small canyon about two miles downstream."

Blusk nodded. "We could build a bridge across it."

Calax looked around. "If there's wood for it. I don't see much here."

"Ropes, then," said Phendour. "There's plenty of suitable grasses about."

Calax shook his head. "A rope bridge, with horses? How's that going to work?"

Phendour nodded. "Right, sorry."

"Maybe we could jump it," said Rhynt. "If the land is flat enough to give us a good start."

"Maybe," said Calax, stuffing the map back inside his breastplate. "We'll just have to wait and see, I guess."

Everyone fell silent and stared at the crackling fish.

"They're ugly as all get-out," said Blusk, "but they smell heavenly."

"Here," said Phendour, pulling the spit off the fire. "They're done by my reckoning. Have at it."

No one needed coaxing. They pulled the fish off the spit and began eating, slowly at first, but then ravenously, juices running down their chins until there were only bones for picking their teeth.

The edge to their hunger smoothed, they settled down on their bedrolls and let the sound of the river sing them to sleep.

In her dream, Phendour was standing on the shore of her girlhood home, the island of Didu in the South Sea. She was young again, no older than Rhynt, and her mother was with her, showing her the ins and outs of fishing with a bow and arrow. Behind them, well inland, she could see smoke rising from the Talmiss Volcano, as it always did.

"Phenny, pay attention," her mother said. "That volcano is all smoke and no thunder. I need you to focus on technique. Here, watch me, and remember, nock, draw, aim, and release."

Phendour smiled up at her mother and watched her as she drew her bow, let loose an arrow, and tugged on the line, which once again had a wriggling fish on the end, the arrow dead center through its silver flesh.

Her mother held up the fish. "You see?"

Phendour nodded. "Yes, mother."

"All right, let's see what you can do."

Phendour nocked an arrow and drew back her bow, just as her mother had taught her.

"Yes, that's it, child. Now remember the water distorts where the fish is."

"Yes, mother." She let loose the arrow and could tell by the wriggling on the line that she had a fish. She pulled the line in and gleefully held up the fish so her mother could see. "Look, I got one!"

But her mother had turned inland, a look of concern on her face as the ground began to shake and the volcano exploded.

In her dream, Rhynt was in a castle, sitting cross-legged on the cold stone floor of the throne room. Lords and ladies walked by her as if she weren't there. They were laughing and applauding about something, perhaps the old jester struggling with his juggling, balls falling and bouncing away. The crowd began gathering around a tall golden throne, which was empty save for a jewel-encrusted crown and scepter resting on a red velvet cushion.

And now she could see a large man striding to the throne, the crowd giving way as he took up the crown, placed it on its head, and lifted the scepter high.

"All hail," they began to cry. "All hail!"

In his dream, Blusk was fighting for his life, fending off swords, pikes, and maces, and dodging arrows, some aflame. No matter how hard he fought, he made no progress. Everyone seemed to be against him, men of every sigil attacking him again and again. They came at him so quickly and in such numbers that even he was not sure which side he was fighting on.

And then there was a roar behind him. A troll had him by the neck and was lifting him off the ground. He could only scream.

In Calax's dream, he was running along a roaring river, the sound of Salibar's shouts growing quieter with each stride. He need only get to the bridge to make good his escape, and then there would be no more cruel lessons. No more rebukes. No more of that awful room. Ever.

He was on the bridge now, each footfall resounding on the boards, the whole bridge shaking from his headlong flight down its length.

And then a new roar replaced the roar of the river. A troll climbed from under the bridge and blocked his way, a sneer growing on its face.

Someone screamed. Calax wondered whether it was his scream, and then the dream collapsed.

He threw off his blanket and reached over to shake Blusk, who was screaming about something. "Blusk, wake up."

Blusk startled and sat up. "By the gods, a troll had me. I could smell his foul breath."

Phendour and Rhynt were now on their feet, striding over to Blusk.

"I had a dream as well," said Rhynt, "but nothing to make me scream like that. I was in a castle, and there was this silly old fool trying desperately to juggle."

Calax shook his head, and smiled. "Sounds like a good dream to me." He turned back to Blusk. "Now, let me give you a hand up, Blusk. I had a dream this night, too, and it was also about a troll."

Phendour looked them over. "Well, you all seemed to have survived, as did I."

"What was your dream?" said Rhynt.

Phendour shook her head. "It doesn't matter. No trolls, though. I think the water fairies had their way with us this night."

Rhynt cocked her head. "Water fairies?"

"Aye, child," said Phendour, "they are the roar of the water and the silence of the mist, and they do play with our dreams."

Calax chuckled. "Pay no attention to her. There are no such things. We need to throw off such imaginings and focus on what's real."

Blusk tapped Calax on the shoulder and pointed away from the river. "Like that, you mean?"

A tall wooden tower was moving silently toward them.

They had all reflexively drawn their swords at the approach of the wooden tower, but after a few moments, dropped them to their sides. What use would they be against a tower of wood so high and so wide? It was square at its base, each side the length of three warhorses standing head to tail. As the structure rose, however, the dimensions grew steadily smaller, though it retained its square shape right to the top, which was taller than the tallest tree but no thicker than a thumb. The tower undulated and coiled as it moved, creating the effect of a moving spiral. Just how it moved was a mystery. No wheels or legs or any form of machinery could be seen at its base. It was in fact floating three feet above the ground, with no apparent means of support or propulsion.

"By the gods," said Blusk by way of understatement.

"Indeed," said Calax. "What manner of magic is this?"

The question hung in the air as the tower slowly dropped down to the ground in silence.

Rhynt began moving toward it, but Calax grabbed her by the arm to stop her. "No, child. We have no idea what this thing is about."

Rhynt struggled free. "I was just going to point out the little windows. See, hundreds of them, no bigger than a thumbnail."

Phendour bent over, peered at the windows, and then suddenly pulled back. "There are *faces* in the windows. Little faces, of people."

Calax took a step closer. "You are right. What in the name of all the gods can this be?"

High-pitched laughter from a thousand souls arose from the tower, and then a little door at its base opened. A tiny man in a wizard's cloak and cowl stepped into the sunlight and peered up at them. He seemed to be speaking, but his words were too soft to be heard. He shook his head, took out a wand, and pointed it at himself. The little man steadily and quickly became a big man, taller even than Calax, but thin and frail. His cloak seemed to be wearing him.

"Sorry," the wizard said. "I've been small for so long, I forget how soft my voice is in miniature."

Calax, Phendour, Blusk, and Rhynt just stood there, mouths agape, staring at him. If he was a wizard, he was an old wizard. His hair was long and white and flowed over his shoulders, and his white beard ended in a point at his waist. His eyes, which hid in layer upon layer of sagging skin, were an icy gray and a bit rheumy. His skin was near translucent. Yes, he was old. Very old.

The wizard laughed. "I see my entrance has no small effect on you."

Rhynt spoke first. "How did you do that? Get big I mean."

The wizard waggled his head. "Sorry, that's a secret."

Phendour stepped forward. "And who are all those people looking out the windows?"

"Ah," said the wizard. "Those are the Elves of Synt, trapped as you see them in this abominable monstrosity of wood."

"Trapped?" said Rhynt.

The wizard shrugged. "A witch's curse, and a strong one. None of the current generation of elves can even remember the why or the when of it, but it's witch's work for certain."

Calax frowned "What manner of curse?"

"Well, a binding curse, obviously," said the wizard with a chuckle that ended in a cough. "They're stuck in there, forever, unless and until they are freed by the same witch or a witch of equal or greater power. Or a demigod, if you can find one."

"And yet you came out," said Blusk.

The wizard rolled his eyes. "Of course I did. I'm not an elf, now, am I?"

"But you are a wizard," said Phendour. "That seems clear, at least from your dress."

The wizard nodded. "Yes, to be sure."

"But you can't reverse the curse?" said Rhynt.

"No, child, though I've been trying for more than twenty years now."

Rhynt looked back at the tower. "What's it like inside?"

The wizard smiled at her. "I love a child with curiosity, and I sense you know more than a few things about wizardry."

Rhynt smiled. "A few, yes."

"Well," said the wizard, "the inside of the tower does not look like the inside of a tower. It is its own world, with forests and mountains and raging rivers, as big as the land we stand in now. Perhaps bigger."

"Really?" said Phendour. "How many elves are in there?"

The wizard waggled his head as he considered the question and calculated the answer. "Lots, thousands, maybe tens of thousands."

Blusk's eyes grew wide. "By the gods."

The wizard gave him a questioning look and turned back to Rhynt. "He seems to say that a lot."

Rhynt laughed. "He does. Yes, he does."

The wizard grew quiet and looked at each of them in turn. "Well, then, why have you summoned us?"

Calax gave him an equally questioning look. "What? We have not summoned you. In fact, we've been trying to avoid you."

The wizard seemed unconcerned. "But I clearly heard a conversation about the best way to cross the river."

Rhynt chuckled. "Distance hearing, yes."

Calax nodded. "Yes, we talked about that, and as I'm sure you heard, came up with a solution."

The wizard shook his head vigorously. "No, no, that won't work. We'll get you across, we will."

Calax cocked his head. "And how do you propose to do that?"

The wizard turned and pointed at the tower. "It's a tower now, but it can also make a fine bridge."

Blusk laughed and started to speak, but the wizard held up a hand to stop him. "Yes, let me say it for you, *by the gods.*"

Phendour laughed. "Well, let's do it. Come on, wizard, let's see what you've got."

The wizard rolled up his sleeves, closed his eyes, mumbled some words, and opened his eyes again. The tower stared back at him, unchanged.

"Hmm, it's been a while, so let me have another go at her."

He closed his eyes once more, mumbled different words, and the tower began to move closer to the river, changing from a tower to a bridge before their eyes and lowering itself to rest on the far bank, the river surging beneath it.

The wizard smiled and pointed at Blusk. "Go on, say it."

Blusk laughed, then shouted, "By the gods!"

"Indeed," said the wizard, hands on hips, marveling at his wizardry. "Now, this spell won't hold forever. Best get to your horses and make your way across. Stay toward the center."

Everyone was still just standing there, looking at the newly formed bridge.

"Come on," said the wizard. "Let's get to it."

They all startled into action at once, each racing for their horses and throwing on their saddles. Then they scooped up their bedrolls and led the horses to the bridge.

Calax led the way with Gash, followed by Rhynt, Phendour, and Blusk. The wizard trailed behind, encouraging them to move quickly. Suddenly, the bridge made a cracking sound and began to rearrange itself back into a tower.

The wizard shouted above the roar. "Run!"

Calax and Rhynt made it to the far bank just as the tower lost its grip and slipped into the raging water. Helpless, Blusk and Phendour let go of their horses and clung to the tower, along with the wizard, who seemed to be shouting something at them. The horses reared, lost their footing, and disappeared under the water. The tower, now fully reformed, began picking up speed in the current.

"Come," said Calax. "To horse."

Rhynt jumped on her horse and followed Calax and Gash at a gallop, racing along the river's edge, trying to keep pace with the tower, which was accelerating away from them around a bend in the river.

When Calax and Rhynt made the turn, they barely had time to pull up to avoid tumbling over a steep cliff next to a waterfall.

Calax dismounted and peered over the cliff to the river below. "Nothing. They're gone."

Rhynt came up beside him and scanned the land and the river below. "There," she said, pointing down the side of the cliff. "A switchback trail to the bottom. Let's go."

They jumped back on their horses and worked their way slowly down the switchback, losing valuable minutes. The tower, whether it was whole or in pieces, was long gone, swept away by the river.

When they reached the bottom, Calax stopped and slid down from his horse. "Look, over there in the brambles."

Rhynt followed his eyes. Phendour's and Blusk's horses were standing in the undergrowth near the river bank, shivering but apparently unharmed.

Rhynt joined Calax as he made his way to the horses and tugged them out of the brambles.

Rhynt looked down the river. "Do you think they made it?"

"I don't know. What do you see?"

Rhynt closed her eyes. "The tower is whole, intact, and it's already five miles downriver."

"What about Phendour and Blusk?"

Rhynt concentrated hard, trying to extend her range, as she scanned the river and the areas on both sides of the banks. "No, nothing. A few bears and, wait—"

"What?"

"Men fighting, about ten of them, some in gray and some in black."

"Enturians and Mystrosians."

"Yes."

"But no sign of Blusk or Phendour."

"No, nothing. It is as if they have vanished."

Calax nodded. "I know it's strange, but I think they're okay somehow. They were there one moment, clinging to the tower, and then they were gone, along with the wizard."

"So you think they made it inside the tower?"

"Exactly, and if they did, I'm sure we'll come upon them further down the river, at the opening to the sea."

Rhynt looked at the roaring, roiling river again and shook her head. "I wonder. It would take a miracle."

Calax nodded. "Or magic."

Calax wondered at Rhynt's abilities as she slowly turned in a circle, scanning the countryside for anything alive—or dead. With fighting ahead, they had decided to spend the day near the waterfall and tend to the horses, which were shaken from their time in the river. Rhynt had built a small fire, and through some other magic taught her by the Red Monk, had made it a smokeless fire, one that would not give away their position in a suddenly crowded and deadly landscape.

Calax was not amused. "Why haven't you done this before? Why not smokeless fires all along?"

Rhynt sighed. "I didn't think of it until just now. Sorry."

"Whatever child. So, what did you far-see?"

"There is fighting everywhere. Here, let's see your map."

Calax pulled out the map and spread it on the ground next to the fire.

Rhynt bent over it and began pointing. The Mystrosian army is here, just past the tavern where we met, and their columns stretch back miles to the west. I'd guess they'd be where we are now in just two days' time, maybe less. They seem to have picked up their pace."

She moved her finger along the road that led directly to the port. "There's a scouting party here, followed by a force of perhaps a hundred swordsmen, all on horse."

Calax nodded. "An advance party to scout and secure the docks, no doubt."

"So it seems." She moved her finger to the spot on the map where they now rested, next to the waterfall. "We're in a pocket at the moment, safe from both sides, but the pocket is collapsing. There are gray warriors and black on both sides of the river, and the Mystrosians seem to be far better soldiers. The Enturians are being slaughtered."

Calax frowned. "Is there no way through them?"

Rhynt stood up and began scanning again. "By the gods!"

Calax leapt to his feet and drew his sword. "What?"

The answer became apparent almost at once. Seven gray warriors burst through the underbrush, swords drawn, racing toward them.

Rhynt took the first down with a dagger to the heart and a second with a dagger to the eye before pulling her sword and engaging a third. Calax took down another one, slicing through him from shoulder to gut, blood spraying.

He turned to engage the next one, but all had sprouted yellow arrows in their chests and had dropped to the ground, dead.

Rhynt dispatched the one remaining gray with a thrust through his chest, the soldier's eyes going wide as he dropped to his knees and then face first to the ground.

She and Calax stood there, back to back, crouched and ready for what might come, whether it be a man or an arrow, but nothing came.

Calax turned to her. "Quick, what do you see?"

Rhynt dropped her sword to her side and closed her eyes. "Nothing, for hundreds of yards."

Calax was dumbfounded. "But the arrows. There has to be someone out there."

Rhynt opened her eyes and sighed. "There should be, but there isn't."

Calax threw his sword to the ground. "Magic, damnable magic!"

Rhynt picked up his sword and handed it to him. "Magic it may be, but it is a good magic. Whoever it is has saved us once more."

Calax peered into the underbrush. "Aye, there's that."

Rhynt grabbed him by the elbow. "Come, let's get back to the map."

Calax took one last look—he could see nothing—and followed Rhynt back to the fire.

"Okay," she said, pointing at the map. "We are here, and there are groups of warriors here, here, and here."

Calax shook his head. "There's no way we can get through that."

Rhynt tapped the map. "Look here. The Mystrosians are moving east, toward the docks, forcing the Enturians back as they go. If we wait until dark, we might be able to get by them by going north, then south, and so on."

Calax smiled. "Like a sailboat tacking in the wind."

Rhynt shrugged. "If you say so," she said. "I've never actually seen one."

Calax suddenly frowned. "But it will be slow going."

"Aye," said Rhynt, "but the only other option is the river, and that's death certain."

Calax looked at the river roaring just a few yards away from them. He wondered whether Phendour and Blusk were safe and whether he would ever see them again—alive or dead.

"We will do as you say."

27

The day stretched on, the sun seemingly reluctant to follow its arc to the horizon. Calax passed the time by pacing back and forth near the river's edge, while Rhynt sat some yards away, drawing stick figures in the ground. By the time the sun gave in, she had drawn a veritable army of figures at war with one another.

Calax finally stopped his pacing and walked over to her. "I've been thinking."

She dropped her drawing stick and looked up at him. "Oh?"

"The horses."

Rhynt stood and brushed the dirt off her trousers. "What about the horses?"

"I'm thinking we should leave Blusk's and Phendour's. They're still weak from their struggle in the river. They'd just slow us down."

Rhynt looked him in the eye. "You think they're dead, don't you?"

Calax shook his head. "No, of course not, but we don't know if we'll ever see them again."

Rhynt looked at the horses. "And you would just leave them?"

"Aye, turn them loose."

Rhynt nodded slowly, then shook her head. "No, I have a better idea. We'll take them. If no one spots us in the night, fine. But if they do, we can release one of the horses and send it away from us."

"A distraction?"

"Yes, exactly."

Calax gave her an appraising look.

"What?" said Rhynt.

"Oh, nothing. Just thinking what a fine leader you'll be one day."

Rhynt chuckled. "Aye, if I'm not skewered by a gray or a black this night."

Calax cocked his head with a smile. "Well, yes, there's that."

"And me," said a voice from the underbrush.

Calax and Rhynt spun in the direction of the voice and drew their swords as a man in bright clothing stepped out into the open and began strumming his lute. "A fine evening for a tune, don't you think?"

Calax grabbed the man by his collar and held his sword at the man's neck. "And who might you be?"

"Now, now," said the man, "no need for arms when a man's about to sing."

Calax released his grip and pushed the man back to get a better look at him in the dying light. He was a head shorter than Calax and a head taller than Rhynt, although to be fair, his tall feathered cap may have distorted the comparison somewhat. Whatever his true height, he was a spectacle to behold, his clothing scarlet from head to foot, save for the sleeves of his tunic, which were yellow and puffed out to make him appear much wider than he actually was. His eyes were green as the forest in spring, set wide over a narrow slice of a nose that seemed to dip and dive like the surrounding hills. A blonde mustache, long and curled upward at the tips, hid whatever lips he had, and waggled with life when he spoke. He carried a lute in one hand and a large weir-deer sack in the other, no doubt containing everything he owned.

"I will ask you again, sir," said Calax. "Who might you be?"

Rhynt spoke up. "I know him. Do you not remember, Calax? He is the very same minstrel who played for one and all at the tavern."

Calax squinted at the man. "Are you sure?"

The man set down his sack and lute and spoke up. "If she isn't, I am, sir. And I am no other than Whelan the Wanderer, singer of songs, teller of tales, and boon companion, if I might ask that favor of you tonight." He swept his hat off his head and bowed. "For a price, that is."

Calax laughed. "Well, you're an odd one, I'll give you that."

"More to the point," said Rhynt. "Why are you here?"

Whelan put his hat back on, taking time to adjust the angle of the yellow feather.

"Like you," he said, "I flee for my life before the Mystrosian hordes."

Calax lifted his sword. "Then perhaps you best be continuing your flight."

Whelan backed away. "Now, now, I only seek the pleasure—and safety—of your company. I assure you I will not be a burden. I seek only a place at your fire."

Calax grunted. "Do you see a fire?"

Whelan shrugged. "Indeed, I do not."

"And why do you suppose that's true?"

"Um, because I have arrived early?"

Calax shook his head. "No, you've arrived too late. We're about to set off."

Whelan looked surprised. "Off? With so many warriors in the land?"

"We plan to avoid them," said Rhynt. "Slip by them in the night."

"Oh? And how exactly are you going to accomplish that?"

Rhynt explained their plan, Whelan listening attentively until the very end, at which point he laughed derisively. "*That* is your plan?"

Rhynt nodded firmly. "It is, sir."

Whelan shook his head. "I'll grant you, that might have worked a couple of nights ago, but things have changed out there."

"Oh?" said Calax. "In what way?"

"The Mystrosians have split their army in thirds and are advancing at quick march toward the docks."

Calax's eyes grew wide. He pulled out his map. "Here, show me while there's still light to see."

Whelan began pointing at the map. "They were here yesterday, but now a third of them have split off to the northeast, a third continue down the main road, and a third are now heading southeast."

Calax turned to Rhynt. "Is it true? Can you see it?"

Rhynt closed her eyes and scanned the countryside. It was as Whelan said, and there was simply no safe direction to go. "It is true. Our plan will not work. They come in all directions, fast, and there is no safe direction for us."

Whelan smiled proudly. "Exactly."

Calax frowned at him. "Well, there's no reason to gloat about it. You're in the same sad fix as we are."

Whelan shook his head. "Maybe, maybe not."

"What do you mean?" said Rhynt.

Whelan cleared his throat. "The Mystrosians are of the d'Porto religion, and are religious in the extreme. They would not think of going anywhere without their white monks."

"And?" said Calax.

Whelan smiled. "And we will join them as such."

Calax laughed. "And how do you expect to pull off such a miracle without being discovered?"

Whelan reached down, opened his sack, and pulled out three white shrouds. "Why, we will be d'Porto monks, my friends. We'll slip in among them as they pass down the main road. Now, quickly, get into these shrouds." He handed one to Calax and one to Rhynt and began putting on the third.

Rhynt looked at her shroud, then dropped it to the ground. "And how is it that these shrouds are exactly the right size for me?"

"Aye," said Calax, once again lifting his sword toward Whelan.

Whelan took a step back. "In truth, I have been following you for days now. When I saw them washing these at the river, I took a chance and made off with them."

Calax dropped his sword. "Are you the man who has been saving us with your yellow arrows?"

Whelan laughed and spread his arms. "Me, an archer? I am only what you see, a poor minstrel."

Rhynt gave him a questioning look. "And why would a poor minstrel be heading to the docks? Why aren't you heading west, to safety?"

Whelan shrugged. "A fool takes chances when there's money or position on the line. In short, I understand that the king of Enturia seeks a new fool for his court. Or at least that's what I've been led to believe."

Calax shook his head. "Well, I can clearly see you as a fool."

Whelan smirked. "I'll take that as a compliment."

Rhynt sighed. "We're losing time. If we're going to do this, we'd best get to our horses and leave."

Whelan cocked his head. "Horses?"

"Don't worry," said Rhynt. "We have an extra one for you."

Whelan sighed. "No, my friends, that isn't what I meant. If we're to do this—and live—we have to do it on foot, to walk alongside the other d'Porto monks."

"What?" said Calax. "Leave my warhorse? Never!"

Rhynt turned to Whelan. "Is there no other way?"

Whelan shook his head. "You've seen what I've described—how, I don't know—but you know in your heart and your head that I am right."

Rhynt nodded and turned to Calax. "Come, I would talk with you alone for a moment."

Rhynt led Calax back to their horses. When she was satisfied they were out of earshot, she turned and began whispering. "Do not look back. Say nothing. Just listen, and act when I say so."

Calax nodded.

"That man over there, if he is a man, is not Whelan the Wanderer."

Calax's eyes grew wide and he started to turn, but Rhynt grabbed him by the arms. "Stay calm. Now, when I scanned to see the Mystrosians, I also saw a man several miles away—the real Whelan the Wanderer. And just before I came out of my far-seeing trance, I saw you and *no one else* standing here."

Calax could bear it no longer, and began shouting. "I will keep my horse." He turned to check out Whelan, who was standing where they left him, smiling.

Calax turned back to Rhynt. "What now?" he whispered.

"Stand between him and me, so he can't see me."

Calax adjusted his position, so his wide body all but hid her from Whelan's view. Satisfied she could not be seen, she slowly reached down to her bedroll and pulled out her bow and a single arrow.

Calax seemed concerned. "Can you make the shot?"

Rhynt nodded, took a step back, and motioned Calax to move away. As soon as Whelan came in sight, she let loose the arrow, which struck true in the man's heart.

He stood there long enough to smile at her, and then disappeared, the white shroud and Rhynt's arrow dropping to the ground.

"By the gods," said Calax.

"A gela," said Rhynt. "The Red Monk told me of such things."

"What is a gela?"

"A shape-shifter created by a powerful wizard, who uses the gela as his eyes and ears while he sits far away in safety."

Calax looked back at the underbrush. "But it's gone now, right?"

"Yes, but we must be very careful now. A gela can take any shape or form. The wizard will come at us again, in a form we would ordinarily welcome. A friend, a loved one. We can't trust our eyes."

"But when you far-see, you can see them."

"Aye, but that's when I'm in a trance state. Otherwise, a gela will look perfectly human to me."

"Well, then, you will just have to scan everyone."

Rhynt nodded. "If I can. Far-seeing is exhausting. It takes its toll."

Calax sighed. "What now?"

Rhynt dropped her bow to the ground and sat down on her bedroll. "Give me a minute. I have to look at the landscape once more."

Calax sat down next to her and watched as she closed her eyes and went deeper in her trance, her body shivering from the effort.

28

Rhynt shivered one last time, and then opened her eyes. "We have but one hope, one path."

"What did you see?"

"More warriors than I care to think about, and they'll be on us within the hour if we don't move."

"Then let's go." Calax stood and helped her to her feet. She was still a bit wobbly. "Are you okay?"

Rhynt nodded. "Yes, it will pass. Here, pull out the map."

Calax took it out and opened it.

"We're here, and we need to be here," she said, pointing at the map.

Calax was confused. "Wait, what? Back on the other side of the river? How are we to do that?"

Rhynt pointed at the map again. "That's where the river narrows. I think we can get across. But we need to hurry."

Calax closed the map and stuffed it under his breastplate. "I don't see how we'll be able to do it, but I trust that your far-seeing saw something I could not imagine."

Rhynt laughed. "Oh, indeed it did. Now, to horse."

Minutes later, they were galloping along the riverbank, each holding the reins of a second horse, those of Blusk and Phendour. The night was moonless and dark, only the roar of the river keeping them on a true path as it snaked through the darkness. Minutes passed, then hours, Rhynt and Calax slowing the horses from a trot to a walk as they neared the spot where Rhynt thought they could cross.

Finally, she slowed to a stop. "Here, this is the place." They dismounted, tied their horses to a nearby tree, and began unsaddling them.

"We must wait for daylight," said Rhynt. "Best get what sleep we can. We will need all our energy on the morrow."

Calax looked into the darkness. "Sleep if you will. I will stand watch."

Rhynt was too tired to object. She grabbed her bedroll, spread it out on the ground, and was soon asleep.

Calax spread out his bedroll next to a tree, so he could sit in the darkness with his back against it. It was quieter than he expected. Even the river seemed distant, its roar muted somehow.

He looked over at Rhynt, who was snoring softly, and smiled. He was more and more astounded by her with each passing day. She called herself a pisspot, but she had powers. He knew that, without her, he would have been captured or killed days ago, perhaps even when they first met near the tavern.

Even with her skills, he wondered how long they would last out here in the wilderness, with warriors from at least two countries after them, not to mention wizards and trolls and who knew what else lay ahead.

The night passed slowly, but after a time, the sky began to brighten enough that he could see his way clear to assess their location. Oddly, even though he could hear it, there was no sign of the river. He stood and stretched and walked slowly toward the sound, being careful not to slip on the grass, which was slick from the morning mist.

As he walked, the sound grew louder, but there was still no river to be seen. And then he saw why. They had made their camp only yards from a chasm, the river a hundred feet or more below them. Calax tried to guess at the distance from one side of the chasm to the other, and his calculation dampened whatever spirit he had. It was too far for man or horse to leap, even with a good head start.

He sighed and walked back to his bedroll and sat down. His first thought was to wake up Rhynt, but if their cause was lost anyway, why not let her get as much rest as she could. She would need her strength. Their only hope now was to outrun the Mystrosians to the docks, and with who knows how many gray warriors in their path.

While she slept, Calax made ready the horses, saddling them as quickly as he could. They'd need to leave as soon as she woke up. No time for a fire. No time for food. Just pure headlong flight.

Once the horses were ready, Calax picked up his bedroll and tied it behind his saddle. Gash whinnied and turned to look at Calax.

"It's all right, boy," said Calax. "But be ready for a quick start to your day."

Rhynt sat up with a start. "What are you saying?"

Calax turned to her. "Good morning. Just having a little chat with Gash here."

Rhynt looked up at the sky. "Why did you let me sleep so long?"

Calax frowned. "You seemed tired, and well . . ."

"Well what?"

He pointed at the chasm. "There's no way we can get across. The gap is too wide."

Rhynt stood and stretched. "Let's just see about that." She walked over to the chasm and looked down. "Wow, that's quite a drop."

"And look at the far side. There's just no way to get there. We need to flee."

Rhynt turned and smiled at him. "No, first I need to far-see. If I'm right, our salvation is almost here."

Calax grunted. "Well, go ahead, but make it quick. I've saddled the horses. We need to go."

Rhynt closed her eyes and dropped into a trance. A third of the Mystrosian army was less than five miles away and heading directly for them. That strange minstrel, Whelan the Wanderer, the real one and not some strange gela, was less than a mile away and running as fast as he could manage. And then there they were, the trolls, not a hundred yards away, and closing the distance with each broad stride.

Rhynt broke from her trance, raced to the edge of the chasm, and began shouting, "Bebo, over here, over here."

Calax raced up beside her. "What are you doing? You'll give away our position."

"Don't worry," said Rhynt, pointing across the chasm. "It's my friend Bebo and some of his fellow trolls."

Calax's mouth dropped open at the sight of the approaching trolls. There must have been twenty of them, some astoundingly tall, and each carrying the trunk of a tree.

Rhynt shouted when she saw Bebo. "Over here, my friend."

Bebo approached the edge of the chasm on the far side and looked down. "Big drop."

"Yes," said Rhynt. "We need a bridge, fast."

Bebo nodded. "You have payment?"

Rhynt laughed. "Yes, a joke for the ages."

Bebo did a little jig, or rather a big jig, considering his size. "Good, we fix."

Bebo turned to his fellow trolls and shouted instructions. One tree was lashed to a second and then a third and then a fourth, and soon the bridge was wide enough for horses to cross. Six trolls hefted the bridge to the chasm, lifted it up on end, and then let it fall. The bridge bounced a couple of times, but then settled down.

Rhynt and Calax raced for their horses and led them to the bridge. As they did so, Bebo ran across the bridge, blocking their way.

"What's this, Bebo?" said Rhynt.

"No joke, no cross."

Rhynt laughed. "As you wish. Lean down, so I can whisper it in your ear."

Bebo leaned down, turning his head so Rhynt could whisper the joke to him. Bebo began to giggle almost immediately and after a minute or two let out a loud guffaw. "That good one. Make happy."

"Then you'll let us pass?" said Rhynt.

Bebo turned and started walking back across the bridge. "Yes, come, must hurry now."

Rhynt turned to Calax. "Let's do this."

Rhynt and Calax started leading the horses over the bridge. Gash and the other horses balked at first, but after some soothing words and a little coaxing, followed Rhynt and Calax across to the safety of the other side.

Bebo was waiting for them, smiling. "We go now."

Rhynt shook her head. "No, you've got to destroy the bridge now. No one else must pass over it."

Bebo crossed his arms. "Payment?"

Rhynt rolled her eyes. "Another joke?"

Bebo chuckled. "Yes, more joke." He leaned down, turning his head so she could whisper in his ear. "Tell."

Rhynt began whispering and Bebo began laughing. "That better one. First good, second better."

"Good," said Rhynt. "Now get rid of that bridge."

Bebo turned to give orders to the other trolls, but Rhynt suddenly stopped him. A man was racing over the bridge toward them: Whelan the Wanderer.

Calax drew his sword and started to run toward him, but Rhynt soon had his arm, tugging him back. "No, that's the real one. Let him come."

But Bebo had also acted, racing to the middle of the bridge, and grasping Whelan with a single hand at his waist, and lifting him into the air, making ready to throw him into the chasm.

Rhynt screamed at him. "No, stop, he is a friend."

Bebo grunted and carried Whelan across the bridge, dropping him to the ground in front of Rhynt. "Here, you take."

Rhynt nodded. "Thank you. Now get rid of the bridge, and quickly. There are warriors not far behind."

Bebo turned to his fellow trolls. "Lift, pull, drop—quick."

The trolls raced to the bridge and did just that, the bridge disappearing into the chasm.

"Bridge gone," said Bebo. "We go."

Rhynt nodded. "Thank you, my friend," she shouted.

Bebo waved at her from across the chasm. "Good jokester, be well." And with that, he nodded at the other trolls and began running, all following in his wake.

Rhynt watched them go, then turned back to Calax and Whelan. "Quickly, to the horses. We must get out of range of their archers."

Whelan nodded at her. "Thank you for saving me."

"You are welcome, but hurry, we need to put some distance between us and them. And then perhaps a fire and some rabbit and some tunes from your lute."

"It will be my pleasure," said Whelan.

They climbed onto their horses and galloped for the treeline, black arrows falling harmlessly behind them.

29

When they galloped into the treeline, they thought at first that they had entered yet another vast forest, but no more than ten strides in, they burst from the trees onto a rocky landscape that forced them to slow the horses to a walk. Finally, the rocks became so large and numerous that they had to dismount and lead the horses through a maze of boulders.

Whelan was the first to complain. "I thought you said we'd stop for breakfast."

Calax chuckled. "You are awfully needy for one so recently rescued."

Whelan returned the laugh. "Aye, I guess, but my stomach calls."

Calax turned to Rhynt. "What say you? Are we safe to stop for a while? My stomach and this man beg to break fast."

Rhynt stopped and closed her eyes, turning in a circle, then stopping suddenly. "Hand me my bow and an arrow."

Whelan looked in the direction she was facing. "What do you see?"

Rhynt stood silently, eyes closed, hands at the ready to receive the bow and arrow.

"Here," said Calax, handing her the bow.

She nocked an arrow, then turned to Whelan, her eyes still closed. "What would you have, rabbit or red-tipped grouse?"

Whelan's mouth dropped open. "Well, rabbit, I guess."

Rhynt turned and let loose the arrow.

Whelan and Calax watched the arrow arc through the air and drop out of sight a hundred yards away.

Whelan turned back to Rhynt. "What is this trickery? Shooting an arrow so far, with your eyes closed. It's, it's—"

"Breakfast," said Rhynt, opening her eyes. "Now, go along and retrieve the rabbit. You watched the arrow's flight, so you should have no problem finding it."

Whelan started to say something, then turned and looked at Calax. "Who is this girl?"

Calax laughed. "She is a mere pisspot—with certain *skills.*"

"Incredible."

"Aye, but you best go fetch breakfast for us. We still have hours of walking and riding ahead of us."

Whelan sighed. "Right, right." He began walking in the direction of the arrow's flight and soon disappeared behind a boulder big as a gross ox.

Rhynt and Calax watched him go.

"What do you think?" said Calax. "Is he real or that gewgaw we encountered back there?"

"Oh, he's real all right. And it's *gela*, not gewgaw."

Calax shrugged. "So long as he's real."

"He is. The question, though, is why he's out here in the first place."

"Minstrels travel, I hear," said Calax.

"Aye, but in the same direction as armies? And along the same path as us?"

Calax frowned. "You have a point. We'll have to coax his intent out of him."

"After breakfast," said Rhynt. "I am already drooling at the mere thought of roasted rabbit."

Calax nodded and then looked around. "I see no firewood, though."

Rhynt drew her sword. "I saw a dead tree not too far from here. Try not to eat the rabbit raw while I'm gone."

Calax laughed as she strode off and disappeared behind a boulder.

Whelan returned first, holding the skewered rabbit out for Calax to see. "Straight through the heart, at a hundred yards. She has skills, all right. Speaking of which, where *is* she?"

Calax pointed in the direction of the boulder. "Off gathering wood."

Whelan shook his head. "Well, good luck with that. I saw nary a twig the whole way there and back. The place is barren."

"And yet she will return with wood."

"Perhaps we should just eat it raw. Getting a fire started will take time, and I'm right famished."

"Ah, yes, time. You forget one thing, though."

"Oh, and what's that?"

"The girl has skills."

Whelan laughed. "From what I've seen, she does, she definitely does."

He heard a sound behind him and turned. Rhynt was coming toward them, her arms filled with firewood. She walked right by them, dropped the wood on the ground, and began sorting and stacking it.

Whelan walked up to her. "I have a flint you can use."

She smiled up at him. "That won't be necessary." She stood, brushed off her clothes, and then raised her hands over the wood, which immediately leapt into flame, the heat so intense that Whelan had to jump back.

She turned to Whelan. "Rabbit, please."

He handed it to her and backed away. "Be you a witch or a wizard?"

Rhynt laughed and shook her head. "The answer is not important. The rabbit is." She took out her knife and began preparing the rabbit for the spit. "It would help if you could find a piece of wood suitable for a spit."

Whelan nodded absently and began sorting through the pile of wood she had brought back, finally selecting a piece thick enough and straight enough to make a spit. "Here, this should do it."

She thanked him with a nod, and skewered the rabbit, placing it over the fire, which had settled down to a good cooking fire.

Whelan smiled at her. "I don't suppose you can magic it to doneness, so we can eat sooner."

Rhynt smiled back at him. "The meat and the fire must conspire. That is the magic. No other will do."

Whelan sighed and sat down next to her at the fire. She gave him a serious look. "So, what have you been doing since I last saw you at the tavern?"

"Ah, that is a long story, and long stories require the meat and the fire to conspire to fill my stomach."

Rhynt laughed. "Then let us watch this conspiracy and husband our words."

They grew quiet and stared at the fire and the spit and the sizzling meat. The smell alone seemed to revive them.

"When I die," said Whelan, "I hope this heavenly scent is in the air. I will surely go in peace."

"It is divine, yes," said Rhynt, reaching out to test the doneness of the meat. "Another few minutes, I should think."

She turned and yelled at Calax, who was feeding what grass there was to the horses. "Almost ready."

He nodded, fed the last handful to Gash, and walked over to the fire, plopping down between Rhynt and Whelan. "Oh, my bones."

"Whelan here is about to tell us a long story," said Rhynt, "a story of his many exploits and adventures since we saw him last at the tavern."

Whelan shook his head. "Not such a grand tale, and I'll let you be the judge of its length. As a storyteller, I tend to run long. People expect length for coin. A short story, however grand, never seems to satisfy them."

"Tell it and trim it to your heart's delight," said Calax. "We seek no grand tale, only the reason that brings you to this fire and this meal."

"Speaking of which," said Rhynt, "it looks and smells ready."

Whelan didn't need further urging. He pulled the spit from the fire and began breaking off and handing out hunks of meat as quickly as he could.

Calax had to laugh at him. "He eats like a ravenous dog."

Whelan almost choked on his meat. "Aye, and don't slow this dog down."

No one said another word, the only sounds the sounds of chewing, the licking of fingers, the satisfied smacking of lips, and the final sucking of bones—the sounds of three ravenous dogs.

Finally, Whelan slumped back with a satisfied sigh. "Gods could not eat better."

Rhynt finished licking her fingers and threw her last bone on the fire. "I will put on some tea, and then we'll be ready for your story, bard."

Whelan nodded with a smile. "I am ready, my lady."

Rhynt stood, brushed herself off, and retrieved the cooking pot from her saddlebag, along with a gourd of water, pouring it into the pot as she returned to the fire. "Please begin. I'll serve it when it's ready."

"As you wish," said Whelan, crossing his legs under him, and picking up his lute.

Calax grabbed the lute away from him. "Without the music, if you please."

Whelan shook his head. "But what's a tale without music?"

"Shorter."

Whelan turned to Rhynt. "How can you live with so crude a man?"

Rhynt smiled. "It takes practice."

"I can see that. Now, where was I?"

"At the beginning," said Calax. "There was the fight at the tavern, Rhynt and I fled, and then what?"

Whelan closed his eyes for a minute and then began. "All was chaos, blood, and gore. The gray men were dead, the tavern keeper and his wife were in shock, and I—"

"Was under a table, bleating like a baby goat," said Calax. "Aye, I saw you."

"Indeed," said Whelan. "May I continue now? Without interruption?"

Calax nodded and Whelan continued with his story. The Red Monk had disappeared, there one moment, gone the next. Whelan, knowing that dead gray men would attract living gray men, all with murder in their eyes, had raced to the barn, collected his meager belongings in a sack, and fled to the countryside.

"I tried to keep off the roads as best I could."

"Yes, I understand that," said Rhynt. "But how did you come to meet up with us?"

Whelan turned his hands palms up. "Luck, fate, a succession of steadily diminishing choices. Who knows? The approach of the Mystrosians has everyone fleeing east."

Rhynt nodded. "Yes, but why was your first instinct to head east? I mean before the Mystrosians appeared."

"Oh, that. Well, as you can well imagine, a minstrel and bard such as myself must always be on the lookout for his next job, and that would be why I headed east, toward the docks by the Great Sea."

Calax nodded. "So you thought to find work in a tavern or brothel there?" He turned to Rhynt. "Makes sense."

"No, no," said Whelan. "To seek passage to Enturia."

Rhynt gave him a puzzled look. "And why would you do that?"

"Ah, well," said Whelan. "Before you skewered the gray men, I had occasion to talk to one of them, who was so impressed by my singing and stories that he suggested I apply for the job of Fool at the king's castle in Enturia. The king's current Fool is, in fact, a forgetful, doddering, gray-bearded old fool, no longer able to perform with any skill."

"That doesn't make sense," said Rhynt. "A minstrel is not a fool. Neither is a bard."

"That is true," said Whelan, "but part of my repertoire includes a story about a king and his fool. Perhaps you've heard it. King Bruthrus and His Dilly-Dally?"

Rhynt and Calax looked at each other, then shook their heads.

"Ah, too bad," said Whelan. "Anyway, as part of telling the story, I act out both parts. The regal king, the silly fool. Here, watch."

Whelan stood and began dancing about, waving his arms insanely, and shouting, "Here comes Dilly-Dally, faster than a Silly-Sally."

30

It took Rhynt and Calax several minutes to stop laughing from the spectacle of Whelan's insane dancing, but finally Calax calmed himself and spoke.

"I am satisfied by your motivation to head east, but a few more questions."

Whelan shrugged, breathless from his dance, and sat back down next to the fire. "Yes?"

"I'm curious about where you were when you realized the Mystrosians were behind you."

Whelan gave him a puzzled look, then retrieved a smoking twig from the fire and began drawing in the dirt.

Calax interrupted him. "Wait, I have a map." He took out the map and spread it out on the ground in front of Whelan. "Where were you?"

Whelan looked down at the map and laughed.

"What's so funny?"

"The map. It can only have been drawn by that little dwarf Zyrx. He's a wonderful blacksmith, but a maker of maps? Oh, no."

Calax blinked. "You know him?"

"Yes, I had the occasion to visit him once."

Rhynt handed Whelan a bowl of tea. "So, what's wrong with it?"

Whelan waved a hand over the map, being careful not to spill the tea. "Why, just about all of it."

Calax grunted. "But it has served us well to this point."

Whelan took a sip of tea. "Has it? If so, tell me where we are now."

Calax placed a finger on the map. "Here."

Whelan glanced over at Rhynt with a quick smile. "The tea is wonderful." Then he turned back to Calax. "Actually, we're here." He put his finger down on the map at a point miles from Calax's spot.

Calax whistled in surprise. "So far?"

Whelan shrugged. "As I said, Zyrx is no map maker. Now, it's not a bad map for a dwarf blacksmith. The major roads and trails are okay, but the landmarks are out of place, and some are missing."

Calax slumped back. "If this is true, we are farther away from the docks than I imagined."

Whelan nodded. "At least an extra day's ride, if we're quick about it."

Calax took a bowl of tea from Rhynt. "We'll finish our tea and be on our way."

"Good," said Whelan.

"Wait," said Rhynt. "You haven't shown us where you were when you encountered the Mystrosians."

"Ah," said Whelan, turning back to the map. "About here."

Rhynt looked quickly at Calax, then back at Whelan. "You were so close to Zyrx's hearth in the hill. Why not seek safety there?"

"That would have made sense, save for three minor details. His hill tigers do not like me. The one time I was there was as brief as it was terrifying. Zyrx could barely control them, and I had to flee for my life. No, I wouldn't have gone there."

"And tell me," said Calax. "Did you see him at all on your way to this spot? Is he also fleeing?"

Whelan shrugged. "I have seen no one but those who would do me harm. If others are fleeing, I have not seen them. The Mystrosians came so quickly, it may be that all have perished. The sky was filled with white arrows."

Calax, who had been taking the last sip of tea, quickly lowered the bowl in surprise. "*White* arrows? I thought the Mystrosians used black arrows."

"They dress in black, yes, but their arrows are white from tip to fletch, an homage to their leader, the White Monk."

Calax turned to Rhynt. "Did your master ever mention a White Monk?"

Rhynt shrugged. "He talked a lot, so maybe. I sometimes paid him no mind."

"I can help with that," said Whelan. "My travels have taken me to most places in the greater world, and where I have not been, I have at least heard tales of such places. Mystrosia being one."

"Good," said Calax, "but first tell me who shoots black arrows? Rhynt and I barely survived an attack, and someone with black arrows was involved."

"Oh my," said Whelan, looking around nervously. "Oh, my."

31

Whelan looked back and forth at them, shaking his head all the while. *How could they not know this?* And then he sighed, knowing full well the answer: they knew nothing of the Teachings.

"Have you ever heard of the Teachings," he said, not surprised that they both looked at him like a Karak cow would look at a new fence.

"I thought not."

"What are these Teachings?" said Rhynt.

Whelan sighed heavily. "The Teachings are the collected wisdom of the greater world."

Calax looked puzzled. "Is there truly such a thing? I have never heard a single man or woman mention it."

Whelan nodded. "Few know about it." He pulled a small leather bag from his belt. "Here, think of this purse as the known world." He tossed the purse to Rhynt, who caught it on the fly.

"Rhynt, if that is the known world, what can you tell me about it?"

Rhynt giggled. "What? This seems a silly game."

"Humor me. Go on, describe that world."

Rhynt looked down at the bag. "All right. First off, it's surface is smooth and brown."

"Yes," said Whelan. "And what else?"

"Um, it has a front and a back and a bottom and a top."

"And a drawstring," said Calax, jumping in.

"Ah yes," said Whelan. "We'll get to the drawstring. Now, Rhynt, have you thoroughly described your world?"

Rhynt nodded vigorously. "Yes, I have."

Whelan nodded back. "Yes, you have. It is all that you can see, after all, and it's a fine world." He turned and looked at Calax. "Except for one thing."

Calax frowned. "Except what?"

Whelan cocked his head and turned to Rhynt. "Rhynt, shake the purse."

Rhynt held it up to her ear and shook it. "Coins, I think, and maybe some odd bits of this and that."

Whelan rocked back and laughed. "My word, I have never heard the Teachings referred to as odd bits of this and that. But it fits, it fits. What we don't know is odd, and odd is the least of it. We don't know what we don't know."

Calax grunted. "You talk in riddles."

Whelan held up a finger. "It may seem so, that's true. But let me make it clear to you. There was once a time when the world was totally unlike this purse in almost every way."

Rhynt gave him a puzzled look. "I do not understand. Are you saying the ground we sit on now was once something else, something different?"

Whelan waggled his head, trying to think of the right words, the words that would set her straight. "I don't mean literally. The ground, the rivers, the sky, all were and are the same. No, what I mean is that being in that world was different. The way people interacted. Their values. The way they worshipped or didn't worship. How they viewed themselves and the gods."

Rhynt nodded. "So it is like we once knew the contents of the bag, but now we don't?"

Whelan clapped his hands. "Exactly, child."

"And you thought of these so-called Teachings because of my mention of the black arrow?"

Whelan looked grim. "Yes, for whatever reason, the drawstring has been pulled and let loose things not seen for ages, the Age of the Six Arrows."

Calax grunted. "And you find this upsetting, because?"

Whelan took a deep breath and sighed. "The black arrow is the arrow of the assassins. Someone wants you dead."

Calax laughed sardonically. "Ah, well, it seems everyone wants me dead. Black arrows, yellow arrows, white arrows. Why am I, a mere sellsword, of such importance that they wish me dead? What I do, I do for coin, and everyone understands that. Who have I harmed? Who have I slighted?"

Whelan threw up his hands. "I don't know, but one thing is clear. We need to keep moving. Here, show me that map again."

Calax handed him the map and watched as Whelan's eyes danced, looking from one corner of the map to the next. "By the gods, Zyrx, you left it out."

"Left what out?" said Calax.

"The cave. It's no matter. I know the way and the landmarks. If we leave now, we will be there by nightfall, whereupon I will regale you with stories of the Teachings. Perhaps hearing what I know will help you unravel your predicament, Calax."

Rhynt gave Whelan a stern look. "You mean *our* predicament, don't you?"

Whelan nodded solemnly, and stood. "Come, we must go."

32

Rhynt wasn't quite sure what to make of Whelan the Wanderer. He wasn't a gela, she knew that for sure, but he seemed altogether too wise to be a mere minstrel and teller of tales. He knew things that neither she nor Calax knew. She was young, so perhaps that knowledge would have been imparted to her by d'Abo Pourcrey, if she had stayed with him. But how could Calax be so old, have fought in so many battles, and sat at so many army campfires without hearing any mention of the Teachings or the Age of the Six Arrows? Could it be that no one knows of these things but Whelan?

Whelan also didn't ask about things he should have. He didn't ask about their fine new armor or the weapons Zyrx had forged for them. And even though he rode beside her now on Blusk's horse, he never once asked about why there were two extra horses. Did he already know? Had he been following them close enough to have seen Blusk and Phendour swept away?

And deep down, she wondered whether Whelan had sent the gela. Were they really going to a cave or was he leading them to the grays or the Mystrosians? She turned and looked at him, perhaps too long.

Whelan wondered at the expression on her face. "What?"

"Nothing."

"Really, that was quite a look you just gave me."

She tried to throw him off. "No, it's just a look I get when I'm in deep thought."

Whelan cocked his head. "Thinking? About what?"

She sighed. Why not just ask? "About *you*."

Whelan smiled. "Good thoughts, I hope."

"Neither good nor bad, but curious thoughts, about you."

"Ha! I have a song about curiosity if you'd like to hear it." He reached for his lute, which was hung over the horn of the saddle.

"No, sir, put that down. I would only have answers, not songs or riddles."

He strapped the lute back down. "Then ask. What about me has so piqued your curiosity?"

"Many things, but one thing is that you don't ask obvious questions."

"What do you mean?"

"You knew me from the tavern, but you did not know Calax, and have yet to ask him his name."

Whelan rolled his eyes. "Everyone who knows of the Battle of Whent Hill knows Calax Halfhand. There are songs about him, my child, songs that describe him from head to foot to wooden hand."

"And yet his hand is metal."

Whelan nodded. "Yes, quite obviously, and also quite obviously the work of Zyrx, just as your fine armor and weapons are his work."

"And how could you tell that?"

Whelan shook his head and chuckled. "You can say many things about Zyrx, but the first thing to know about him is that he always leaves his mark."

"His mark?"

Whelan pointed at her breastplate. "See there, between the images of the hill tigers, a little "Z" tooled into the metal. And I dare say, you'll find that mark on everything he's made for you."

Rhynt looked down to see a little upside down "Z" just where he said it was. "All right, I'll give you that, but what about the horses. Why haven't you asked about the extra horses?"

"Ah," said Whelan, "good point. Well, I knew Calax was Calax, so when I saw the extra horses, I put one and three together and came up with Phendour and Blusk, and I ride on his horse now."

"How could you know that?"

"Almost every song ever sung about Calax includes mentions of his friends and comrades, Phendour and Blusk chief among them."

"So you picked out those names from songs?"

"Partly, yes. Then I studied the horses themselves and their saddles and tack. Blusk's horse is wide, like the man, and slumps a bit in the middle from carrying his weight. The saddle on the horse that trails behind us now is too small for most men, so I guessed—and truly it was a guess—that it must be a horse ridden by a woman. And that can only be Phendour."

Rhynt pondered his answers, and then shook her head. "So if you knew about the horses and their riders, why haven't you mentioned it to me or Calax? Why haven't you asked about them?"

Whelan nodded. "A good question, with an equally good answer, at least to my mind. You and Calax are grieving. I can see it in your faces every time you look at their horses. I would not dare intrude on a person's grief. It would be up to you and you alone to tell their story, whatever happened to them."

Rhynt looked puzzled. "I guess."

Whelan cocked his head. "So, is that the end to your questions?"

"For now, though I'm sure I'll have others when we reach the cave, if there *is* a cave."

Whelan laughed. "Questions are good anytime. And yes, there is a cave, as you can plainly see." He pointed ahead of them to a dark spot on the side of a mountain. "There, just above the trees. Do you see it?"

Rhynt smiled to herself. It was a good question with a good answer. "Yes, I see it."

33

Rhynt pulled Calax aside as they unsaddled the horses, and told him of her questioning of Whelan.

"I must admit I had similar questions," said Calax. "Tell me, though, did you believe his answers?"

"Yes, I think so. He answered them directly, without hesitation. I believe we can trust him, and trust what he says."

Calax nodded. "Even that business about the Teachings and the Age of the Six Arrows? I never heard of such things."

"Aye, I should have asked more about that. You'd think someone your age would have heard of such things."

"My age? You say it like I'm a graybeard."

Rhynt smiled at him. "No offense, I just meant—"

Calax interrupted. "Yes, yes, that a person of my *advanced years* likely would have heard of such things just through common gossip."

"Indeed."

"Well, I haven't, so we'll have more questions for this Whelan the Wanderer."

Whelan walked up behind them. "Did I hear my name being bandied about?"

Rhynt recovered quickly. "Oh, we were just curious about your knowledge of this cave."

Whelan sighed. "I must say, I've never met a more curious girl who was so curious."

"I guess I am," said Rhynt, "but questions are questions."

"And I shall always have an answer for you, if there is one. Now, come along, both of you, and see the wonders inside this cave. You will be amazed."

Calax and Rhynt grabbed their bed rolls and followed Whelan up a steep graveled slope to the mouth of the cave, which was large enough to swallow an army.

Whelan stopped briefly at the entrance and picked up a large stick. "I don't suppose you can set this afire so we might see our way?"

Rhynt fell silent, closed her eyes, and mumbled the words of the Red Monk. The end of the branch burst into flame, much to the delight of Whelan. "Curious, wondrous girl!"

Whelan led the way inside the cave, the light flickering on the walls, where Rhynt could just make out some sort of drawing.

"Just down here we should find firewood set out for us to light. Ah, here it is."

A stack of kindling and wood sat in front of them, and as Whelan had said, it was ready to light.

"I don't understand," said Calax. "Why is this fire set ready for us?"

Whelan dropped the torch into the firewood and watched as the flames made the cave grow brighter. "It is a custom, a rule, a command. *Whosoever enjoys the cave shall leave the cave ready for the next.* Or at least I think that's how the rule goes."

He turned and held out his hands as the cave grew still brighter. Rhynt and Calax were awestruck. A painting yards and yards wide by yards and yards high filled one wall of the cave. There were dwellings and castles, mountains and streams, and wild beasts beyond imagination. And at the center, a circle of men and women standing before a cluster of arrows of different colors.

"Behold the old world and the Age of the Six Arrows."

34

Rhynt took the last bite of cave rat and passed around bowls of tea. They had eaten in silence, Calax and Rhynt rapt by the painting before them. The flickering of the fire made the men and gods and beasts painted in it seem to come to life, as if they were watching.

Whelan had paid no attention. He was more interested in wolfing down the last of the seven rats they had killed and roasted. Finally, he found a small bone and began picking his teeth. "My two everlasting memories of this cave are that painting and these rats. There is nothing like them in the known world."

Calax broke away from the trance of the painting. "Is it truly as you have said?"

Whelan nodded. "Oh, yes, these are the best rats anywhere."

"No," said Calax, "I meant the painting. It truly depicts our past?"

"Yes, of long ago. Rhynt, may I have more tea. As tasty as these rats are, they bring a thirst."

Rhynt stood and walked over to Whelan, filling his cup and then turning her attention back to the painting. "Six gods, a people living in harmony, in and around this cave, right here on Paudia?"

"Truly," said Whelan. "And now they are spread far and wide, some here on Paudia, others in Mystrosia, Ichthia, Olasia, Enturia, and Didu. Although not on Didu anymore. The volcano saw to that."

"It is a marvel," said Calax. "I thought Enturia a myth."

"As did I," said Whelan, "till the gray men arrived. I can't tell you how much they boasted about Enturia while they drank at the tavern."

Calax shook his head. "And for some reason, they want me there. I think, alive or dead."

"Ah, yes, the note," said Whelan, looking down at his bowl, which looked back to him in emptiness. "A curious business."

Rhynt walked over to Whelan again and poured the last of the tea into his bowl. "And the arrows again. I forget which is which."

Whelan stood and began pointing at the painting, where the six gods stood side by side, each with a bow over their shoulders and an arrow in their right hands. "Okay, pay attention. Starting from the left we have the god Porto and his white arrow. Then comes Canto and his blue arrow, followed by Bedo with the green, Abo with the red, Dado with the gray, and Indo with the black."

"So my master, d'Abo Pourcrey, is associated with the god Abo and the color red. Why did he not tell me this?"

Whelan chuckled. "More to the point, why did you not ask?"

"Why would I? There are a hundred hundred gods now, and all without names. Everyone just says *by the gods*, and that's that."

"Well, known to you or not, it is so. He is the last monk of Abo, and a practitioner of that god's skills."

Rhynt shook her head, incredulous. "And he was teaching me. But for what purpose?"

Whelan threw up his hands. "You will have to ask him the next time you see him."

Rhynt cringed. "See him? Well, I hope not. He was always swift and harsh with his punishments. My running away is not sitting well with him, I'm sure."

Calax frowned. "Speaking of which, I think it is time for you to do some far-seeing before we rest for the night."

Rhynt nodded, set down the empty pot next to the fire, and walked to the mouth of the cave, hoping she would see nothing but land and mountains and rivers and the wild beasts that roamed far and wide. She closed her eyes and said the words.

Behind her, at the fire, Calax noticed a detail in the painting he had missed, what looked like a young girl in green armor, running up a hill with three hill tigers. A chill went through him.

Part II

"Yes, yes, I know you have questions, particularly about the Cave of the Six Arrows, but we will get to that, sir. We will. But first let me have a sip of tea to revive my voice, which has grown gruff in the telling. Ah, that's better. Now, where were we? Oh, yes, but no. Let's leave Calax and Rhynt and that curious fellow Whelan alone for a time. Let them wander, let them fight, let them seek. Oh, sir, that look on your face says you are beyond confused, which is troubling. Do they not teach history in Enturia anymore? Whatever, no matter. I'll tell you all you need to know. Enturia, Enturia, fairest of lands, but with a sinister past, and you must know it to understand any of it. Let's start with Bookins, the king's fool."

The thing about a castle, particularly a small room like the one occupied by the king's fool, Bookins, is that it is never a place of comfort. You're either too hot or too cold, or both. Stand in front of a fire and your backside freezes. Turn around, and frost forms on your brows. It is a place of sweats and shivers, and this morning was no different. And Bookins was getting too damned old for it.

He had been fooling since he was a boy, and at the time had counted himself lucky to be selected as Fool to the king, who was himself but a young man. But the years had come and gone, and now the king had grown frail, as had Bookins.

He had once been lithe and muscular, able to perform every wheeling dance, along with feats of tumbling and juggling, but now even the king called him "slow and creaky." His days as Fool were numbered, and the number was growing smaller each day as the king's health declined. There was already talk of succession, and succession could only mean one thing for an old fool: the end. The best he could hope for would be a job at a tavern, telling ribald tales in exchange for mead and a bed.

Bookins shook off the thought as well as his blanket, which was warm on one side and cold on the other. Rising from bed had become an ordeal, but with some effort and a swing of his leg, he was able to force himself into a sitting position. He scanned the room, looking for the piss pot, which should have been right under his bed, but wasn't. Then he spotted it across the room.

"May the gods help me," he said, rising from the bed and shuffling to the pot as quickly as he could manage, arriving just in time to direct his golden stream into the pot, more or less.

"What fool moved my pot?" His own sigh was answer enough. He knew it was he and no other. He seemed to grow more forgetful by the day. If it weren't for routine, he knew he would just wander off one day, muttering to himself about inanities, a trail of urine marking his exit.

He shook off that thought. He had work to do, and the first order of business was to get dressed. The selection was easy, in fact, proscribed, the king demanding a different outfit for each day of the week. To make sure he got it right each day, Bookins had come up with a method to keep things straight in his room and in his mind. Each outfit was suspended from a rope he had strung across the room, the Monday outfit first, followed by Tuesday's, and so on. The previous day's outfit would be left on the floor for the maid to clean, a system that aided Bookins in determining which outfit came next.

The green outfit with white diamond patches was on the floor, which meant yesterday was Wednesday, so he moved to the hanging clothes and suddenly stopped in horror. Someone had replaced his Thursday outfit—a scarlet one featuring golden suns—with a midnight black one. Had the king died in the night?

No, that can't be, thought Bookins. The king had rallied the previous day, had even laughed aloud at Bookins' ribald tale of the girl with three ribbons.

No, this new outfit must be the work of Chancellor d'Mander, the king's advisor, a man who seemed to be scheming for nothing less than a quick death for the king. Bookins had seen him huddled in a corner with the bone wizard, whispering fervently. The chancellor had already instructed everyone who came in contact with the king to wear black, and this new outfit must be part of that scheme to kill whatever hope the king had to survive.

Bookins sighed. Still, perhaps he *had* died. Although he had rallied yesterday, his health overall was on a downhill slope, each day a slide toward the bottom.

Well, thought Bookins, *until I see him dead, I will be his fool and act his fool, whatever punishment d'Mander might think to mete out. I am the king's fool and answer to no one but the king.*

He pulled the black outfit down and threw it on the floor. Today was a good day for scarlet and golden suns. He tugged off his sleeping gown and set about getting dressed. The king's attendants would be helping the king through breakfast, and Bookins wanted to arrive at just the right moment, when the trays and tureens were moved aside and the king was propped up on pillows to better see the entrance of his fool.

Bookins adjusted his outfit, pulled on his belled boots, grabbed his tasseled staff, and shuffled from his room. A long walk lay ahead, through stone halls and vaulted rooms, and worst of all, a staircase with a well-counted flight of fifty steps, each more painful than the last.

As he climbed, he mumbled to himself, "*Please don't be dead, please don't be dead.*"

36

Breakfast, a gray tasteless slop prescribed by the bone doctor, was not sitting well with King Braque. Not even the weak tea could take away the slop's flinty aftertaste. He had tried to object when the tray had been brought in, but he was too weak to raise a hand or even say a word. All he could do was grimace as the young maid levered the spoon into his mouth, again and again, and dabbed at the slop that oozed back out.

In another time, he would have been dancing with this maid, cajoling her to this very bedroom with promises of jewels. The irony of his present situation—in bed with her, in this very room, but not in any way he had once hoped—was not lost on the king.

His world, it seemed, had narrowed to the confines of the royal bedroom. Not a small place, mind, with its large bed, where he had once made love to five women at once; its huge fireplace, which even now crackled with a fire large enough for a spitted pig; its fine tapestries, which hung from the sills of twenty high windows that had become the nesting places for doves; its fine carpet depicting the Battle of Whent Hill in full detail; its chandelier, which hung above everything, big as a wagon, aflame with the light of a hundred candles day and night; and its vast array of chairs and sofas, large and small, which he could see were now occupied by a dour collection of royals, maids, and attendants, all dressed in black. Still others scurried about the room or stood in small groups, whispering to each other and casting glances at him.

I'm surrounded by ants, he thought, *and they all think I'm dead.*

The sound of jangling bells drew his attention to the door, where a brightly colored old man was attempting to dance into the room. The king couldn't help but smile as his fool made his way to his bedside and gave him an appraising look.

"What, not dead yet?" said Bookins, turning to the mourners in waiting. "Who's responsible for this outrage?"

The king forced out a chuckle, which followed quickly with a fit of coughing that brought the bone doctor and Chancellor d'Mander quickly to the bedside.

The chancellor was livid. "Away, fool, have you no respect?"

Bookins attempted a jig, but his knees objected. "Respect implies there was once a *spect*, and I can see in your eyes that there was none. No spect, no spect at all."

The chancellor screamed in Bookins' face. "Insolent fool!"

The king, who had recovered from his coughing, managed to find his voice. "Hold, chancellor, and come closer so that I might have your counsel."

The chancellor turned away from Bookins and moved closer to the bed.

"Closer," said the king in a whisper.

The chancellor complied, coming up to the bed and leaning down to place his ear near the king's mouth. "What is it, Majesty?"

The king bellowed his answer. "Get out! All of you, get out!"

The chancellor turned away in anger, wiping spittle from his face. Everyone else began scurrying for the door, at speeds appropriate for their ranks, maids and pages quickly, royals more deliberately to suggest both rank and offense.

Bookins likewise turned and began his slow shuffle toward the door, sad that he would miss his time with the king.

But the king had other ideas. "Not you, Bookins. I would speak with you."

Bookins stopped and smiled, pleased. "As you wish, Majesty. What shall it be? I have a new story, if you will, and I think it will be to your liking."

"Perhaps, but first pull up a chair. I would speak of other things."

"Yes, your Majesty." Bookins grabbed the closest chair and attempted to drag it toward the bed, but the chair seemed to be rooted to the floor. "Um."

"Never mind the chair, fool. Come, climb into bed next to me."

Bookins couldn't believe his ears. "Majesty?"

"Oh, come on, there's room enough for a hundred fools. I'm sure two old fools won't be a problem. Here, there's steps on the other side. Otherwise, I dare say you will need a siege ladder."

Bookins nodded, shuffled his way to the other side of the bed, and made his way up the steps, dropping down breathless beside the king. "Oh, my. I tell you, if the world is flat, why are there so many steps?"

The king attempted a laugh but ended up coughing for some moments. "Damnable maladies. They take my breath."

Bookins looked at him with deep concern. "Perhaps we should save our talk for another time, Majesty."

"No, I have more words than time, and would have them out, spilled upon this bed if need be, covered with blood and phlegm if I must."

"As you wish. What words, Majesty?"

"Ha! In case you haven't noticed, everyone seems to be wearing black these past few days. I can only assume that I am dying, or have already died, and that the whole world has turned into carrion vultures."

Bookins frowned. "Alas, word of your health has not been good, Majesty. They even set out a black costume for me this morning. When I awoke, I thought you must already be dead."

The king sighed. "I feel it, Bookins, this slow release from life. The aching recedes and a deep slumber beckons. My mind seems to be separating from my body. My newest thoughts are of things old."

Bookins could barely hold back tears. "Majesty."

"No, no, Bookins, it is all right; all is as it should be, this passing. But, as I said, I would have a word or two with you about other matters."

"Yes, Majesty."

"Now, tell me, has the Gathering begun?"

Bookins let out a sigh that seemed to buffet the tapestries on the wall.

"Come now," said the king. "Tell me."

"Yes, the Gathering has begun. Messengers have been sent far and wide. Seven or eight of your children are already here, and of course, your son d'Bedo Brendyl has always been here."

"Yes, yes, our ambitious Green Monk. And the others? There must be, what, another twenty or so."

Bookins chuckled. "You had quite a run with the ladies, Majesty."

The king smiled. "I did spread my seed, did I not?"

"Indeed, Majesty. You were quite the farmer."

"And how are they proceeding with this Gathering?"

"Proceeding?"

"Who's doing what?"

"Oh, yes, I see. Chancellor d'Mander has sent many men to gather them in, some sent far and wide across the Great Sea."

"That's all? Just d'Mander?"

"No, Majesty, I have myself sent more than a score of birds to my network of fools and players in the faraway lands."

The king shook his head. "Good, may your friends find my children first. I do not trust my dear chancellor. He's a schemer, that one."

Bookins held his tongue. When it came to intrigue, Chancellor d'Mander had no peer.

"Okay," said the king with a sigh. "Now let's talk about you."

Bookins seemed taken aback. "Me?"

"Yes, what will you do when I am gone?"

Bookins puffed out his cheeks and shook his head in dismay. "Wander, I suppose. Although on these old legs, I may not get that far. And there's no market for an old fool."

"Just as I thought." He leaned over and patted Bookins on the hand. "That is why I have come up with a plan."

"A plan? What kind of plan, Majesty?"

"Ha! I call it The Fool's Plan."

"As well you should, Majesty. But I am all ears."

"Here, reach your hand under the pillow there."

Bookins ran his hand under the pillow and pulled out a large, heavy leather pouch with a drawstring. "Majesty?"

"Enough gold to see you through to the end."

Bookin's eyes grew wide. "Majesty!"

"Now, now, don't thank me yet. There's more. Do you remember the lodge in the wood?"

How could Bookins forget? When the king was in a randy mood, which was always, he would take his leave from Queen Milanda, now long dead, and travel on horseback to the lodge, where a score or more nubile maidens awaited. "Yes, Majesty, I well remember."

"Well, in that bag there, you will also find title to the lodge, in your name, and a barony in the bargain."

Bookin's eyes grew wide. "What, me a baron? Baron Bookins?" He couldn't help giggling. It seemed so absurd.

"Indeed, good fool. And I have also made plans for a retinue of servants and hang-abouts to serve your every need for as long as you live. Fully paid for from the treasury."

Bookins sat there, stunned, mouth agape.

The king laughed at him. "Well, fool, if your mouth is already open, how about a story for a dying king? Something as funny as it is ribald."

Bookins found his voice. "But Majesty, how can I thank you?"

The king smiled at him. "A story. One last story to beat them all. The story you have saved all these years for just such a moment. And if I should close my eyes in the telling and rattle off to another world, continue on to the end. I would have every word of it, whether in this world or the next."

Bookins thought for a moment, and then began. "There was once a baker who had three comely daughters . . ."

"Ah," said the king. "Ah."

The king's son, d'Bedo Brendyl, the Green Monk, picked up the pace. He was late, again, and knew that Chancellor d'Mander would be angry with him. He must play the part of a loving son for all to see at the king's deathbed. It would help with the transition of power. All they had to do was get through this ridiculous Gathering ceremony, and the kingdom would be his.

He continued down the long hallway that led to the king's chamber, but suddenly stopped when the door to the chamber burst open and servants and royals alike poured out, some in headlong flight and others at a more measured pace. He could not gauge what had happened from the looks on their faces. Some looked frightened, some looked angry, and some looked mystified.

And then he saw Chancellor d'Mander, a scowl on his face, heading directly toward him.

"What news? Has he died at last?"

The chancellor rolled his eyes. "If only. He clings to life like a pauper clings to the skirts of a queen, begging for alms."

"But why is everyone leaving?"

"The king has sent us out, all save his fool."

"Bookins? Why just him?"

"I don't know, and it doesn't matter, anyway. The efforts of our bone doctor, what with his slop and his leeches and his blood-letting, will have you on the throne before the week's end."

The Green Monk tried his best not to smile too broadly, but it was a struggle. "I cannot wait."

Chancellor d'Mander nodded. "But you must. We're down to hours now, I'm sure of it. So come, I must needs talk with you about the Gathering."

"What, again?"

The chancellor grabbed him by the shoulders and gave him a little shake. "One last time is all. It must be done right, and convincingly."

The Green Monk nodded, resigned to it. "One last time, then."

38

Bookins continued on with his story until the king's soft snore gave him leave to struggle back to his room, a journey that required several stops along the way, the bag of gold hidden under his garments taxing his strength and will.

Finally, he made it to his room and shut the door behind him. The king had given him gold, a lodge, a barony, and servants, but he knew it would all be lost if anyone discovered the bag. He scanned the room, looking for just the right place to hide it, and then he stopped and laughed. Who would search the room of an old fool? Not even the maids wanted to spend so much as a minute in this foul room, which smelled more and more like piss as the days passed and his bladder lost its will to retain its contents.

He spotted the spare piss pot in the corner, made sure it was suitably empty, and dropped the bag in.

"Where to put it, where to put it," he said, turning in a circle. "Ah."

He moved to a little table he had placed just so to catch the morning sun. On it was a little pot, with a tiny plant with delicate blue flowers, his only touch of nature in an otherwise bleak room. He lifted the little pot and set it, too, down into the piss pot. The bag of gold and documents gave the plant just enough lift that the blooms flowed over the edges, making it look nothing like a piss pot.

Satisfied, he shuffled over to his desk and chair and sat down on the soft blue cushion a maid had kindly given him to soften the blow of falling back into the chair.

"Ah, that's better."

He looked around the room, wondering what to do next, the coo of a pigeon in the high window drawing his attention.

"A bird at last," he said, struggling back on his feet and moving to the center of the room, whistling as he went, beckoning the bird.

The pigeon took flight, circled the room, and landed on Bookins' outstretched arm. Bookins grabbed the bird with his free hand and tugged off the message scroll attached to its leg before releasing the bird. "There you go."

He watched the bird fly directly to its cage, where its mate waited, along with enough food to celebrate the homecoming.

"Let me see now," said Bookins, unrolling the little scroll and holding it up to the light. The message sent a chill through him. "By the gods."

He crumpled the scroll and threw it into the hearth, which had been revived during his visit with the king. He would have to thank the maid for the fire he needed now to hide the contents of the message forever.

"Rest, now, and eat your fill," he said to the pigeons. "I must send you off again on the morrow. There is evil afoot in this land, and it comes this way."

The knock at his door startled him. "Ye gods, what now?"

The door swung open and Chancellor d'Mander strode in, along with d'Bedo Bendryl. Bookins looked at them both and shook his head. It was hard to believe that d'Bedo was the king's son, let alone that he was the most powerful. If anything, he looked more like the son of the chancellor. Both were tall and muscular, with sharp features. Their noses were too long, their ears stuck out, and they both wore their black beards short on the cheeks and pointed on the chin. Where they differed was their eyes and their clothes. The chancellor's eyes were as gray as the castle walls, while d'Bedo's were a deep brown, quite unlike the king's blue eyes. While the chancellor wore a gold-studded black tunic and matching cape, d'Bedo wore the emerald green cowl and shroud required of the Green Monk, a position that had come to him following the curious death of his predecessor. Not a single person at court thought the death had been natural, and most thought the death was the work of d'Bedo himself.

Bookins sighed. "What is it, my lords?"

Chancellor d'Mander looked around the room. "You really should do something to brighten this place up." He sniffed. "And it stinks of piss."

Bookins rolled his eyes. "Perhaps one day I will have a fine dwelling of my own."

The chancellor laughed. "More like a pole and a sack and a kick on your arse to get you started."

Bookins set his jaw. "Perhaps, but is this why you come to me now?"

"No, of course not. I would hear of your private discourse with the king."

The Green Monk cleared his throat. "Was there any discussion of the Gathering?"

Bookins nodded. "Yes, he is aware that steps have been taken to gather his children."

"And what else was discussed?" said the chancellor.

"My, my," said Bookins, "you really care what a fool says to a king or a king to a fool?"

The chancellor drew his dagger. "Yes, yes I do. Now tell me, and don't leave out a single word."

"Put away your dagger. You have nothing to fear from me. The king simply wanted to say his goodbyes to me in private. We have been together so many years, you see. We talked of the good old days, particularly his randy days, and he asked for one final story."

The word *final* startled the chancellor. "Final? Is he dead, then?"

Bookins shook his head. "He now snores like a baby, but I fear your wait will not be long. The life flows out of him."

"And that is all you discussed?" said d'Bedo. "Did he say anything about me?"

Bookins held a finger to his nose and looked at the ceiling as if deep in thought. "Let me think, let me think." Then he turned back to d'Bedo. "No, no he didn't."

"Nothing else at all?" said the chancellor. "No talk of succession or final decrees?"

Bookins shrugged. "Nothing."

The chancellor looked at d'Bedo. "Come, let's go. As I said, I think you are a fool to think a king would share anything of consequence with a fool."

The Green Monk nodded sheepishly and followed the chancellor to the door.

"As for you," said the chancellor, turning back to Bookins. "If I were you, I'd start packing."

Bookins smiled at them and gave them his best fool's bow. "Oh, I shall, my lords, I shall. You should not fear that."

The chancellor grunted and strode from the room, followed by d'Bedo, who slammed the door behind them.

Bookins shook his head. "What a pair."

He looked at the black ashes of the little parchment he had thrown into the fire. "This may not turn out well. I must to the king."

The thought of climbing back up those steps made him sigh, but he gathered himself up and started shuffling to the door.

"Okay, pigeons, you may have your privacy now. Don't do anything the king wouldn't do." He turned to go, but then turned back to them. "On second thought, behave. You've a long flight on the morrow."

He continued on his way, the pigeons cooing behind him.

39

The steps, the steps, the steps, each one an ordeal, his knees cracking, his breath flowing from him, his very will to live coming into question. But then he was at the top. He leaned against the cold stone wall to rest and gather his strength. He must get the message to the king before he passes. No one else would know better what to do. Left to the vultures who circle his bed, nothing but tragedy lay ahead.

A maid passing by with a tray and a pitcher caught his attention. "Here, lass, do that be water, or for that matter, anything wet?"

The maid stopped and smiled at him. "It is but warm water, to bathe the king's body."

Bookins was at her side in an instant. "Has he died, has he died?"

The maid backed away from him, thinking him crazy. "Why, no. I was merely asked to fetch it for the bone doctor, so it be ready in the event of, of, the king's death."

"Here, lass, let me take a look." He lifted the pitcher off the tray and peered inside. It looked like water, all right. He then stuck in his finger, pulled it out, and tasted it tentatively. "You are right. It is water."

The maid reached for the pitcher, but Bookins pulled it close to his chest. "No, a fool needs a drink, and a drink needs a fool." He lifted the pitcher to his lips and drank until water flowed around his face to the floor.

"Here now," said the maid, alarmed. "I shall have to fetch more now." She tugged the pitcher away from Bookins and walked away, grumbling to herself.

Bookins watched her go and then, refreshed by the water, set off again for the king's chamber. *At least there are no more stairs*, he thought.

As he walked, he played a childhood game, avoiding the cracks in the floor. *Step on a crack, won't get a snack.*

So it went, step after step, crack after crack, until the door to the king's chamber came into view at the end of the last long hallway. Strangely, guards had been posted outside. As he drew nearer, they drew their swords, forcing him to stop abruptly a few steps and cracks away from them.

"What is this?"

The guards said nothing, but stood their ground.

Bookins persisted. "Step aside for the king's fool."

One guard, the taller of the two, sheathed his sword and stepped aside, alarming the other guard, who waved his sword menacingly at Bookins. "You shall not pass. We has our orders."

"Orders? What orders? Whose orders?"

The answer came quickly, when d'Bedo Brendyl opened the door. "Guards, what's going on here?"

Bookins threw up his hands. "These *gentlemen* are preventing me from seeking access to the king, as is my right and his everlasting desire. Now, let me in."

The guard looked to d'Bedo for guidance. "Your holiness?"

The Green Monk sighed and looked up and down the hall, as if he were expecting an army to come charging down its length. "All right, let him in. But no one else." He turned to Bookins. "Come, and be quick about it. The king is failing."

Bookins gave him a quick nod and moved into the chamber as quickly as his old legs could carry him. Since he had last seen the king snoring peacefully, someone had had the bright and cheerful idea of erecting a black canopy over the bed, with curtains to block any view of the king.

Chancellor d'Mander gave Bookins a look of utter disgust and annoyance when he saw him approaching the king's bed. "You? What now, fool? Can you not see that death is close?"

Bookins shuffled up to the bed and gently nudged the bone doctor aside, so he could peer in through the curtains to see the king. The king looked back at him and smiled weakly. "Hello, my dear friend. The time comes."

The chancellor took Bookins by the arm and pulled him away from the bed. "Now that you've seen, go."

Bookins wrested his arm away from the chancellor with a force that surprised even him. "I shall not move. There is news he would hear. News he must hear. News for all of us, our very lives depend on me giving him—and you—this news."

The chancellor stepped away from him. "What?"

Bookins ignored him and went back to the king's bedside. "Your Majesty, I would have a word with you."

The king managed to blink his eyes open, and smiled again. "Ah, my fool, here to tell me a story."

The chancellor elbowed Bookins aside. "Majesty, ignore this fool. We have important matters of state to discuss."

"Yes," said d'Bedo. "*Real* matters of state." He turned to Bookins. "Not the state of fools."

The king gave the chancellor and d'Bedo a look that suggested the king was about to growl. Instead, with some effort, he managed to force himself into a sitting position. Then he looked up at them and sneered. "I would hear from the baron first."

The chancellor looked around. "Who?"

Bookins cleared his throat and smiled. "He refers to me. I am now Baron Bookins, if you please, thanks to his Majesty's largesse."

The chancellor sputtered to get out any words at all, and finally, completely flustered, turned to go. "Come, d'Bedo."

"Hold, the both of you." said the king. "The baron says he has words we should all hear, and I suggest—no, I *demand*—you stay."

The chancellor and d'Bedo complied, returning to the king's bedside.

"Now," said the king, "what is this news?"

Bookins cleared his throat. "Majesty, you know of my friend in Paudia . . ."

That's all that the chancellor needed to hear before interrupting. "Paudia? *Paudia?* Communication of any kind with the outside world is forbidden."

While the chancellor was angry, d'Bedo Bendryl, the Green Monk, was incensed. "That is a violation of the First Word of Bedo. *Seek not the word of others.*" He turned to the king. "Majesty, this man must be arrested and punished."

The king held up a hand. "Silence. I will hear no more from either of you. What Baron Bookins did was with my permission, and was innocent in the extreme. From time to time, he sends pigeons to a friend of his in Paudia. A minstrel of some sort, I believe. Is that right, Bookins?"

Bookins nodded. "Yes, Majesty. And the man knows not where the bird comes from or where the bird returns. I simply send a request for stories, tales, and songs, and he sends them to me."

The Green Monk had been shaking his head nonstop as Bookins spoke. "But how did the first pigeon know to fly to this man?"

The king cocked his head and turned to Bookins. "An interesting point, baron. What say you?"

"Majesty, as you will recall, when I first proposed this idea, you raised the same question. The answer is on the first occasion, I sent out twenty birds, not knowing if any would even reach a man capable of reading the message. But one bird did return."

"And I suppose," said d'Bedo, "it then knew to fly back to that very same man the next time. How is that possible?"

Bookins threw up his hands. "Birds, sir, birds. There is no end to their mysteries. How do they know anything? But this time, for whatever reason or magic or bird sense, it did."

The chancellor spoke up. "How long has this been going on?"

Bookins tapped his finger to his nose and looked at the ceiling. "Oh, well, ten years or more, I would say."

"What," said d'Bedo, "does a bird even live that long?"

Bookins shook his head. "No, so as the bird aged, I would send a second bird along with him, so that the knowledge would be transmitted from bird to bird over time."

The Green Monk flapped his arms at his sides and turned to the king. "This is all too ridiculous to believe. I mean, really, your Majesty. Birds training birds? How can we believe this?"

The king moved his legs to the edge of the bed and forced himself into a sitting position, which greatly alarmed the bone doctor, who had retreated to a chair along the far wall to avoid the heated argument.

Now, though, he rushed forward. "Majesty, I must insist that you lie down."

The king pointed a finger at him. "Stop where you are, you menace. I shall do what I wish."

The bone doctor said nothing more, but backed away and returned to his chair.

The king looked at Bookins and smiled. "Whatever the message is, I thank you. I seem to have found my last reservoir of energy. How long it will last, I do not know, but for now, while I am fit to hear it, tell me." He waved his arm at d'Bedo and Chancellor d'Mander. "And them."

Bookins looked back and forth at them. "Very well. Some minutes ago—though it now seems like hours—I received a bird from my friend in Paudia. I was expecting a new story for you, Majesty, but instead there was only a brief message."

"Which was?" said the king.

"That a great army approaches the eastern docks of Paudia, along with a great fleet, all headed to Enturia."

The king blinked, hard. "Army? What army? Whose army?"

"He said the army comes from a land called Mystrosia, wherever that is, and that it is the army of the White Monk."

The Green Monk gasped. "The White Monk?"

"Yes," said Bookins, "and yet he said to look for an army clothed in black."

The Green Monk began to pace back and forth nervously. "This can't be possible. Mystrosia and the White Monk are myths. Scary tales you tell your children so they'll behave."

The king nodded. "I have heard the same, but always wondered about it. Even stories are sometimes true, or partly true, is that not right, Bookins?"

Bookins shrugged. "Yes, I suppose, but more to the point, Majesty, an army approaches. What are we to do?"

The king paused, then looked at them solemnly. "Chancellor, convene a council of war on the hour."

"Yes, your Majesty," said the chancellor.

The king turned to d'Bedo. "My son, please attend. We shall need your wisdom and, more importantly, your blessings for what is to come."

The Green Monk nodded. "Of course."

The king turned to Bookins. "Your words have steeled us all. Let us hope the news has come in time to save us."

"Yes, Majesty."

The king slowly lowered himself to the floor to test his legs. "Ah, that's better. I was turning into a puddle of flesh in that damned bed. Bookins, I wish you to attend as well. As baron, you have earned that right."

Bookins looked so astonished, the king had to laugh. "Don't look so surprised. There is wisdom in humor, and we shall all need it."

"Yes, Majesty."

The king looked around the bedside. "Who has made off with my clothes? I can't fight a battle in a sleeping gown."

Bookins chuckled. "Have a seat, Majesty, I will see to it."

Bookins, d'Mander, and d'Bedo bowed to the king, and turned to leave.

"Oh," said the king, calling after them. "I think the blue shoes will be just the thing." He looked over at the bone doctor. "And take this damnable man with you."

40

Bookins couldn't keep up with d'Bedo and the chancellor, and that was just fine with him. As they accelerated down the corridor, obviously in an animated, aggravated conversation, each man gesticulating wildly, Bookins shuffled up to the tall guard and passed on instructions to clothe the king and see to it that he made it to the counsel hall.

"And there should be wine. It restores him."

The guard grunted and went back to the other guard to explain things to him before he went in search of a maid who might know about the king's clothes.

Bookins turned and called after him. "And make sure to get his blue shoes."

The guard waved his hand in the air without turning around or slowing down. *Good*, thought Bookins, *good.*

He looked down the corridor and sighed. So many steps to take, and that just to reach the staircase down to the next corridor, and then on to his room. He wondered whether he could make it, but seeing no other alternative, put one reluctant foot in front of another.

He'd just have time to get back to his room, change into something more appropriate for a war room, and launch another bird. He thought of his answers to the king and shook his head. He didn't like lying to the king, but he didn't see any other way around it. Yes, what he had told him was true, at least as far as it went. But he had left out half the message. He had wanted to tell the king, but not in front of the others. That would just raise alarm bells in their minds, and probably be the end of him. Perhaps he could linger in the counsel hall and get the undivided attention of the king. Then he could tell him all.

Satisfied with his plan, he picked up the pace and soon reached the dreaded staircase. Going down was just as painful as going up, with the added fear that he would topple forward and break every bone in his body. The steps and walls were slick, and there was nothing to grab onto to help him along the way. He had to press his palms on the walls to either side of him and hope that he could gain enough purchase not to perish.

And then he was down on the landing, his shins and knees aching from the descent. As he walked down the corridor to his room, he could hear the sound of trumpets. *The call to arms*, he thought. But would the call amount to anything?

Enturia was a small island nation that had cut itself off from the outside world centuries ago. A fortified wall had been built around its entire circumference, which was effective against small raiding parties in the early years. But eventually the raids decreased in frequency and then stopped. Centuries passed and Enturia became a myth to the outside world.

But now they had been found, and there was no telling whether they would have the strength of numbers or the skills to hold off an entire army and its fleet.

The sight of the door to his room brought a smile to his face. He took the last few steps, opened the door, and set about writing out a message. It was one word: *faster!*

41

The war room, if you could call it that, because there had never been a war, was far too large for the table that sat along one wall. It had once been part of the tallest gray oak tree in Enturia, a tree that was said to be a thousand years old, but perished nonetheless by a lightning strike in a brief thunderstorm. The table was four feet wide by thirty feet long and eight inches thick. The pattern of light and dark striations that ran through the wood resembled a child's notions of a ghost rising from a cemetery.

Sixty-one chairs sat around the table, thirty on each side and one, which was much larger, at its head. That was for the king and no one but the king. Eight men sat on either side of the table, bunched up near the king's end, all still dressed in mourning black, each with their own shouted ideas about what to do about the Mystrosian threat. Their voices echoed through the vast hall, making them sound more like a murder of crows than counselors to the king.

Then all conversation ceased when the guard at the door rapped the end of his spear hard on the floor three times, indicating the approach of the king. They all sat there quietly as the sound of a squeaky wheel grew louder and the king appeared in the doorway, being pushed in his wheeled chair by a soldier.

Unlike the rest of them, the king was dressed in blue trimmed in gold, his lightest crown, a mere band of gold, twinkling in the sunlight that streamed into the room from the single high window.

The guard stopped, pulled the large chair away from the table, and rolled the king into place at its head. The king surveyed the room, nodding at each of them in turn. Chancellor d'Mander, as was custom, was just to the king's right, looking pensive and impatient. The Green Monk, d'Bedo

Bendryl, sat to d'Mander's right, avoiding the eyes of the king. The king feared there was something not quite right about his son, and that the kingdom would fail in his hands.

To d'Bedo's right was the Chancellor of Coin, Besbo d'Arc, a hunched-over man with tiny hands and bulging eyes well suited for counting even the smallest coin. To Besbo's right was someone unknown to the king, but from the ribbons and medals on his chest was clearly a soldier, as were all the other unknown men on the other side of the table, save for General Boh, High Commander of the Forces of the King, seated directly at the king's left and giving him an obsequious smile.

The king shook his head. "Look at you, all in black, as if I am already dead."

Everyone looked straight ahead and down, avoiding the king's sharp look.

"Where's Bookins?"

Bookins, who was seated along the far wall of the hall, stood and waved. "Over here, Majesty."

"Here now, come closer. How can we hear you from way over there?" The king turned to the guard who was attending him and waved in the direction of Bookins. "Please, a chair for my fool, at the end of the table, if you will."

The guard moved to the far wall and dragged a chair over to the far end of the table, dropping it down facing the king. Bookins shuffled over to it, smiled at the king, who seemed miles away, and sat down.

"Now," said the king, "we have serious business to discuss. Plans to make. Orders to give. But first I would speak of my condition."

He looked at them and sighed. "Your manner of dress is appropriate. I fear that whatever we discuss today and whatever decisions we make, I shall not be here to see them play out, at least not until the end. Death is pulling me in like a fish, and no matter how hard I struggle, no matter how much I want to stay in these waters, I fear the hook is firmly set."

Everyone looked down at the table.

"So, before we discuss the Mystrosians, I think we need to discuss the Gathering."

The Green Monk was startled. "The Gathering? But Majesty, that is something done after your death, not before."

The king nodded. "Yes, yes, that is true, but this time, I fear, the Gathering must take place as soon as possible. I don't want it happening in the middle of a battle."

The chancellor cleared his throat. "We will need a few days to prepare, but I take your point, Majesty. I will see to the arrangements."

"Good," said the king. "Have you gathered them all? Are they all here?"

The chancellor smiled. "You were quite prolific, Majesty. We have eight so far and an additional three should be here by the morrow."

"Eleven? I thought there were more."

The chancellor shook his head. "No, Majesty, several died in childbirth, along with their mothers. Only eleven remain."

"I see."

"Would you like to meet with them, Majesty?"

The king thought about it. The only child he'd ever seen or known was d'Bedo, his child with Queen Milanda, who died in childbirth a year later, along with their second child.

He shook his head. "No, it is better that I don't. I cast my seed freely and wildly, but know nothing about the plants that grew from them."

He turned to the men at the table. "Now, let's discuss the topic at hand—*survival*." He turned to General Boh. "General, what is the status of our forces?"

General Boh puffed out his cheeks and cocked his head, not sure where to start. The king had often wondered how such an indecisive man could have risen through the ranks. He gave every appearance of a general—stiff back, a tendency to bluster, a scowl fitting for the job, a fastidiousness of dress bordering on obsession, and a deep voice that sounded just right when shouting commands, however foolish. "Well, Majesty, as you know, we have never engaged in battle. We have trained for it, yes, but I'm afraid our best skill is marching in parades."

The king sighed. "I don't think a marching competition is what the Mystrosians have in mind."

The general looked down at the table and folded his hands together. "No, Majesty."

"And how many men do we have in arms?"

The general looked up, glanced around, and smiled. "More than seven hundred, Majesty."

The king turned to Bookins. "And how many Mystrosians did your pigeon say were coming, Bookins?"

Bookins grimaced. "Thousands, Majesty."

The general visibly blanched. "Thousands, you say?" He rubbed a hand through his hair. "Still, we are well positioned defensively. If we met them in the field, yes, that would be a problem, even a disaster, but here, behind these walls, the advantage goes to us." He rapped his knuckles on the table for emphasis.

The king stroked his beard. "And how would you conduct this defense, general?"

The general beamed, warming to the subject. "They will be coming by ship, so first we will hit them with volley after volley of flaming arrows. Those that grow still closer will be met with boulders and flaming bails thrown by our trebuchets. Any who make it to the beach will then have to pass through a thicket of pikes, making them easy targets for our archers and spearmen."

The general licked his lips and looked around the room, almost giddy. "And then, if they make it to our walls, they will be met with boiling pitch from our kettles."

He turned to the king. "All will be chaos, and we shall carry the day."

The king smiled. "That is the answer I hoped to hear, but one question if you don't mind?"

The general looked puzzled. "Majesty?"

The king sighed and looked around the table. "I just wonder what will happen if they do manage to breach our walls. Will your men be ready for that as well?"

The general slumped back in his chair. "As I have said, they have been trained in hand-to-hand combat."

The chancellor interrupted. "But with wooden swords."

"Yes," said the general. "What they will do when faced with bloody steel is unknown. None have been bloodied or seen their comrades dismembered or killed."

The king shook his head. "Then we best make sure our defenses are as strong as you say. Do we have enough boulders and arrows and such?"

"Aye," said the general, "plenty of boulders, and our blacksmiths and fletchers are hard at work making more arrows and swords."

"Good," said the king. "Is there anything else we need to cover?"

The room fell silent, but then Bookins cleared his throat. "A minor point, Majesty."

"Yes?"

"The last time I took a stroll, which I assure you was some years ago, our defensive wall stretched for hundreds of miles around our fair island."

"Yes, so?"

"How much wall can seven hundred soldiers defend?"

The king looked stricken and turned quickly to the general. "Well?"

The general shrugged sheepishly. "A mile, perhaps two."

The king was crestfallen. "We are doomed."

Bookins clapped his hands together. "A thought, Majesty."

"Go on," said the king.

"Ah," said Bookins, "have you heard the story of the spider and the ant?"

The chancellor threw up his hands. "A story? By the gods, we don't need a story."

"He's right," said the king. "What's your point?"

"Oh, all right then. I'll skip the story, although it's a good one."

The king motioned him to continue. "Please, Bookins, please."

"Yes, Majesty." He looked around the table. "The enemy could land anywhere, right? But they know nothing of Enturia. No one does. I think they will attack at first sight of land."

The general grunted, annoyed. "So what's your point, then?"

Bookins leveled his gaze at the general. "My point, general, is that all we need do is lure them in where our walls are strongest."

The general threw up his hands. "And how do you propose to do that?"

Bookins cocked his head, glanced around the table, and giggled. "I have a plan."

General Boh turned to the king. "The fool has a plan. Must we listen to it?"

The king waved a dismissive hand at the general. "We will listen, yes, because I don't hear anyone else coming forward with a plan. Go on, Bookins. What is this plan?"

Bookins stood and started to do a little jig, although badly. "I calls it the Smuggle-Buggle Plan. *When Enturia was in struggle, Bookins the Fool knew to smuggle.* And so on and so on. The rest of the verse will come to me, I'm sure."

The chancellor was on his feet. "This is ridiculous!"

The king rubbed at his temples, then turned to Bookins once more. "Bookins, less verse, more plan."

Bookins bowed. "Yes, Majesty. Well, then, if you'll all stand—not you, Majesty—and follow me over to the map, I'll explain what I have in mind. Guard, would you be so kind as to roll the king this way."

They all pushed back their chairs and walked over to the far wall, where a floor-to-ceiling map of the known world was displayed. Bookins waited patiently until the king was rolled into position at the center of the group.

"Now," Bookins began. "Here we have the known world. To the west, two days' sailing from Enturia, we have the easternmost coast of Paudia, also known as the Wild Lands or the Free Lands, a country without government or religion, filled with tigers, witches, wizards, and trolls, not to mention every variety of hang-about, sellsword, cutthroat, pickpocket, and scamp."

The chancellor nodded, impatient. "Yes, yes, we know that. Go on."

Bookins rolled his eyes. "Yes, of course." He turned back to the map. "Now, to the north we have the little island country of Olasia."

The Green Monk groaned, exasperated. "What's your point?"

Bookins was about to reply, but the king interrupted him. "How can he get to a point when everyone is interrupting him?" Silence, everyone. Now, go on, Bookins."

Bookins gave the king a quick bow and proceeded. "Now, as you all know, we do some trading with both countries, but not as Enturians. Our fishing boats trade in Olasia under the guise that they're Paudians. Likewise, when we trade in Paudia, we do so under the Olasian flag."

"I'm sorry," said the king, "but I have to join my lords on this one. What exactly is your point?"

"Yes, Majesty, I'm getting there. Firstly, no one really knows much about Enturia, particularly the Mystrosians. When they get to the Paudian docks and ask which way to sail, all the locals will be able to say is that we're out here somewhere to the east."

"Okay," said the king. "Is there a secondly?"

Bookins smiled. "There is, indeed. Okay, so now let's look at the coast of Enturia. You see there, the cove?"

"Yes," said General Boh. "That's the harbor used by our fishing fleet."

"Precisely," said Bookins. "Now, what we want to do is get the Mystrosians to attack there."

The general stroked his chin. "I'm sorry, why would we do that?"

"A number of reasons, general. First, look at the shape of the harbor. To get to the docks, you must first pass through an opening in the land no bigger than the width of three ships."

"Ah," said the general, "so we attack them in the narrows."

Bookins shook his head. "No, general, what we want to do is trap them all, every last Mystrosian ship, in our harbor. If I'm not mistaken, the harbor is big enough for a hundred ships, perhaps more."

"Yes," said the general. "That's right, but how will we fight them in fishing boats?"

"Ah," said Bookins, "you miss my point. We will hide our fishing boats behind the cliffs, here to the north of the harbor. Then, when the last of the Mystrosian ships enter the harbor, our fishing fleet will sail around this cape and seal it off. It's shallow enough there that if we just scuttle a few fishing boats, the harbor will be sealed and the Mystrosians will have nowhere to go. We will then pounce on them from every direction."

The king smiled. "That's brilliant!"

The chancellor nodded. "As far as it goes, yes, but how are we going to get them to land at that exact spot."

"Ah," said Bookins, pointing a finger at the ceiling. "We will station our fastest fishing boats at intervals just over the horizon. When the Mystrosians spot one, they will not be able to yet see our coastline and will think they've come upon an Enturian warship."

"But they're just fishing boats," said the general.

Bookins waggled his head. "Yes, yes, but with a little work, flags and so forth, we can fool them into thinking they've come upon a warship."

The king seemed confused. "Then what?"

"Then, Majesty, our warship turns and flees."

"Oh, so the idea is to lure them to our fishing harbor?"

"Yes, exactly."

"Wait," said the chancellor. "What if they catch our ship?"

Bookins smiled at the chancellor. "Good question, and I think the answer is, they won't. Our fishing vessel will be empty of all cargo, whereas the Mystrosian ships will be loaded down with men and, no doubt, siege machines. They'll sit heavy in the water. My guess is our fishing vessel will have to take care not to outrun them too much."

The Green Monk cleared his throat. "Okay, I'm with you so far, but why would you think they would all just sail straight into the harbor?"

"Again, a good question. Correct me if I'm wrong, general, but isn't one of the key tactics of battle to surprise your enemy?"

The general nodded. "It is."

"Well, then, the Mystrosians want to get to our so-called warship before it can sound the alarm. They want to take us by surprise, in great numbers, overwhelm us."

"Makes sense," said the general.

Bookins looked around the room. "Any other questions?"

The king raised a hand. "Yes. Isn't it also a known battle tactic, or rather caution, not to concentrate your forces at a single point?"

"Yes," said the general. "The king makes a good point."

"He does," said Bookins. "It's true. If they split their forces, we are lost. But, it would depend when they split their forces."

The Green Monk, who had mostly stood silent throughout the meeting, spoke up. "Why is that?"

"My guess, my hope, is that if they do split their forces, it won't be until they've caught sight of land and had a chance to study the coastline."

"And?"

Bookins pointed at the channel in front of the harbor. "See here, our fishing fleet uses this channel because it's the only safe passage into and out of the harbor. If the enemy decides to split its forces while they're in the channel, they'll have to deal with the reefs and rough waters to either side."

Bookins laughed. "In some respects, it might be *good* for us if they split their forces there. They'll lose ships and men on those treacherous reefs, which will have the added effect of forcing the other ships straight into the harbor." He shook a fist in the air. "And then, by the gods, we'll have them."

He turned to the king, who was beaming. "Majesty," he said, looking around and smacking his lips, "I thought there was to be wine."

Part III

"Yes, yes, a war approaches, a war on a vast scale, Mystrosia on one side and Enturia on the other, and now only the Great Sea separates them. I see you are confused and—may I say it?—a bit alarmed, but tarry a while longer with me. The tea is hot, we are out of the elements, and most important, we are safe here. Good, good. Now, your confusion takes us back to the Cave of the Six Arrows. As I recall, a chill was running through Calax's bones. Something about the painting on the cave wall. Ah yes. I remember now. So then . . ."

42

Rhynt stared at the painting, mouth agape, Calax and Whelan at her side. "How can this be? She looks just like me. The armor, the hair." She pointed at her breastplate. "And see here, it is the very same scene Zyrx hammered into my armor, and exactly as it was in my dream."

Whelan's eyes grew wide. "You dreamed this?"

"Yes, and when I awoke, this armor with this scene was at my bedside."

Whelan shrugged. "I can explain the armor. Zyrx has been here before."

"Yes, of course," said Calax. "Your red hair and the way the hill tigers took to you must have jogged his memory about the painting."

"But then there's the dream," said Whelan. "That's the part that worries me."

"Oh?" said Rhynt.

Whelan gave her a concerned look, and turned to the painting. "See here in the painting, her position in it in relation to the gods. While all before them kneel and pray, she and the tigers flee."

Rhynt shrugged. "So?"

"So, this painting represents the Great Unraveling."

"The what?"

"The *end* of the Age of the Six Arrows."

"What happened?"

Whelan sighed and pointed at the girl in the painting. "There are many stories. It is said that she was the child of a beautiful peasant woman and one of the gods. No one knows which."

Calax laughed. "Whelan, don't fill her head with nonsense. There are no gods, and never were."

Whelan turned on him. "There were, there *are*."

Calax shook his head. "We have opposite ideas. Go on, finish this wild story of yours."

"Please," said Rhynt. "I'd like to hear it."

"Very well. Anyway, when it was clear to the other gods that the child was indeed the daughter of one of them, a great argument ensued."

"Wait," said Rhynt. "How did it become clear to them?"

Whelan sighed. "I was afraid you might ask that. According to all the songs and tales I know, the union of a god and a mortal never goes well. Babies are born with unusual skills, certainly. That's the good part. But the bad part is that they are often deformed or malformed in some way." He hesitated, and then pressed on. "Like your foot."

Rhynt gasped, but Calax began laughing. "Minstrel, please, if that were true, Rhynt and I would be demigods."

Whelan nodded. "Well, all the songs say you fight like a god in battle."

Calax scoffed. "I am a berserker, nothing more, and what skills I have are from long practice and long experience. There is nothing godly about me, or I dare say, Rhynt. We were each malformed, but what brought us here to this spot, on this day, is nothing but mortal toil, not godly gifts."

Whelan shook his head, smiling. "You really are quite the skeptic, aren't you? Well, I'll have to work on you. You'll see the light one day."

"Speaking of which," said Calax, "if we don't get some sleep, daylight will be upon us, and we have a long way to ride."

Rhynt balked. "No, I would hear the rest of the story. Go to sleep if you wish." She turned to Whelan. "Will you finish the story?"

Whelan nodded, which made Calax throw up his hands. "Suit yourself, I'm going to find a soft spot near the fire. See you in the morning."

He started to go, but then turned back. "By the way, what did you far-see before I beckoned you back to the painting?"

"The Mystrosian army moves closer, in great numbers, scattering men and beasts before them. There are great fires behind them, the villages burned."

Calax nodded. "Are they even moving now, at night?"

"No, they have camped for the night, as we have. But they are less than five miles from us now. It is as you say. We will have to ride hard on the morrow."

Calax looked at her and then at Whelan. "All right, I'll leave you to your story, but don't be long. We leave at first light." And with that, he turned and walked toward the fire.

Whelan watched him go. "He is a strange man, don't you think?"

Rhynt shrugged. "Not to me. He is what he says he is, and does what he does. No tricks with him, at least not like my master."

"The Red Monk, aye. Do you sense him out there?"

Rhynt shook her head. "No, and that worries me."

"Because?"

"Because I never want to be his pisspot again."

Whelan chuckled. "No, I guess not. Now, where were we in the story?"

"A great argument among the gods."

"Ah, yes. Okay, so order in the kingdom, the harmony that the gods had provided for eons, was lost. All was chaos. Here, come closer to the painting."

They walked closer, and Whelan pointed to a place high on the painting. "Do you see that chasm?"

Rhynt nodded.

"That is what came to be known as the Chasm of Chaos. Now, several of the gods sought to kill the girl, thinking her an abomination. Some even thought she might be a risk to them."

"What?"

"She was a demigod, you see, and had powers in some respects as strong as those of the gods themselves."

Rhynt giggled. "Sounds like it would be fun to be a demigod. Are they immortal?"

Whelan shook his head. "No, unlike gods, though they might live forever, demigods can be killed just like you and me."

Rhynt smiled. "Okay, the gods are angry with her. Go on."

Whelan started to continue. "The girl—"

"No, wait," said Rhynt. "You keep calling her the girl. What's her name?"

Whelan raised a finger. "Ah, I see what you mean. Yes, she most certainly had a name. Unfortunately, the name is lost to history."

"Really? You'd think a demigod's name would be known through word of mouth, carrying forward in tales."

Whelan gave her a quizzical look. "That's very perceptive of you, but there's a good reason the name remains a mystery, which I will get to in a moment."

"All right, go on."

"The dissolution of the Age of the Six Arrows did not happen overnight. The girl lived. The argument continued for fifteen years, the anger and bitterness eroding the Age by the day."

"Until?"

"Yes, there is always an *until*. Until the child reached her fifteenth birthday. No one knows the significance of that, but on that very day, the scene you see depicted here, the girl running with her hill tigers—that was the last day."

"What happened?"

"No doubt something horrible. Some think there was a coordinated attack by several of the gods. Some think the event was sparked by something the girl said or did, an exercise of her power, perhaps. In any event, the girl and her tigers rushed to the chasm and disappeared for all time."

Rhynt was incredulous. "What, they jumped into the chasm?"

Whelan shrugged. "It is not known. They could have jumped, I suppose, but none of the tails mention that. And there's no mention of bodies being found either. The chasm could be navigated top to bottom using trails along its cliff faces, so it is just as possible that they simply made their escape, never to return."

"Okay, so they're gone. Then what?"

"Ah, the screaming and finger-pointing began, each god distrustful of the others, until they could no longer stand to be in each other's company. They dispersed, then disappeared themselves. All that remains is a succession of monks, the monks in their colored robes and hoods, each trying to retain the teachings of the god that meant most to them, not that they do that very well. And the argument among the gods continues in the monks, each certain that their god is the true god, and more than willing to kill monks of a different color and whoever follows them."

Rhynt nodded. "Like now. My master is the last of his kind, all his followers gone. He seeks revenge, but has no means."

"Aye," said Whelan. "And now we have the Mystrosians, followers of the White Monk, seeking to wage war against Enturia, followers of the Green Monk."

They grew silent for some moments, each wondering at the painting. Finally, Rhynt spoke. "Wait, why do we not know the girl's name?"

"Ah," said Whelan, giving her a wink. "When she and her tigers disappeared, the gods decreed that her name should never be spoken again. It was said among the people that a simple whispering of her name would bring tragedy to a person, their loved ones, or the entire village. Some thought that was ridiculous, of course, and used her name freely, but over time, the curse of saying her name out loud became the dominant theme. And so the name was lost."

Rhynt sighed. "I don't like that. A person should have a name. And demigods, too."

Whelan smiled at her. "I agree, and in another story, she has a name."

"Really?"

"Yes, but I must not say it, for it is the story that I believe. If I say her name, I may curse her return."

"Return?"

"Yes, in this story, she and her hill tigers return, and a new age begins."

"I like the sound of that better."

Whelan laughed. "I thought you would."

She looked down at her breast plate and then back at the wall painting. "Do you think it could be me?"

Whelan laughed even louder. "Ha! Are you the child of a god?"

Rhynt frowned and shook her head. "No, but I have some skills."

Whelan put a hand on her shoulder. "Which were taught to you by your Red Monk, who would like nothing more than to make people believe you are that very demigod."

Rhynt spat. "And he would use me for his own ends."

Whelan nodded. "Yes, I believe so. I'm sure when he came upon you he thought just that, a way back, a way to restore his power and his following."

Rhynt clinched both fists. "That man!"

Whelan patted her on the shoulder again. "Don't get so worked up. You are rid of him now."

"I guess. I hope."

Whelan sighed. "The hour grows late. Time to get some rest. And you'll be happy to know that we travel into the chasm tomorrow."

Rhynt's eyes grew wide. "Really?"

"Yes, it's the only way to get to the port now. All other roads lead elsewhere."

Rhynt looked back at the painting and the chasm. "Do you think she's still there? I mean, if she is a demigod?"

"Perhaps," said Whelan, patting her on the shoulder. "You never know with demigods. She could be anywhere. Come, let's to sleep."

She dreamed of running, the tigers bounding along beside her, racing free with her across the plain, their speed ever increasing as the chasm came into sight and all went black.

43

King Merek the Mighty sat on a pillow within his tent, wondering why he had allowed d'Porto Saleen, the White Monk, to talk him into this invasion. Mystrosia had all the land and wealth it needed after the defeat of Alamaria. No, this new venture, a war against a land most thought mythical, was about religion. It always was with d'Porto.

The first days in Paudia had been exhausting. So much marching, so much killing and mayhem. But that was what Mystrosian armies always did, killing everyone lest they attack from behind as the army moved on.

King Merek looked around the tent. They had packed light for the journey, but the royal tent was still luxurious enough to make the end of each day pleasurable. There were carpets to block the cold, tapestries depicting Mystrosian victories, and large, plump pillows to ease the pain of the ride. Food and wine sat on silver trays within reach, and a well-tended fire warmed the whole tent. His seven concubines helped as well, although after days on the road, they now snored softly beside him, exhausted. Not that he had the energy to enjoy them.

He patted his stomach and frowned. He was growing round, no longer the robust warrior who had succeeded his father. His once thick black hair was also gone, making him look like a small round ball sitting on a large round ball sitting on a pillow. But as decrepit as he was becoming, he still had the same black eyes that could fix a man in place with fear.

He plucked a grape from a tray and popped it into his mouth. There was nothing better than an Alamarian grape, unless it was an Alamarian wine, two bonuses that came with the victory over them in the previous year.

Merek looked at the concubines around him, wondering which one's rump to rest his head on for the night, but then the flap to the tent was thrown open and d'Porto Saleen strode in, followed by two guards dragging a prisoner between them.

Where the king was round and squat, the White Monk was tall and gaunt. Dressed in white robes, cowl, and hood, with a long white beard to match, he was an imposing figure. And for all his whiteness, like the king, it was his eyes that you remembered long after he had left the room. Not black, like the king's, but an icy blue.

The king frowned. "What's this?"

The White Monk approached and bowed. "A prisoner, your Majesty, one of the grays with the diamond sigil I told you about."

The king shrugged. "And?"

The White Monk cocked his head. "You had expressed disbelief in the idea that Enturia was more than a myth."

The king nodded and looked at the prisoner. "And he is Enturian?"

"Yes, Majesty." He turned and smiled at the prisoner, who had clearly been tortured. "And he has given us a wealth of information."

The king's interest was piqued. "Such as?"

"Enturia's exact location and an estimate of their army's strength." He laughed. "They have but seven hundred men, Majesty. Seven hundred against our seven thousand."

The king brightened. "Well, that is good news. Here, d'Porto, have a seat and enjoy a glass of wine with me."

The White Monk shook his head. "I don't touch wine, as you know, and besides, there is more news to discuss."

"Oh?"

"Yes, Majesty." The White Monk pulled a small scroll from his robes and handed it to the king, who read the message silently.

"What does this mean?"

The White Monk pointed at the prisoner. "This note was found on the prisoner. He is one of an elite guard sent into Paudia to retrieve Calax Halfhand."

"The hero of the Battle of Whent Hill?"

"The very one."

"But why?"

The White Monk sighed. "That is the puzzle. The prisoner claims not to know, and as you can see by his appearance, I have done everything to get him to reveal that reason."

The king looked at the prisoner and then back at d'Porto. "Yes, I'm sure you've done everything to get an answer. But is an answer really important? I know Calax is a valiant, formidable warrior—a berserker even—but the odds are still no better than seven hundred and one of them to seven thousand of us. Even a berserker can't improve those odds much."

The White Monk nodded. "That is true, but this man's quest to find Calax Halfhand may mean that the Enturians know of our intent and are reaching out to sellswords for assistance. There numbers may have grown beyond seven hundred by now, but most important, we may have lost the element of surprise."

The king had to laugh. "Surprise or no, we have the numbers."

"We do."

The king popped another grape into his mouth. "On the other hand, perhaps we should try to find this Calax Halfhand ourselves. We can always use another berserker, and price is certainly no object."

"Yes, Majesty, I have been tracking him—and others—with gelas, so it shouldn't be too difficult to find him again. My first attempt was thwarted, but I will be more circumspect the next time."

"You've been tracking him? Why am I the last to hear about it?"

"I've been tracking everyone to the east of us, to make sure our path is clear and that no one escapes our march to the sea."

"I see. Well, then, find him."

"Yes, Majesty."

The king pointed at the tray of food. "Are you sure you won't join me. The Alamarian grapes are wonderful. In my mind, the best part of our victory."

The White Monk shook his head. "I appreciate the offer, Majesty, but I have other things to attend to. Speaking of which, what would you have me do with the prisoner?"

The king sighed, looked at the prisoner, and then nodded at d'Porto. "Just don't bloody my tent."

The king cringed as the prisoner was dragged screaming from the tent. "Oh, bother." He rolled over and leaned his head against a plump rump. Sleep came quickly.

44

Calax was back in the room, a boy again, staring into the angry face of Salibar, who was screaming at him. Phendour and Blusk, full grown and alive, stood by the hearth, laughing at him as Zyrx's three hill tigers circled, their growls echoing around the room.

He looked around for Zyrx, but he was nowhere to be seen.

"Pay attention, boy," said Salibar, hitting him hard in the leg with his stick.

Calax retreated in pain.

Salibar was shouting at him again. "Get back here, boy, to this spot or there will be no dinner this day. You will get this right, and you will get this right now."

Calax could take no more. "No, no, no!"

"Here, now," said Whelan, "wake up."

Calax startled awake and immediately went for his dagger, forcing Whelan back. "No, Calax, no. It was but a dream. You are safe and well, and thankfully awake."

Calax lowered his dagger and looked around the cave. Light was streaming in, illuminating the painting, which seemed to dance in the morning light.

Calax sighed heavily. "Why did you not wake me sooner? It is well past dawn."

Whelan nodded. "Yes, I thought to, but the girl was having a fitful dream as well. Being rested is far more important than being early. We have a difficult trip this morning."

Calax got to his feet. "Where is she?"

"Saddling the horses."

"What, shall we not eat?"

"No, I have already reset the fire pit with fresh wood, as is the custom. We may have but one fire in this cave, and no more."

Calax cocked his head. "So many customs. I tell you, I would give up all your customs for another cave rat."

Whelan laughed. "Don't worry, I have already cooked up three fat ones. We'll eat them as we ride."

Calax smiled. "All right, then, let's go."

"Great, get your bedroll."

Calax kneeled down, grabbed one end of the bedding and rolled it up tightly, lashing it closed. He stood up, looked around the cave one last time, and followed Whelan to its mouth, where Rhynt was waiting with the horses.

Gash whinnied in greeting as Calax grabbed the reins and climbed into the saddle. "I hear you had a bad dream last night?"

"Aye," said Rhynt, climbing onto her horse. "And you as well, I hear."

Calax nodded. "A dream that comes again and again most nights."

"Oh?" said Rhynt. "What's it about?"

Calax sighed. "About my struggles as a boy. It's nothing." Calax turned to Whelan, who had come up behind them on his horse, trailed by the empty-saddled horse. "Where's these plump cave rats you were talking about."

Whelan laughed and pulled a bag off his saddle horn. He handed a roasted rat to each of them. "You'd best eat it before we get to the chasm. You'll need both hands—and your wits—to make the descent."

They began their descent from the cave, the horses moving gingerly, their hooves spraying loose rocks and pebbles as they tackled the slope. Calax and Rhynt ate their rats greedily, Whelan laughing at them and singing a tune whose words were lost in the stiff breeze. The graveled slope soon gave way to rolling hills, and then the hills were gone and they were on a vast plain, the horses eager to run, horse and rider becoming one as they galloped toward the horizon, where a deep gash in the land loomed.

As they drew closer, Whelan held up a hand, motioning them to slow down and then to stop just feet from the chasm. Whelan got off his horse.

"We'd best rest the horses a while," he said. "They will need their strength for the descent."

Rhynt and Calax jumped down from their horses.

"I will need my strength, too," said Calax. "I don't suppose you have another rat."

Whelan laughed. "No, but I have hard bread."

Calax turned to Rhynt. "Are we safe here? Are they getting closer?"

"I'll check," she said, closing her eyes and turning slowly in a circle. "Interesting," she said, finally.

"What?" said Calax.

"The main army is about four miles away, and heading straight this way, but they've sent out groups of scouts in all directions."

"They're looking for something," said Calax.

"Yes, us, I fear," said Whelan. "That gives us less time than I thought."

"No," said Rhynt. "The scouts are not yet headed our way. We'll have time to feed and water the horses."

Calax looked around. "What? On this barren plain?"

Rhynt laughed. "Not so barren. See that hillock there. There's a pond surrounded by grasses just beyond it."

Whelan smiled at her strangely. "What a wonder you are."

Rhynt giggled. "Just a trick of the Red Monk is all."

She took up the reins of the four horses and tugged them in the direction of the hillock, Whelan and Calax following.

Calax turned to Whelan. "On second thought, now that we have water, I'll have some of that hard bread of yours."

"Aye," said Whelan. "There will just be time enough, I think, if we can avoid the scouts."

"Will they be able to follow us into the chasm?"

Whelan shook his head. "I think not. Even if you know the trail down, as I do, it is a treacherous business. You'll understand as soon as you look over the precipice." He looked ahead, where Rhynt had let loose the reins of the horses to allow them to drink from the pool. "Ah, that water looks good."

"Indeed," said Calax.

They moved to the pond, where Rhynt was already spooning up handful after handful of water into her mouth.

"Hey, leave some for us," said Calax.

Rhynt spit the water out, laughing. "Ha, there is plenty, sir."

Calax and Whelan kneeled down next to her and scooped up water, first in their hands and then, when they had slaked their thirst, with gourds for the trip to come.

Finally, all three sat back and watched the horses nibbling on the grass. Calax was the first to speak. "So, once we're at the bottom of the chasm, what then? None of this is on my map."

Whelan frowned. "It's curious, isn't it, that our friend Zyrx would leave off first the cave and now the chasm. They are both important features for any map of Paudia."

"Aye, so it seems." said Calax. "So what next?"

Whelan picked up a stick and drew a winding streak in the sand. "This is the chasm." He stuck the stick into the ground. "We are here." He moved the stick forward and stuck it in the sand again. "Here is where we must climb out of it."

Calax nodded. "How far is that?"

Whelan chuckled. "It is not the distance; it is the difficulty. Although we may ride the horses down, the rest of the journey must be on foot."

"Can we make it there by nightfall?"

Whelan laughed heartily. "Oh, no. At best, we will make it to the bottom by nightfall. The walk and ascent will take yet another day."

Calax was crestfallen. "Another day?"

"Do not worry," said Whelan. "The army and its scouts will not be able to follow us into the chasm, and a mountain now lies between them and the port. Our shortcut should have us there at least a day before they arrive."

Rhynt suddenly spoke up, her face ashen. "Riders!"

Calax leaped to his feet and drew his sword. "How close?"

"Two miles, but they're coming fast."

"Come," said Whelan, standing and grabbing the reins of his horse. "This way."

As he strode quickly away, Rhynt and Calax followed with their horses.

Whelan led them back to the chasm and peered over the edge. "Ah, here it is." He mounted his horse and rode it slowly, carefully over the edge, along a trail no wider than a maiden's waist. He turned back to them. "Hurry," he said, "but slowly."

Rhynt climbed into the saddle and moved toward the edge, her first view of the chasm and its depth taking her breath away. She shuddered, held the reins hard, and coaxed her horse over the edge.

45

Bookins sat in a chair beside the king's bed and listened to the king's soft snore. The council meeting had exhausted them both, but the king more so. Bookins even wondered whether the king would last the day. And he was beginning to wonder about himself as well.

The trip from the counsel room to the king's chamber had been easy enough for the king, who was wheeled through the corridors and lifted up the stairs. Not so for Bookins. He had trailed behind, moving slower and slower with each step. When he had reached the dreaded staircase, his first thought was to sit down and die. After a few deep breaths, though, he had trudged up the stairs, stopping to catch his breath ten times before he reached the top. When he had finally reached the king's chamber, the sight of the king being lifted into bed made him wish that he was a dying king. He had had a strong urge to crawl into bed beside him, and just die.

The king coughed.

"Majesty?"

The king opened one eye and managed a grin. "Ah, Bookins. Are we dead yet?"

Bookins smiled back at him. "No, Majesty, it just feels that way."

The king's laugh was interrupted by a fit of coughing. "Water," he finally managed to say.

Bookins shuffled over to a small table and brought back a cup of water. He lifted the king's head and gently put the cup to the king's lips.

The king took a sip and Bookins eased his head back onto the pillow.

The king cleared his throat. "What of the preparations?"

The king had apparently lost track of time. "Just beginning, Majesty."

"Beginning? Has it not been days?"

"No, Majesty, but a few hours."

"I see, I see. Well, what has been done?"

Bookins sat back down in his chair, his knees cracking, prompting the king to chuckle. "You're getting as creaky as me, Fool."

"Aye, Majesty."

"So, tell me. The preparations."

"For the Gathering or for war?"

The king seemed annoyed. "I care not about the Gathering. I wish it weren't our tradition, but it is. Now, as to war?"

Bookins took a deep breath. "The general is arranging for the scout ship and has already begun fortifying the battlements around the harbor. The fishing fleet will make one more catch to supply us for any siege, and then go into hiding according to our plan."

"And the weaponry?"

"As we discussed. If you were to go outside, you would see the smoke from twenty forges."

"Twenty? Do we really have twenty blacksmiths?"

"No, Majesty, we have four. They have recruited apprentices, and are supervising five forges each, moving back and forth between them. Their first swords should be in the quench about now, and many more will follow in rapid succession."

"Good. And they are of our finest metal, the one with the green hue?"

"They are, Majesty."

The king sighed heavily.

"Majesty?"

"Nothing. I just worry about our chances. Your plan is clever and bold, but I know that battles often do not follow any side's plan. Will our warriors stand strong, Bookins? Will they take the fight to the enemy?"

Bookins wondered the same thing. His plan would have to go perfectly, or near perfectly, for them to have a chance. And once the battle began, the ruling force would not be any plan, but the chaos and sweep of battle.

"Aye, Majesty, I have looked into their eyes and seen nothing but steel."

"Good, Bookins, you have put me at ease. Perhaps I shall die now."

Bookins grabbed the king's hand. "No, Majesty, at least not without a story first. Have I told you the one about the mermaid and the shepherd?"

The king managed a smile. "No, please do. It sounds enchanting. Is the mermaid pretty?"

Well, thought Bookins, *he's not dead yet.*

46

When they reached the bottom of the chasm, Rhynt dropped down from her horse and slumped to her knees on the banks of a slow-moving river.

"By the gods," she said. "I would not do that again."

Calax got down from Gash and pulled Rhynt to her feet. "Nor would I."

Whelan laughed at them both, still astride his horse and strumming on his lute. He began to sing. "Up when we go, and down when we went, such was the hill at the Battle of Whent."

Now Calax had to laugh. "I have heard that one, minstrel, and I assure you, Whent Hill was neither as tall nor as steep as this chasm."

Whelan stopped playing and jumped down from his horse, lute still in hand. He strummed the lute. "Up we went, and the arrows went down, swatted away by the berserker of Whent."

Calax rolled his eyes. "Enough, enough."

Whelan nodded, bowed, and strapped his lute back to the saddle on his horse. "It is a grand tune, one I sing at the conclusion of every performance, on those lucky days when I get coin for my songs."

Rhynt had been looking up and down the river. She turned to Whelan. "Is this the same river?"

"Can't be," said Calax. "It is too calm."

"But it is," said Whelan. "If you listen carefully, you can hear the sound of the waterfall that dumps the river into the chasm."

Rhynt gasped. "Nothing could survive such a drop."

Calax watched as her lips quivered and she began to cry. "There, lass, we don't know that for sure. And remember, it was a magic tower, charmed for eternity. I doubt the witch would have left out any possibility of its destruction."

Whelan walked up to Rhynt and put a hand on her shoulder. "I agree, child. They say the tower can neither be breached nor broken."

Rhynt looked up at him. "Is there a song about the tower?"

Whelan nodded. "There is, but I would not sing it now. Now is the time for drying tears and moving on. We will want to get to the cave before the setting of the sun. You can't imagine how dark it gets here at night."

Rhynt looked up at the jagged slice of blue that was all that was left of the sky. "I see what you mean."

"Okay," said Whelan to them both. "Walk the horses as close to the cliffs as possible. The river may be calm, but it is said to harbor beasts."

Rhynt moved quickly away from the banks of the river, her eyes wide. "What?"

Whelan chuckled. "Not to worry. For the most part, they are creatures of the night."

Rhynt was not reassured. "For the most part?"

Whelan cringed a little and gave her a smile. "Yes."

"Then let's go," said Calax, grabbing the reins of Gash. "Come on, boy, nothing like a good walk by a calm river."

Whelan and Calax began to move away. Rhynt took one last look at the sky, where a flight of birds seemed to be diving toward them. A white-feathered arrow struck her square in the breastplate and bounced away as a score of arrows hit the ground beside her. An arm reached out and tugged her to the side of the cliffs.

"By the gods," said Calax, tugging her to safety.

The rain of arrows continued but the frequency began to diminish, and then stopped.

Calax took a step out into the open. At first, he could see nothing but the slash of blue sky, but then a large object appeared over the edge of the chasm and began dropping toward them.

Calax screamed. "Back."

They all flattened themselves against the wall of the chasm, and watched as the body of a warrior hit the ground in front of them, the impact so great that his head ripped off and rolled into the river, gouts of blood pouring from his severed neck.

They waited, and waited, but no other bodies fell before them. Calax stepped out into the open, and looked up at the sky. Nothing. Then he walked over to the body.

A yellow arrow protruded from the man's heart. "A yellow arrow again. What's going on?"

Whelan shrugged. "I don't know, but I'd have to say this mysterious archer is a friend."

Rhynt walked over to the body and then peered into the sky, shielding her eyes with her hand. "Why won't he show himself, then?"

"Perhaps he thinks it's better to hold back," said Whelan, "to see the enemy approach, and then do him or them in."

"It's curious," said Calax, turning back to the body. "As curious as I am about this body."

He kneeled down next to it and drew the man's sword. "A common enough metal. I would say Ichthian in origin. I remember it well from Whent Hill. They were strewn everywhere at battle's end."

He took out his own sword. "You see, the Icthian blade is a full hand's span shorter. A definite disadvantage in hand-to-hand combat."

"Unless the Ichthians have longer arms," said Whelan.

Calax grunted. "Aye, but the thing is, they didn't and they don't. The Ichthians are thick as bulls, but their arms are no longer than my half arm."

Rhynt had been looking around nervously during this exchange. "More to the point. Why would Ichthians be pursuing us? I thought we were dealing with Mystrosians."

Calax nodded. "Aye, but alliances come quickly at the point of a sword."

"And the Ichthians have every reason to pursue you, Calax Halfhand. Perhaps it was a group of Ichthian assassins."

Calax nodded. "Aye, a fair point."

"On the other hand," said Rhynt, "perhaps the Ichthians are trying to flank the Mystrosians."

Calax gave her an appraising look. "How do you know about flanking?"

Rhynt shrugged. "I must have heard it somewhere." She turned to Whelan. "Perhaps from one of your songs, minstrel?"

Whelan nodded. "Yes, the word is in many of my battle songs."

Rhynt pointed at the slice of sky above them. "A storm is coming. Shouldn't we go?"

Whelan looked up. "She's right, clouds are gathering, and I fear we will be full wet by the time we reach the cave."

Calax shook his head. "A moment, and then we'll go." He reached into the man's boot and pulled out a dagger. "Yes, Ichthian for sure." He looked at the man's boots and clothes. "The boots are Ichthian as well, but his garments are Mystrosian."

Whelan nodded. "Assassins often take on disguises."

"Even down to the white arrows?"

"Perhaps they jumped a group of Mystrosian scouts," said Rhynt.

"Aye," said Calax. "But it's still curious."

A bolt of lightning flashed across the sky, followed by rolling thunder.

"That was close," said Rhynt.

"Aye," said Calax. "Let's go."

They grabbed the reins of their horses and started walking them down river, sticking close to the walls of the chasm. They had only gone a few steps when a hard, cold rain began to fall.

47

King Merek the Mighty awoke in a tangle of arms and legs, his head resting comfortably between the bountiful breasts of one of his concubines, whose name escaped him.

The White Monk, d'Porto Saleen, was hovering over him, looking disgusted. "Majesty, we are ready to march."

The king rubbed a hand over his face and looked around. "I must have had a fine night, I think, though wine clouds my memory."

"Majesty, from the smiles on your concubine's faces, I would say you had an extraordinary night." He cleared his throat. "But now we must leave."

The king nodded, and sighed. "Yes, I'm sure you're right." He turned to the guards. "Strike the tent!"

The sound of his voice woke the concubines, who gathered themselves and their clothing up and scrambled out of the tent, giggling and whispering as they went.

The king smiled, watching them go. "Yes, a *very* good night."

The White Monk nodded. "Indeed. Now, if you will, Majesty, I'll fetch your attendants so that you might dress more quickly."

He turned to go, but the king stopped him. "Wait, any news on Calax Halfhand?"

The White Monk frowned. "Several scouting parties have returned, but none have encountered him."

"Are others due back?"

"Majesty, all but one scouting party has returned, and it is long overdue."

The king grunted his concern. "Perhaps they'll join us along the way."

"Yes, Majesty."

"And d'Porto, send more scouts out. I will have this man on our side, or no side at all."

The White Monk bowed, backed away, and then turned and left the tent. Outside, an army in the thousands was already marching away to the beat of drums.

48

The cave was somewhat smaller than the Cave of the Six Arrows, but it shared two important qualities: it was out of the blasted rain and firewood had been set for the lighting. Rhynt had immediately closed her eyes and shivered out the words that would bring the fire to life, the cave suddenly alight, and most important, warm.

Rhynt and Calax saw to the horses, pulling their saddles and wet blankets off and setting them near the fire to dry. In the process, the horses shook themselves dry, an act that would have annoyed Rhynt and Calax, except they were already too wet to care about an extra shower. Then they joined Whelan by the fire. He was turning in circles, like meat on a spit, drying his clothes.

Rhynt and Calax tugged off their armor and set it by the fire, and then sat down. Rhynt untied her mechanical foot and set it near the fire as well. Seeing that, Calax unlashed his arm and dropped it down next to her foot.

Rhynt smiled at him. "We are quite a pair." Her lips were trembling so hard she could barely get out the words.

"Here," said Calax, "get closer to the fire. I've always found that if you dry your back first, the shivers will diminish quickly."

They both turned and moved their backsides as close as they dared to the fire. It only took a few minutes before they could turn around and dry their fronts. And when they did, Whelan was handing them each a surprise: a cold but roasted rat from the Cave of the Six Arrows.

"I thought we might be needing this right about now."

Calax and Rhynt grabbed the rats and ate them greedily.

"You're welcome," said Whelan. "The thing is, the rats in this cave are as elusive as they are stringy and foul tasting. Always best to bring along spare rats."

Calax and Rhynt nodded, but continued chewing and making appreciative grunts.

Whelan laughed. "Any rat in a storm, eh?"

Whelan moved away from them and picked up several torches, lighting each in the fire and placing them in holders affixed to the walls of the cave.

Rhynt looked up from her well-picked rat and gasped. "What wonders!"

Calax turned and looked as well. "What magic is this?"

Whelan raised both arms. "Welcome to the Cave of Randall, also known as Randall's Reach. Here are the runes he set down eons and eons ago, what we refer to now as the Teachings."

Rhynt threw the bones of her rat into the fire and crawled as best she could to get closer to the wall and run her fingers in the grooves made by the runes. "They are a marvel, but what do they say? And who is this Randall person?"

Whelan beamed. "I love your curiosity, Rhynt. No wonder escapes you." He moved to the wall and ran a hand over the runes. "Let's take your second question first. Some think Randall was the seventh god, some think he was just a wise man, and some think he was an insane hermit. Depending on your view, these runes are holy, wise, or ridiculous."

"And your view?" said Rhynt.

"I lean toward the godly, but no one really knows."

"And what do they say? I have never seen the like."

Whelan smiled at her. "Oh, but you have."

Rhynt was incredulous. "What?"

Whelan turned back to the wall. "Here, this square with the two dots above it. Do you not recognize it?"

Rhynt gasped. "My master's sigil. It is on a medallion he wears round his neck on a gold chain."

Whelan nodded. "Indeed. And what about this diamond shape here?"

Rhynt laughed. "The sigil of the gray men."

"Yes," said Whelan, glancing over at Calax, who was drop-jawed. "And if you look carefully, you will find the sigils of all six gods here, each preceded by their names."

Whelan began pointing at various runes. "Porto, Canto, Abo, Bedo, Indo, Dado."

"Yes," said Rhynt, my master, d'Abo Pourcrey, the Red Monk, is a follower of the god Abo."

"Yes, the symbol for *d'* can be found in various places among the runes. It means *of the*."

Rhynt nodded and grew silent for some moments, then turned back to Whelan. "You said these were the Teachings. How is that possible if no one knows what these runes say?"

Whelan laughed. "You are right. Once, back in the Age of Randall, everyone knew, at least the gods, or so the story goes. If the stories are true, Randall was the first god, and created the six others."

Rhynt frowned. "Why would he do that?"

Whelan cocked his head. "My guess is that he was lonely, but the story is that he was a somewhat lazy god. There was so much to do, you see. So, he created the six gods as more or less assistant gods, and gave each of them a portion of his knowledge and powers. They were to go into the land and tend to the sheep, meaning us."

Rhynt frowned. "Humph."

"*Humph?* Is that the best you can do?"

"Well—"

Whelan waved a hand at her. "No matter, child. So, where was I? Oh, yes. So, Randall sent the gods into the land to work as a team, providing for and punishing the people as they saw fit, with an ultimate goal of universal harmony. What I like to call peace and prosperity."

"But it didn't work."

"Oh, no, it worked fine for a time, until that one god's indiscretion, which created, you know."

"The girl in the painting who looks like me."

"Yes, the demigod. The gods scattered to eight points of the compass, followed by the people who most valued their knowledge and powers. Some became warlike. Some became isolationist. Some became nothing at all. I think they may have been the happiest, those few who settled Paudia. Wild and free, right up to this day—"

Calax interrupted them. "With the invasion by the Mystrosians, followers of the god Porto and the White Monk."

"Exactly," said Whelan. "I fear we are entering a whole new era as far as the gods are concerned."

Calax scoffed. "You can keep your gods, minstrel. I have never seen them on the battlefield, when men's heads were separated from their bodies or their limbs were lopped off. What god creates such misery?"

Whelan sighed and shook his head. "And what do you believe, Rhynt?"

She seemed surprised by the question. "I don't know what to think. I do know that my master, the Red Monk, is cruel and merciless, and has the darkest piss I've ever seen."

Whelan chuckled. "Well, I don't know about the piss, but perhaps the god d'Abo was in charge of cruelty."

Calax couldn't contain himself. "Ha! And why would a god have such powers. To what purpose, minstrel?"

Whelan smirked at him. "It's difficult to explain. With cruelty comes pain and anguish, correct?"

Calax nodded. "In full measure."

"Well, there is another side to cruelty, and that is how we handle cruelty. Do we tolerate it? Do we recover from it? Do we condone it? Do we punish it? Do we allow it to change us?"

"Good questions, minstrel, but why have cruelty in the first place?"

Whelan sighed heavily. "It is all about the Teachings. Cruelty and how we deal with it is just one lesson. The idea is that we must understand the whole—the good and the bad—to live in harmony."

"And yet we do not," said Calax, moving away from them to look out the cave entrance.

Whelan called after him. "Because the gods are no longer in harmony. We live in a time of chaos."

Calax didn't turn around. He just threw up his hands and continued walking.

Whelan turned back to Rhynt. "I think he is lost where the gods are concerned."

Rhynt shook her head. "No, he is as godlike as any man I have ever met. He is a warrior, yes, and fierce, but there is a kind side to him. He feels pain and seeks to ease it."

"No," said Whelan, "he is just a man, a man who kills for coin."

Rhynt turned and looked at Calax silhouetted in the fading light at the mouth of the cave. "I think there is more to him than that. Stay with us and you will see, I'm sure of it."

Whelan looked at Calax, who was now returning to the fire. "Oh, I'll stay, child. My guess is that there will be more than one tale or one song to sing after we reach Enturia."

"Speaking of that," said Rhynt, "I shall need my strength for the rest of the journey. I don't suppose you have another rat."

"Oh, child," he said, laughing, "I have a sack of them, but no more to share with you tonight. In the morning we will have rat and tea and hard bread. The day will be long and arduous, so we will have double portions."

Rhynt beamed. "Yes!"

"Now," said Whelan, "we'd best to bed."

Rhynt nodded.

"And don't think to do your business outside this cave. The beasts come in the night."

Rhynt chuckled and lay down on her bedroll. When she closed her eyes, she could hear Whelan and Calax settling down with grunts from the pain of a long day, and sighs from the pleasure of easing that pain in sleep.

Outside, in the river, a beast surfaced, searching for food.

49

King Braque of Enturia fathered nineteen children over half a century of farming the local maidens. Two were stillborn, leaving seventeen. Four were malformed at birth and put to the sword, leaving thirteen. One died of red fly disease, leaving twelve. And one was killed in an accident, leaving eleven, including the Green Monk, d'Bedo Brendyl, the only child born of King Braque and Queen Milanda, now dead these thirty years.

A grand tent had been erected in the courtyard to accommodate them, all but d'Bedo that is. He had grand quarters of his own, befitting his rank. The others would have to make do on straw beds and second rations from the kitchens. Not that second rations were bad. In fact, the servants preferred the overcooked meats and gray vegetables that made up the second rations. It changed from day to day, new old ingredients added to the pot.

The Green Monk watched as five half-brothers and two half-sisters gobbled down their food at the large table that had been supplied for the center of the tent. Some seemed to have manners, but most had no idea how to use even a spoon, scooping up stew with their hands and forcing it into their mouths. The other three siblings, when they arrived, would no doubt be just as slovenly.

Most still wore the clothes they had been wearing upon arrival, but a few had changed into the formal white tunics for the Gathering.

The tent flap flew open, and Chancellor d'Mander strode in, followed by two guards. The chancellor caught sight of d'Bedo, and walked over to him.

"I see you have met the others," he said.

The Green Monk shrugged. "More or less. They are an ugly lot. Father must have been drunk when he dropped his seed in those maidens, for surely beauty was never part of the mix."

The chancellor looked at the children at the table. "Yes, I see what you mean."

"Only a few are younger than me. Perhaps mother's death changed him in some way."

The chancellor laughed, perhaps too loudly. He quickly put a hand over his mouth. "No, no, it would be nice to think that, but the king couples at least once a week, even now, though I hear he has difficulties."

"As well he should, a man in his eighth decade."

The chancellor gave d'Bedo a serious look. "Are you ready? Do you think you will be able to perform your function at the Gathering?"

The Green Monk snorted. "Of course, I'm all about ceremonies. You should know that by now."

"Oh, I do, I do," said the chancellor. "It's just—"

"What?" The Green Monk seemed annoyed.

"No, no, don't get me wrong. I am sure you will do fine. I am more concerned about them."

The Green Monk scoffed. "Oh, by the gods, you need not worry about them. I'm sure they can at least follow instructions."

"Do none concern you?"

The Green Monk scanned the table, and clucked. "Not a one. The Gathering will go as expected." He paused. "Still."

"What?"

"I don't like the fact that father will be there. That is all wrong, against every formality and tradition."

The chancellor put a hand on d'Bedo's shoulder. "What matter, really? He will just be one of many in attendance, and what he thinks will not matter."

"I fear he will try to insert himself into the ceremony."

"I assure you, he is so weak now I doubt he could even insert himself into a maiden."

The Green Monk laughed. "Aye, I guess you are right."

"Of course I am. He will be on a litter, and probably will sleep through the whole ceremony."

The Green Monk nodded. "So, the preparations here are on schedule. What of our defenses?"

The chancellor frowned. "I fear the clock will run out before we are ready, but things are moving apace. The blacksmiths are doing wonderful things at the forge. Their output is astounding. The question is whether our army, such as it is, will stand up to a battle-hardened horde."

"Indeed," said d'Bedo, looking back at the table. "Ye gods, there manners are so bad we should have probably just used a trough instead of a table."

"Never mind them," said the chancellor. "Let me show you the state of the defenses. Walk with me."

50

In the dream, the beast had come upon her suddenly, wrapping its tentacles around her, making it hard to breathe. And what breaths she could take in smelled of river rot and sulfur. The life was slowly going out of her. She made one last desperate attempt to free herself from its grip, and then . . ."

Whelan was jostling her awake. "Here now, you've wrapped yourself in your bedroll. Wake up, girl."

Rhynt opened her eyes and stared into Whelan's face, his breath smelling of river rot and sulfur. She pushed him away. "I'm all right, just a dream."

She scrambled to her feet, or at least one foot, and hopped over to her mechanical foot, which was still warm, even though the fire had died hours ago. "Is it time to go?"

Whelan pointed at the cave entrance, which was dark as pitch. "What do you think?"

She looked at him skeptically. "Then why are you awake?"

Whelan snorted. "It's hard to sleep when a girl is screaming right next to you."

She looked over at Calax, who was still in a deep sleep, snoring loudly. "I was louder than that?"

Whelan nodded.

She rolled her eyes. "Whatever." She looked at the cave entrance. "How long, do you suppose?"

"Not long, time enough for you to put on your foot and your armor and rekindle the fire."

She stared at him, hard. "Seriously, why are you awake?"

Whelan threw up his hands. "Nothing gets past you, does it?"

She smiled. "I have an eye for detail, aye."

"All right," he said, walking over to the wall. "I was studying the runes, hoping to understand more."

"And?"

"And they defeated me once more."

She looked at the runes. "It seems to me that if you could find the right scholar, a man or woman of great intellect and patience, the riddle would unravel."

Whelan shrugged. "Maybe."

"No, not maybe. If I had any say in it, anyway."

Whelan laughed. "You could always do it yourself. Stay behind, avoid the war to come, eat the stringy rats here until you've solved the puzzle."

She had to chuckle at that. "No, no, I may be small, but I have skills that may be of use."

"Your far-seeing?"

"Aye, and more. And besides, I would not leave Calax's side."

Whelan gave her a curious look. "And why is that? You have only known the man for a matter of days."

Rhynt sighed. "I know, but there is something about him. I can't really put it into words, but I think we were destined to be together."

"As husband and wife?"

Rhynt laughed out loud. "Oh, my, no. I meant as comrades in arms."

Whelan smirked. "Seriously? I doubt he would share your feelings."

"Oh, and why is that?" She realized her response was too strident. She tried again, more calmly. "I mean, our skills seem to complement one another."

"I know what you mean, child, but I think you know deep down that Calax Halfhand, Calax the berserker, Calax the hero of the Battle of Whent Hill, is very much a loner."

Calax was suddenly beside them. "What goes here?"

Rhynt, embarrassed, waived him off. "Nothing, we were just talking."

Calax cocked his head. "Just talking? Well, child, when someone mentions your name three times in one breath, something is going on."

Whelan shook his head and chuckled. "We were just talking about your snoring and whether it sounded more like a pig or more like the snort of a bull."

"We decide on the pig," said Rhynt, giggling.

Calax looked back and forth at them. "Ah, whatever." He looked around. "Why are we even awake?"

Whelan and Rhynt stared back at him blankly.

"Oh, come on, I don't snore that bad."

They both rolled their eyes.

"Seriously?"

"Oh, yeah," said Rhynt. "On the bright side, I have no doubt you scared the beasties away."

Calax smiled. "Well, then, I'll continue to snore like a pig."

Calax looked at the entrance of the cave. Sunlight was beginning to stream in. "Shall we have breakfast or go?"

Whelan followed Calax's eyes. "I think breakfast." He turned to Rhynt. "Could you see to the fire? There's extra kindling and logs behind that boulder over there."

Rhynt nodded. "I'll put on my foot and get to it." She made her way back to the fire, which was now only embers.

"Now," said Whelan, "While she's doing that, you tend to your hand and armor, and I'll see to the horses. We'll have breakfast, but we'll have to make it quick."

"Aye," said Calax, "and while we eat, can we discuss the path ahead? I don't like surprises, and I'd know the route you'd take us."

"Of course," said Whelan.

Everyone set about their tasks, Rhynt gathering wood and starting a fire, Whelan tending and saddling the horses, and Calax, once he'd affixed his hand, digging into his saddle bags for Zyrx's incomplete map.

Although Calax didn't like surprises, he made an exception for the bonus roasted rats Whelan produced with a flourish. Warming them took only a few minutes, just enough time for the tea water to boil. They ate greedily, as before, not so much from hunger, but from haste—and taste. There simply was nothing like a sweet cave rat to set a person drooling, and always wanting more.

Finally, Calax slumped back and sighed. "I could eat a thousand thousand of them and still want more."

Whelan nodded agreement. "Aye, there's magic in their flesh, at least these ones from the Cave of the Six Arrows."

"You keep surprising us with these," said Rhynt. "How could you possibly have so many?"

Whelan held a finger in the air triumphantly. "Minstrels, we have our ways."

"Well, keep those ways coming," said Calax. He reached down and picked up the map. "Now, before we go, could you please explain exactly where we are on this confounded map, and where we go next?"

Whelan took the map and spread it out in front of them. "Let's see now." He laid a finger on the map. "We are here, and our goal—the port—is over here."

"Can we reach it today?" said Whelan.

Whelan waggled his head. "Maybe. Possibly. But it will depend on how fast we can make the ascent from this chasm. Once out, the path is clear, the land flat and barren all the way to the port."

"Once up," said Rhynt, "can we make it in one go, or will we have to stop to rest the horses?"

Whelan set his head to wobbling and waggling once more, considering what lay ahead. "Unknown. We'll have to keep an eye on the horses and make a decision once we're on the plain."

He looked back and forth at them. "Are we ready to go, then?"

Calax and Rhynt nodded.

"Then we're off," said Whelan.

They stood and walked to their horses, Rhynt stopping briefly at the fire to say the dousing words. "Should we not lay a new fire?"

Whelan, who was already halfway to the horses, turned and answered, "Normally, yes, but under the circumstances, I think the gods will forgive us for not being hospitable to the next strangers who find and use this cave."

"Okay," said Rhynt. She turned away from the fire and ran to her horse, grabbing its reins and tugging it out of the cave.

They made their way along the river, keeping an eye out for beasties until they came to a wooden bridge.

Calax stopped in alarm. "Be there trolls?"

Whelan laughed. "Not in the chasm. Trolls are afraid of heights and holes, so they would never come here."

Calax looked over at Rhynt. "If they did, I'm sure Rhynt here could tell them a joke and send them on their way."

Rhynt giggled. "Aye, I could."

They began walking the horses over the bridge.

"Could you tell us one of those jokes?" said Whelan. "I can always use a good joke to please a crowd."

Rhynt's laugh was almost a guffaw. "Oh, no, minstrel, a troll joke is for trolls only. You'd lose your crowd sure if you told a troll joke."

Whelan cocked his head. "And why is that?"

Rhynt smiled at him. "Well, troll jokes usually involve disemboweled cows and humans on pikes. They think that's hilarious."

Whelan raised his eyebrows. "Whoa."

They continued across the bridge, Calax stopping suddenly once they'd reached the other side. "Wait."

"What?" said Rhynt.

Calax frowned and handed Gash's reins to her. "I see something in the river."

Whelan and Rhynt watched as Calax made his way around the edge of the bridge and reached into the flowing water. He pulled out a scarf and held it into the air.

Rhynt screamed and dropped to her knees. "No!"

Calax twirled the scarf around his wrist and climbed back up.

"What is it?" said Whelan.

"It's Phendour's scarf, or rather her mother's. She wore it at her belt for luck in battle."

Whelan looked over at Rhynt, who had let go the reins of the horses, and lay on the ground, bawling. He turned back to Calax. "They are gone, then?"

Calax nodded. "It seems so."

He turned away from Whelan and stared at the flowing river. "Farewell, my friends."

51

King Merek the Mighty had been warned about the east-west road that cut across Paudia from the Sea of Dros to The Great Sea, but he hadn't appreciated just how bad it was until he had actually had to traverse it by horse or royal wagon. In dry weather, you had to deal with hardened ruts and potholes, and in wet weather, the rain and dirt conspired to create a sucking mud that swallowed boots, hooves, and wheels.

Thankfully, the road was dry today, so they could make some progress. The pain of riding the previous day had forced him to opt for his wagon today. Even with all the pillows to dampen the shock of the road, he felt like he was being slowly torn apart as the wagon did its best to handle the ruts and holes.

They had already stopped six times to deal with injuries sustained by soldiers and horses. The men had to be carried to the rear of the column to be attended by bone doctors. The horses were another matter; they had to be put down by spear, a grizzly business. The king shuddered just thinking about it.

The royal wagon suddenly stopped, again. Another injury perhaps, or a hole too large to traverse without first filling it in. Whatever the reason, the king was quick to pour himself a goblet of wine, an act that was impossible when the wagon was moving. He knew, because he had tried, wasting half a bottle. And what wine made it into his glass had soon found its way to his chest as he attempted to get the goblet to his lips.

He quickly downed the first goblet and poured another. With any luck, its effects would soon carry him off to sleep and he could then wake at the end of the day, safe in his tent with his concubines.

His attention was drawn to the sound of the door being opened. The White Monk, d'Porto Saleen, smiled up at him and climbed into the wagon, dropping down on a pile of pillows opposite the king.

"Why have we stopped?" said the king.

The White Monk could see that the king was out of sorts and already into his cups. "A scheduled stop, Majesty, to rest the men and horses."

"Will there be food?"

"Yes, of course."

The king was pleased. "Good, good. I rather enjoyed that Paudian sausage we had yesterday. Is there more?"

The monk shrugged. "Perhaps. I will check."

"Wonderful," said the king, motioning him to leave. "You may go, then."

The monk didn't move.

The king sighed. He was hoping not to speak to the monk at all. The man was a bother at times, and when the king was tired and sore, he could barely stand the man. "Is there something else?"

"Yes, Majesty." He held up a large scroll. "I would share a map of Paudia with you."

The king watched as the monk unrolled it and spread it out in front of the king. "Here now, how did we come by this?"

The White Monk beamed. "I have been working on it for some time now, and it is finally complete." He cocked his head. "I think."

"Working how?"

The monk was more than happy to discuss his wizardly skills. "As you know, I have skills. In this case, I sent gelas far and wide, posing as minstrels to gather information about this land."

"Minstrels, you say. Why minstrels?"

"To avoid suspicion. Minstrels are known travelers, and would draw little attention from the population. Going from village to village would be normal for them, you see."

The king did see, and gave the monk a smile. "Ah, well done."

The White Monk gave him a quick bow. "Thank you, Majesty. Now, to the map."

"Yes, where are we, by the way?"

The White Monk pointed to a spot along the east-west road, which made the king clap his hands with delight. "So close! Are we really almost done with this damnable road?"

The monk nodded. "Today's march and maybe part of another day and we'll be at the port."

"Good. No, better than good. Excellent, d'Porto. Now, if you wouldn't mind sending for my food."

The White Monk shook his head. "But Majesty, there is more."

"More?"

"Calax Halfhand, Majesty. You asked that he be found."

The king beamed. "You have found him?"

"No, no, Majesty, but I have a good idea where he might be."

"Have the scouts returned, then?"

The White Monk shook his head. "All but six, and that is why I know where he might be." He pointed at the map. "See here, where the river flows into a giant chasm?"

"Yes."

"I sent a gela, who reported finding the bodies of five of our men. I know them to be battle-hardened warriors, and yet all were dead. The only single man who could stand against them would be a berserker, and I think that berserker is Calax Halfhand."

The king whistled through his teeth. "I could use such a man, d'Porto. Imagine him at the head of our forces."

"That would be wonderful, but I imagine him opposed to our forces. If he were inclined to work for us, why is he fleeing like all the rest, or worse, heading to Enturia for the sole purpose of joining up with them?"

"Yes, I see what you mean."

The White Monk began tapping on the map again. "In any case, he shall not escape us. There is only one way he can get to the port, and that is over this mountain. I'll have men follow him and there will be more men to greet him when he comes down on the other side."

"Good, but do your best to capture him, not kill him. Perhaps he will listen to reason." The king looked back at the map. "Now, tell me about this port."

"Ah, yes, Port Ochno, a small village but a big prize. They are said to have the largest fishing fleet in the known world. We will be well supplied."

The king seemed concerned. "Do our men really like fish?"

"No, not really, but it's better than an empty stomach, and it is said that the fish in The Great Sea are tastier than fish from the Sea of Dros."

The king shook his head. "Why would that be so? The seas are one, distinct only by their names. Why would fish in one area be tastier than the fish in another area?"

"I don't know, Majesty." He tapped on the map. "Shall we get back to the village?"

The king continued reflecting on the sea. "I do not like it, the sea. Too many mysteries, and who knows what lurks in its depths? I tell you, d'Porto, I do not look forward to our next time aboard ship."

The White Monk tried his best to move on. "Yes, Majesty, and as to the ships, my gelas with the fleet report smooth sailing, and just as we planned, we shall arrive at port within hours of their arrival."

The king looked concerned. "But we'll get there first, right?"

"Yes, Majesty, to secure it and put down any lingering resistance. I don't really expect that to be a problem. The Paudians are not ones to stand and fight."

"Excellent, and when will we be there? I am running low on wine and sore of limb."

The White Monk looked back at the map. "If we are not slowed further by this damnable road, we should be there by midday tomorrow. And if the fleet continues its progress, we'll be aboard ship and on our way by nightfall."

The king wasn't sure how to respond to that. On one hand, he would be off this damned road, but on the other, he'd be aboard ship, dealing with a queasy stomach or worse.

"Well, then, shall we get on with it."

The White Monk nodded, bowed, and turned to leave, the king calling out after him, "but I'd enjoy a meal first."

52

Rhynt was still in shock from the discovery of Phendour's scarf, so much so that she barely remembered the ascent out of the chasm. She had simply been crying one moment, the scarf clutched in her hand, and standing on a vast plain the next, the scarf tied around her waist, as Phendour had done in homage to her mother.

Calax came up to her. "Are you all right?"

She nodded, then shook her head. "Yes, no, I don't know. Poor Phendour, poor Blusk, they did not deserve such an end."

Calax began rubbing her back. "No, child, they did not." He kneeled down and looked directly into her eyes. "I have been thinking about the scarf. When the tower fell into the water, I remember a wave coming across it, washing over Blusk and then Phendour. Perhaps that is when the scarf was lost."

She looked into his eyes. "So you think they are still alive?"

Calax smiled weakly. "No, but it is possible."

"But the waterfall, the depth of the chasm, who could survive that?"

Calax ran a hand through her hair. "If anyone could, they could."

Rhynt nodded and wiped a tear away. "Okay, let us not discuss it further." She looked around. "Where are we?"

Calax turned away from her and shouted at Whelan, who was standing apart with the horses. "Where are we, and which way do we go?"

Whelan tugged the horses over to Rhynt and Calax. "Well, the tender of horses thinks we're on the Plain of Morthos, and given our slow ascent out of the chasm, I don't think we can make the port by nightfall. In fact, I'd suggest we not even try. I think it would be better if we arrived at the port shortly after dawn. There will be fewer people about and perhaps we can find Marthe and his boat and be on our way."

Calax nodded. "Sounds right. And do you know a place where we can camp?"

"Yes, there's a high bluff overlooking the port. We won't be able to have a fire, of course, so I think we should stop about halfway there to rest the horses and cook up as much game as we can find. Speaking of which, Rhynt, do you far-see any game out there?" He pointed to the southeast, in the direction of the port.

Rhynt gathered herself and closed her eyes. There was so much to see! Game by the hundreds: rabbits, weir deer, molfrumps, and diddle mice. She gasped at what she saw next. A group of twenty Mystrosian horsemen racing across the plain about five miles in front of them, heading toward the mountains. She looked back toward the mountains. Another group on the far side of the chasm was heading up the mountain.

She broke from her trance. "Mystrosians!"

Calax wheeled around, scanning the horizon. "Where?"

Rhynt pointed. "They're coming from the west, but they're well out of sight and heading toward the mountains, not us."

Whelan chuckled. "Bravo, Mystrosia, Bravo."

"What?" said Calax.

"They think we are on the other side of the chasm, climbing the mountain."

"Yes," said Rhynt. "There's another group of them doing just that."

Calax was puzzled. "What?"

"They think we're heading to the port by way of the mountain," said Whelan. "They don't think we could have possibly come by way of the chasm."

Calax turned to Rhynt. "Are you sure of what you saw?"

Rhynt sighed. "Yes, but let me look again."

She began far-seeing, the horsemen still on a path to the mountain. She scanned further, looking for the main force. "They have just crossed the route we will take to the port, and the main force is still proceeding down the main road. My guess is that they will arrive at the port by midday tomorrow, perhaps sooner."

Whelan clapped his hands. "Perfect. If all goes well, we'll be long gone. Let's go."

"No," said Rhynt. "We should wait here another few minutes till the horsemen are well out of range."

Calax sighed, relieved. "Good, good. Now, did you see any game out there?"

Rhynt smiled. "Lots. We could feast for days. There are even molfrumps."

Whelan's eyes went wide. "Molfrumps? Fat, juicy molfrumps. I can taste them already."

53

The sound of the bed chamber door being opened and closed startled Bookins awake. A maiden with a tray was making her way toward the king's bed. From the slant of the sun through the high windows, he knew he must have slept for hours at the bedside of the king.

The king!

He turned to the king with alarm. Was he dead? The sound of the king's snoring said otherwise. Still, the king looked weak and ashen.

The maiden smiled at Bookins in the dismissive way that young maidens smile at old men. "I have brought grimble cakes and ale."

Bookins brightened. "Ale, you say?"

"Yes, Baron Bookins."

Bookins couldn't help beam at her. The news of his ascendancy had spread throughout the castle, no doubt. And that was good news for him. Now, no one could challenge his claim. The king had spoken and the word had spread. "Here, then, let me have a cup."

The maiden nodded and poured, lifting the cup with both hands and offering it to Bookins with a bow.

They bow before me now, he thought. *How wonderful!*

Bookins took the cup and smiled at her. "Thank you. You may go now."

She seemed reluctant to leave. "I was instructed to wait until the king had had his cakes and ale."

Bookins looked at his cup of ale and quickly handed it back to her. "No, that won't be possible. Take the cakes and ale away."

The maiden looked fearful. "But the monk said . . ."

Bookins reached out and grabbed the maiden by the arm. "The monk said what?"

The maiden tried to wrest her arm away, but Bookins held her fast. "He said that I must wait until the king had had a cake and a cup of ale. He said it was important for the king to regain his strength."

Bookins let go of her arm. He could see that he had left bruises. "I'm so sorry, my dear. You are right, of course. Please have a seat, and we shall wait together."

As she moved away toward the chairs along the wall, he walked quietly to the tray, set his cup of ale down, and then flipped the tray off the table, the sound startling the maid.

"Oh, my," she said. "What have you done?"

Bookins did a little dance. "Oh, Bookins is a clumsy fool, a clumsy fool is he."

The maiden gave him an exasperated look and then turned to go. "I'll fetch more."

Bookins called after her. "No, wait, I would change the menu somewhat."

She stopped and walked slowly back to him. "Yes, Baron?"

"The king is really not a devotee of grimble cakes and ale." He screwed up his face to show her just how much the king hated them. "Not at all."

"Oh, but he has had just that every day for the past weeks."

That does not surprise me at all, thought Bookins. *A slow poison would be just the thing.* "And yet he just this morning told me of his distaste for it. I guess his tastes are changing even as he fades away from us."

The maiden rolled her eyes. "Well, then, what *would* he eat?"

Bookins started to speak, but couldn't find the word. *Damnable old age!* "Um, let me see. Yes, do you know the tall flowers that grow alongside the castle walls?"

"Yes, the moonflowers."

"Moonflowers, moonflowers, yes. Cut me off a blossom and its seeds, and bring it to me here, along with enough hot water for tea."

The maiden looked concerned. "But moonflower tea is forbidden."

Bookins nodded. "Yes, yes, I know, but in the king's condition, the restorative nature of the tea far outweighs the hallucinations that will follow."

"Are you sure about this? I don't want to get into trouble."

"Quite certain, and there would be no trouble for you. In fact, if you've a mind to tend to an old fool like me, there will be a position for you when I move to my new estate."

She frowned.

"With a much better wage, of course."

A smile grew on her face. "I'll be back with it as quickly as I can." She turned and ran for the door.

He called after her. "Make it a big flower with many seeds."

And then she was gone, leaving Bookins alone with the king. "What have they been doing to you, Majesty?"

He moved back to the bedside and patted the king's hand. "Whatever it was, whatever they were attempting to do, I shall seek to undo." He chuckled to himself. "Oh, and what visions you shall have."

54

Marthe stood on the deck of his ship and watched the chaos on the docks. Everywhere he looked people were racing about, loading their belongings and themselves into ship after ship. Even the women in the brothels and the barkeeps were fleeing, most in small fishing vessels headed for Olasia.

Marthe had been more particular in allowing passengers and cargo aboard his ship, the Marthe, a cargo barge he had named after himself when he won her in a game of driddles. He really wasn't that good at cards, but it was one activity where his ugliness was a good thing. The other card players never looked at his face. If they had, they could have seen his blinking blue eyes and known in a nonce whether his cards were good or bad.

Not that he could blame them. His face was pocked and disfigured by a bad case of the droops when he was a child. It was a face now that only a mother could love, or some mothers anyway. Marthe's mother had abandoned him on the steps of a brothel and had fled to the interior of Paudia, never to be seen again.

Other than his face, he was a fairly normal young man, with a barrel chest and enough muscles to handle even the heaviest cargo, including stubborn livestock. That strength had come in handy just hours ago when he had helped load the wild animal cages of a traveling carnival. They had paid good coin, and there was room for them all, including their sixteen workers and five freaks. The manager had given Marthe a onceover and immediately asked if he had any interest in joining them. He could always use another freak, he had said. Marthe had turned him down as politely as he could manage, cuffing him upside his head and dropping him to the deck.

Marthe began pacing, wondering where his last passengers were. A messenger had paid for their passage in advance, with the promise of a second payment once they were safe at sea. Marthe glanced at the horizon, where the sun was beginning to set. If they didn't come soon, he would have to abandon them, good coin or no. Word was that the Mystrosians were getting close and would be upon them by tomorrow midday.

And then it would just be too damned late.

55

They rode on, the three of them and the one empty horse still saddled for the unlikely appearance of Blusk or Phendour. The land was thankfully flat, so the horses could gallop at a good pace and the riders could lose themselves in the rhythm of their steads and think of what might lie ahead.

Rhynt kept wondering about Blusk and Phendour and created elaborate scenarios where they miraculously escaped harm and appeared suddenly at the edge of the river, laughing at the concern in Rhynt's face. Calax thought of the confrontation ahead. Who in Enturia had sent the assassins, and why? And once he knew the answers, what then? Was he just racing to his own death? *A sellsword always was*, he thought. Whelan thought to sing, but the wind tore his words to silence, so he just stared ahead, the horizon seemingly not getting any closer at all.

And then there it was. An oasis in the middle of nowhere, with six trees for shade and enough grass around the pool to satisfy the horses. Whelan signaled them to slow down. "Easy," he said. "This is not on any map known to me." He checked the angle of the sun. "Still, I know we are going the right way."

"It seems a good place to stop," said Calax. "We can rest the horses and then make a go for the coast."

"Aye," said Rhynt. "Let's stop."

Whelan looked worried. "I don't know, but I guess it's all right. Be on your guard in any event."

"Always," said Calax.

They slowed to a walk and stopped just within the shade of the first tree. Rhynt was the first to jump down. "If you'll attend to the horses, I'll far-see to make sure we're okay to stop."

A voice suddenly came from behind a tree. "You won't have to far-see to find me."

Rhynt had nocked an arrow and Calax had drawn his sword before the man could say another word.

"Come out," said Rhynt. "Slowly."

A small man in shimmering green clothing came out from behind the tree. "Greetings of the day, me lords."

"And who might you be?" said Calax.

The man smiled nervously. "Just a fellow traveler, a minstrel as you can see, come to refresh myself before moving on to the port. In case you didn't know it, there be Mystrosians upon the land, swarming like ants and headed straight this way."

Rhynt kept her arrow pointed at the man. "We know, so who are you?"

The man gave them a dramatic bow. "I be Japsin Jopsin, minstrel and storyteller extraordinaire. Ah, I see you have a spare horse. Might I buy it from you or at the least join you on your journey?"

Whelan walked over to the man and began circling him, sizing him up. "A minstrel, you say?"

"Yes, one of the finest, or at least I hope so."

"Strange that I have never heard of you in all my travels."

The man shrugged. "Sometimes paths cross and sometimes otherwise."

"Possibly," said Whelan. "Tell me, what's your favorite village to play?"

"Village? Posh, I usually play in palaces and at grand estates."

"Really? But there be nonesuch in Paudia. Paudia is a poor land and a free land. There be no kings here, or even royalty."

The man looked nervous. "Well, of course not. No, I meant the castles of Ichthia, Alamaria, once even in Mystrosia. Paudia is just a land to be crossed to get to the next performance."

"And where would that next performance be?"

The man smiled, gaining confidence but wary of the arrow and blade pointed at him. "Why, in Olasia."

"Olasia? Olasia is no more than a small island populated by fishermen."

The man seemed saddened. "They said there be a castle, and that I would perform every day for good coin."

Whelan shook his head. "Well now, don't worry, perhaps they have built a castle since I was there last." He gave the man an appraising look. "I am also a minstrel, as you can plainly see."

The man nodded.

"Well, then, as minstrels, you and I, we have a vast repertoire of songs and tales, learned at the knee of a master minstrel, am I right?"

The man nodded again.

Whelan smiled at him. "You are suddenly quiet for a man claiming to be a minstrel."

The man seemed offended. "I be a minstrel, all right, or my name isn't Japsin Jopsin."

"Well then, Japsin Jopsin, answer me this. What is the First Tale?"

The man seemed confused. "What?"

Whelan moved closer to him. "The first song taught to all apprentice minstrels, as is the custom throughout the known world."

The man began shaking his head and backing away. "I don't know." And then he turned and ran.

"Shoot him," said Whelan. "Now!"

Rhynt let loose her arrow, which found its mark in the man's back.

And then the man and the oasis disappeared.

"By the gods," said Calax. "Another gela?"

"Yes," said Whelan. "One controlled by someone with enormous power."

Rhynt closed her eyes. "Let me have a look." She dropped into her trance state and began turning in a circle. Halfway round she stopped. "Riders!"

They had just enough time to ready their weapons before a cloud of dust appeared on the horizon.

"How many?" said Calax.

Rhynt sighed. "Thirty at least."

"We could use the cover of an oasis right about now," said Whelan. But there wasn't a tree or even a pool of water, just the vast plain.

Rhynt turned to Calax. "Shall we try to outrun them?"

"Yes," said Calax. "Whelan, which direction?"

"West," said Whelan. "There's a place, but we'll have to be quick about it."

They jumped on their horses and galloped west, leaving their own cloud of dust for the riders to follow. Rhynt did her best to far-see, and when she saw it, she nearly fell off her horse.

56

Bookins stood guard over the king for as long as he could, but when his bowels began to rumble, he knew he'd have to shuffle off to his quarters. Using the king's piss pot would have seen his head separated from his body and displayed on a pike.

He and the maiden had managed to pour a few drops of moonflower tea into the king's mouth, which had prompted his eyes to pop open. He was soon babbling like a child who had not yet learned language and then had leaped out of bed and raced around the room, shouting for his dead queen. And then he had jumped back on his bed and fallen into a deep sleep.

Throughout this escapade, the maiden had stood in the center of the room, flapping her arms, mouth agape like a bird hatchling. Bookins was barely able to move her to a seat before she collapsed in tears. "What have we done?"

Bookins patted her hand. "Now, now, it will be all right. See, the king sleeps peacefully."

She looked at the bed. "But will he do that again?"

Bookins chuckled. "Possibly, which is why I need you to stay here and watch over him while I, um, tend to some business in my quarters."

She clutched his wrists. "Don't leave me alone with him."

"There, there, girl, it will be all right. I assure you, he will sleep now for several hours. You need only sit here and make sure no one tries to wake and feed him. He is not to have any further food or drink unless I am present."

The maiden let go of his wrists and wiped away her tears. "All right, but be quick about your business. Oh my, oh my, what have we done?"

Bookins patted her shoulder. "We have done nothing less than save his life, such as it is. He may still die, he is certainly weak enough, but if he does, it will not be by poison."

The maiden leaped to her feet. "Poison?"

Bookins pushed her gently back down into her seat. "Look at me, child. There are many in this castle who would see him dead, and I fear the cakes and ale you've been serving him have been laced with poison. Just a little at a time, so as not to draw attention."

The maiden's mouth dropped open and she began to shake her head. "But I didn't know, I didn't—"

"Yes, yes, you are innocent, I'm sure. Now don't fret about it."

"But the monk," she said, suddenly putting it all together. "It must be the monk. I was following his instructions."

Bookins nodded. "Possibly, probably, or it could be someone else who knew about the grimble cakes and ale."

The maiden looked puzzled. "Someone in the kitchens, you mean?"

"Yes, perhaps." His bowels rumbled, prompting him to move to the door. "Be quiet about this for now. I shall be back as quickly as I can."

He shuffled to the door and walked out into the hall. Oddly, there were no guards about. "By the gods."

He turned and shuffled back into the king's chamber, startling the maid. "Quick, another moonflower."

"What?"

"Don't argue, girl. Get me another moonflower, now."

She gave him a curt nod and ran from the room. He waited until he could hear her footsteps receding down the hall, then turned and headed for the king's chamber pot.

Any pot in a storm, he thought.

57

The White Monk screamed at the heavens, startling the horse and rider next to him. "I had them, I had them!"

He dropped back into his trance and was suddenly seeing the world through the eyes of his gela, the minstrel Japsin Jopsin. He could see two clouds of dust, one heading toward the location of the now-gone oasis, and a smaller one headed west.

The White Monk broke the trance and thought about it. Why would they be headed west? His maps of Paudia were comprehensive, and there was no safe haven in that direction. Plus, they were now headed away from the port. What could it mean?

He dropped into a trance state once more, the rush of horses turning as he pointed them west. "I shall have them!"

He watched the horses race away, then broke the trance once more and turned his horse back toward the royal wagon. He looked up at the sun. The king would have finished his dalliance with one or more concubines by now and should be sleeping. He wondered briefly whether it would be wise to wake him, but then quickly decided that the king would want to know.

The White Monk motioned the wagon driver to slow to a stop so he could climb aboard. The inside of the wagon was dark, as it always was. King Merek the Mighty could not abide daylight, so it was only natural that the sudden burst of light upon d'Porto Saleen's entrance would have the king screaming.

"Shut those curtains, you fool."

It took a moment for d'Porto's eyes to adjust to the darkness, but eventually he could make out a pile of people at the back of the wagon.

Apparently, he had interrupted the last throes of one of the king's recurring orgies.

Concubines scrambled away from the king, clutching their silken clothes to their breasts, and headed for the front of the wagon, where they sat whispering.

Satisfied that he now had the king's undivided attention, he stepped forward and bowed. "Majesty, I have news."

The king grunted. "And it couldn't wait, I see."

The White Monk glanced at the concubines, then looked back at the king. "I am most sorry, Majesty. I judged by the passage of the sun that now would be a good time."

The king snorted. "The position of the sun, you say. Could you not hear the moans and screams of my concubines? Was that not enough to stay your hand on the curtains and wait for a better time?"

"Majesty, I did not think—"

"Exactly," said the king, adjusting the pillows around him and tugging on a robe. "Now, what is it?"

The White Monk bowed again. Perhaps a sign of obeisance would calm the king. "Majesty, we are this very minute in pursuit of Calax Halfhand and his companions."

The king clapped his hands with delight. "How wonderful. Companions, you say?"

"Yes, Majesty, a minstrel named Whelan the Wanderer—I have used his likeness as a gela to no avail—and a small girl all got up in armor."

The king chuckled. "Armor? A girl? What nonsense is that?"

The White Monk shook his head. "She is accomplished, Majesty. She broke my gela spell with an arrow well placed in my gela's back."

"Really, well who could she be?"

"I have no idea, Majesty, but we will have her and the rest of them soon enough."

"Are you certain? We've been down this road before. This Calax seems to be very resourceful and elusive."

The White Monk smirked. "He has been, but we have him now, Majesty. I am certain of it."

The king sighed. "I wish I had a concubine for every certainty that has proved otherwise."

"If you will allow me, Majesty, I will send a gela to their exact location and verify that we have them."

"Of course. Why didn't you say that before?"

The White Monk ignored the king's comment and dropped into a trance. His first image was a bloody sword swinging for his head. He ducked and screamed, startling the concubines, who also began screaming.

The king clutched at his pillows. "By the gods!"

58

Calax swung his sword, hard, but the minstrel disappeared before his eyes. "Another blasted gela," he screamed, but no one replied. Rhynt and Whelan both had their hands full, fighting off Mystrosian swordsmen.

He turned and raced back to them, striking down three men before he reached Rhynt and Whelan. "Back to back. Let them come to us."

Rhynt and Whelan, still fending off strokes, positioned themselves so they were back to back, each facing out to fend off the swordsmen, who came in waves now, the clang of steel taking on its own song as blood sprayed around them. Then Calax let loose a roar and raced away, charging a group of seven swordsmen, the last of the Mystrosians.

Rhynt and Whelan, exhausted from the fight, watched as Calax changed from warrior to berserker, showing no mercy as he lopped off heads, arms, legs, killing everyone in his path. When the final Mystrosian dropped to the ground, Calax continued swinging at them, chopping at their lifeless bodies until they no longer looked human.

Rhynt screamed at him. "Stop, Stop!"

He turned to her, blood in his eyes, and roared once more.

Rhynt took a step back, frightened by the look he was giving her. Then she screamed again. "Calax, stop!"

Calax blinked as if coming out of a trance and looked down at the bodies, finally letting his sword drop to the ground. He dropped to one knee, exhausted. "Did we win?"

Rhynt nodded. "We did."

He looked up at her. "What? Why are you looking at me like that?"

Rhynt shook her head. "I did not know what a berserker was until now."

Calax looked down at the ground. "So now you know. It comes over me. It is not pretty to see, I know, but it is me."

Whelan came up beside them. "Enough of that. Rhynt, anything else out there?"

Rhynt continued shaking her head in disbelief, then dropped into a trance. "No, we have a clear path to the sea."

"Good, but we will have to ride faster now to reach the bluff by dark." He turned to Calax and helped him to his feet. "Come, there is no time to rest."

They slowly climbed on their horses and galloped away.

59

Bookins arranged the king's hands so that they were folded over his chest and adjusted the covers to better present a dead king for viewing. He could hear the hurried steps of many people racing down the corridor to the king's chamber. He kneeled beside the bed and clasped his hands in prayer, so the news would reach them as soon as they entered the chamber.

And the news hit hard for some, who gasped and cried out in grief. The news seemed not to affect Chancellor d'Mander or d'Bedo Brendyl, who exchanged smiles before solemnly approaching the bed.

Bookins turned to them. "The king is dead."

The chancellor moved around Bookins and leaned down over the king's face, looking for any sign of life. "Yes, it is true, the king is dead."

"We must perform the Gathering at once," said d'Bedo.

Bookins nodded. "It is as you say, but the body must first be prepared, and you must perform the ceremony for the dead. I will see to preparing the body."

"Fine," said the chancellor. "How long will that take?"

"For a king? No less than two days, I would say."

The Green Monk seemed exasperated. "Two days? Two days? Can't we do it faster?"

Bookins shrugged. "These things take time. His body must be prepared just so by the mortuarian, and there's the matter of a royal coffin, and then there's—"

"All right, all right," said the monk. "A ceremony for the dead in two days, and then the Gathering immediately afterward."

"Yes," said Bookins. "Yes, that seems right."

60

The shadows of horses and riders stretched long in front of them as they galloped across the plain in the setting sun. The horses were spent and slowing on their own, no amount of coaxing moving them faster. And finally, as if on signal, they slowed to a trot, then a walk, and then stopped.

Whelan was the first to jump down. "We'll be fine. We can slow walk them to the bluff, which I reckon to be no more than a mile."

Calax and Rhynt jumped down and began walking their horses alongside Whelan.

"Fine with me," said Calax. "My arse has had enough for one day."

Rhynt chuckled. "Aye, me too."

They walked on silently, the horses reluctantly following until they came over a small rise in the land and saw the bluff ahead. The closer they got, the louder the sound of the sea became, waves crashing on an as yet unseen shore.

Rhynt turned to Calax. "Do you hear it, the waves?"

"Aye, and it is always a pleasing sound."

"You have been here before?"

"No, but I expect the sea here is much like the Sea of Dros back west."

"I can't wait to see it. I have never seen an ocean before?"

"Really? Well, it is a wonder to behold. Vast and deep, with creatures you'll not find on land."

Rhynt scoffed. "Oh, I have seen fish and eaten them."

Calax laughed. "I am not talking about fish. There are things girl, gigantic things with many arms and suckers big as a bowl that will take even ships to the bottom of the sea."

Rhynt's eyes went wide. "No."

"Oh, yes," said Calax, "and even if there were only fish, you have to remember that big fish eat little fish, and bigger fish eat big fish, and still bigger fish eat—"

"I get your point."

"Good, because there are fish in that sea ahead that could swallow you and me and even the horses whole."

Whelan, who had been walking ahead, slowed to a stop and turned back to them. "Stop your yammering. We're here." He pointed at the bluff and beyond it a sea darkening in the dying light.

Rhynt handed her reins to Calax and raced to the edge.

"Be careful," Whelan shouted after her. "It's quite a drop."

Rhynt stopped just short of the edge and peered over. Whelan was right. The drop must have been more than a hundred feet, and below it a narrow strip of beach alive with crashing waves.

She turned back to them and shouted, "Come see."

Whelan and Calax tethered the horses to a small bush, and walked to the edge.

"How will we get down?" said Rhynt.

Whelan looked to the south, where the beach widened. "See there, you can just see the town."

Calax turned but saw nothing. "Where?"

Whelan pointed. "Over there? See the light?"

"Ah, I see it now. But just one? Shouldn't there be more?"

Rhynt had dropped into a trance beside them, scanning the town and the sea. "All but a handful have fled. There is but one ship left in the harbor. The rest of the ships are at sea, scattering in all directions. And the Mystrosians are but a mile away from the town and picking up speed."

Whelan frowned. "It is as I feared."

"What shall we do?" said Calax.

"We will have to get to that last ship. If we're lucky, it will be the man you say is waiting for us."

"Marthe."

"Yes."

Rhynt looked over the edge again. "But how do we get down?"

Whelan pointed to the south. "There should be a path about a hundred yards that way. It will be treacherous in this light, but if we don't get down by sunset, we have no hope at all."

"But the horses," said Rhynt. "They can barely stand."

Calax turned and began running for the horses. "They will have to do what they have to do. Come on and be quick about it."

They raced for the horses and against the looming darkness.

61

Bookins could hardly contain himself. He had pulled it off. The king would be safe, at least for now. Both the chancellor and the monk had thought the king dead and not under the spell of the moonflowers. A few seeds lead to hallucinations, but a few more lead to a deathlike sleep. Bookins had only to pray that the king would remain so through the Ceremony for the Dead and the Gathering Ceremony. Then, if he awoke, there would be no need for anyone to kill him. Or at least Bookins didn't think so.

The one remaining obstacle, of course, was the mortuarian. He would have to be dealt with. Bookins thought immediately of the gold coins the king had given him and did a little jig, which ended in him bending over in pain.

I really must stop dancing, he thought. He shuffled over to the king's bed. "Don't you worry, Majesty. If you are to die, it will be on your own time and not at the hand of another. Now, let's see to the preparations."

He looked around the room. The maiden sat along the wall, staring into space, still in shock over what they had done.

"Come here, girl."

It took her a moment to realize that someone was talking to her.

"Yes, I mean you, girl."

She stood and walked over to him. "Is he really not dead?"

"Oh, truly not dead. Just under the influence of the moonflowers."

She looked down at the king. "Are you sure?"

"Yes, yes, now pay attention. I have to go to my chambers and then have a chat with the mortuarian."

Her eyes went wide. "Oh, he must not touch the king."

"Exactly. Now, while I am gone, it is very important that you stay with the king. If he wakes—and he shouldn't—calm him as best you can and send a guard for me. There are two just outside the door, who have instructions to admit only me, the mortuarian, and his assistants."

She nodded. "All right, I think I can do that."

He grabbed her by the shoulders and looked her in the eye. "The king will be most happy with you when all of this is over, as will I. And there will be gold in the bargain for you."

She gave him a weak smile. "I do this for love of our king, not for gold."

"And that is why I have chosen you to help. I know you seek only the welfare of the king, as do I. Now, pull up a chair and wait. I shall be back with the mortuarian within the hour."

He gave her a quick squeeze of the shoulders, then turned and shuffled for the door. He could hear her dragging a chair to the king's bed as he left the room.

The guards seemed surprised by his sudden appearance and made to draw their swords, but soon realized their mistake with a hearty laugh, Bookins joining in.

"Yes, yes, it is only the king's fool. Now, remember your orders. Only I and the mortuarian's team may be admitted to the king's chambers. Preparing him for the grave must be conducted solemnly, in privacy, and without interruption. Do you understand?"

The guards nodded.

"Not even the chancellor or the monk."

The guards nodded again.

"Good. Now, I shall return with the mortuarian within the hour. Then perhaps we can get you some refreshment for your steadfast labors on behalf of a dead king."

They gave him big smiles.

"Okay, then, here I go."

He shuffled down the corridor, headed for the dreaded staircase down to the corridor that led to his chambers. He could hear the guards laughing, but paid them no mind. What are fools for if not laughter?

By the time he made it down the staircase, his legs were screaming from the effort and the lower corridor seemed longer than it had ever been, as if a team of masons had added a hundred steps to its length.

His chamber was a welcome sight. He looked longingly at his bed but turned instead to the flowers atop the chamber pot. He pulled out the bag of gold, took five coins out, and returned the bag to its hiding place. *Five coins should be more than enough,* he thought. *No, wait, I forgot the assistants.*

He took three more coins out of the bag and replaced it once more.

"That should do it."

He tucked the coins in his pocket and turned to leave the room. The sound of a cooing pigeon distracted him.

"What now, bird?"

The pigeon had just come in through the high windows, and now fluttered to the floor.

Bookins scooped him up and removed a small scroll from the bird's leg. He read the message and then slapped his knee. "By the gods, what wonderful, perfect news. Thank you, bird. Well done!"

He released the bird and shuffled for the door, laughing. "To the mortuarian!"

62

They were halfway down the trail to the docks when they saw it, the last ship in the harbor unfurling its sails, getting ready to depart. A man at the stern was waving a torch frantically.

Whelan, who was in the lead, turned and shouted back at Rhynt and Calax. "Faster!"

He urged his horse on, horse stumbling, rider lurching as they picked up speed, Whelan nearly thrown as they reached the bottom, where the land leveled out, the horse nearly dropping to the ground. Whelan managed to get her upright, urging her on, Rhynt and Calax right behind him, racing for the ship.

The man on the ship was shouting something and pointing to the east. The Mystrosian army was pouring into the town, charging toward the docks.

Rhynt could make out a score of archers readying their bows. "Arrows!"

She turned to the ship. The sails were beginning to billow. They only had seconds before the plank would be pulled. She rammed her metal foot hard into the side of the horse, who responded with a burst of speed, taking her past Calax and Whelan. In three long strides, the horse was up the plank and jumping onto the deck, its hooves sliding on the polished wooden deck.

Whelan and Calax followed, leaping from their horses as they hit the deck and nearly slid off the other side.

The man with the torch, a hulk of a man, was soon standing at their side, the torch still in his hand. "You make a grand entrance."

Calax nodded, trying to catch his breath. "We only hope for a grand exit."

The man laughed and held out his hand. "They call me Marthe. Like my ship, I'm not much to look at, but I'll get you where you're going."

Calax laughed. "You are the loveliest thing I've seen all day, friend." He reached out and shook the man's hand. Each gave the other a nod of appreciation at the strength of the other's grip.

An arrow thumped into the deck next to them, followed by another and another.

"I think we best seek cover, friend," said Marthe. He pointed to the rear of the ship. "We'll be fine up against that bulwark. Bring your horses along, too."

They all retreated to safety, Marthe urging them all to sit with their backs against the bulwark. Then he pointed up at the sails. "They've taken hold. We'll be out of range soon enough."

They sat there, watching arrow after arrow hit the deck.

Marthe laughed. "Well, we'll have a fine supply of arrows. I bet I can get good coin for them in Enturia."

"How long will it take to get there?" said Calax.

"About two days," said Marthe. "Maybe less if the wind holds."

The arrows soon stopped. Marthe was the first to stand, peering back at the docks. "By the gods!"

The others stood and looked back. The docks were teeming with men and horses.

Whelan whistled. "Well, we certainly cut that one close."

"Aye," said Rhynt. She dropped into a trance to have a look. "There are thousands of them. And I see wagons and siege engines by the score. It's a formidable force."

Calax nodded. "But no ships for them to board."

"Let me look," said Rhynt. She scanned the sea to the south. "A great fleet approaches. A hundred ships or more, many bigger than this one."

Marthe stepped up beside her, amazed by her far-seeing skills. "If this be magic, fine. How many masts on the ships, and do they sit low in the water?"

Rhynt looked again. "The ones at the front are two-masters and smaller than the others, which are three-masters. The big ones sit low in the water, aye, but not the two-masters. They're moving fast and I think they've spotted us."

"By the gods," said Marthe. "How far away?"

Rhynt shook her head and dropped out of her trance. She moved to the rail and pointed at the horizon. "There."

Marthe and the others squinted at the horizon.

"I don't see anything," said Calax.

"I do," said Marthe, "and I don't like what I see."

He turned away from them and yelled at his crewmen. "More sail, more sail, and be quick about it!"

63

King Merek the Mighty had been pacing for some minutes, occasionally glaring at d'Porto Saleen. The monk was insufferable at times and just didn't listen to instructions. The flagship was supposed to be ready to board hours ago. The monk knew that and yet he had let the troop ships enter the harbor and board first. Worse, after all his promises to the contrary, the monk had failed to produce a single woman for him from the bordellos. They had all fled, he said. And there was no food ready for him upon his arrival.

He stopped and jerked a finger at the monk, who uncrossed his arms and walked slowly over to the king, all the while looking back at the men boarding yet another troop ship.

"It is going well, don't you think?" said d'Porto.

The king grunted. "No, it is not. No food, no women, no flagship. How long am I expected to wait?"

"Majesty, as you can see, your flagship sits third in line now. It will be but an hour more and then you and I and your concubines will be aboard. I have sent instructions for the preparation of your cabin and have laid in delicacies beyond compare."

The king raised an eyebrow. "Delicacies?"

"Yes, Majesty, of three kinds. Remember that fish you so enjoyed when we marched into Paudia?"

The thought prompted the king to smile. "Yes, such delicate flesh and sweet in the bargain."

"We have a store of it for you."

"Wonderful."

"Next, we have laid in several cases of Alamarian wine, both a red and a white."

"Ah."

"And the greatest delicacy of all, Majesty."

"Yes, yes, what?"

"Our fleet captured a vessel not three hours ago, a vessel carrying the women of that empty bordello behind you."

The king's eyes went wide. "All of them?"

The monk nodded. "So it is said."

"How many in all, then?"

"I think they said twenty-one, but it could be a few more."

"And how long will we be at sea?"

"I would think two days, Majesty?"

The king smiled. "That shall do nicely."

"Indeed."

The king suddenly frowned. "But what about this Calax Halfhand business? He's gotten away, hasn't he?"

The monk sighed. "For now, yes, but it is of no matter. He will be ours in two days, as will Enturia."

"So you've let him escape."

"Majesty, we tried to catch his ship, but it was devilishly fast. We had to break off."

"So now he flees to Enturia, where he will undo any surprise we had hoped to have in this attack."

The monk smirked. "Our numbers are overwhelming. Surprise or not, we'll win the day."

The king grunted. "So you say."

The monk rolled his eyes. "Majesty."

"Seriously, is there nothing that can be done to stop Calax from reaching Enturia? Can you not send a gela to make him an offer or kill him?"

The monk sighed. "He and that girl with him have thwarted me three times already."

"Well, send a fourth."

"Yes, Majesty, but . . ."

"But what?"

"The girl, Majesty. She has powers unlike any I have seen before."

"Powers? What kind of powers?"

"Do you remember the Tale of the Six Arrows and the peasant girl who brought the gods down, sundering the harmony of the known world?"

"That's a myth. You just worship your god Porto so you can raise yourself up over others."

The monk glared at the king. "Do not say such things, Majesty. Do not anger the god of the white arrow."

The king screamed back at him. "I shall do what I please and say what I please. Your so-called god means nothing to me."

The monk strained to calm himself. "So, as I was saying, I think the girl can far-see, just as it is set forth in the tale."

"Yes, so she will see us coming. So what? You said surprise wasn't necessary."

"True, Majesty, it's just that I wonder what other powers she has."

The king chuckled. "You worry too much, monk." He turned away from him and looked at the flagship, which had worked its way closer to the dock. "The whole bordello, you say?"

64

Calax stood beside Rhynt, rubbing her back as she heaved over the side into the rushing waters. "This will pass. You just have to find your sea legs."

She attempted a laugh. "Or more precisely, my sea leg."

A young woman walked up to them, reaching out with a cloth for Rhynt. "Oh, dear, I fear we have someone new to the sea aboard."

Rhynt took the cloth and wiped her mouth. "Yes, and thank you."

The woman reached out her hand to Calax. "They call me Dimura. I'm with the carnival. A dancer."

Calax took her hand, which was warm and small and smooth. "Calax. I guess you could say I'm a warrior."

Rhynt snorted. "I guess you could say you're a right berserker." The last word came out garbled as she quickly turned and heaved over the rail once more.

"What?" said Dimura.

Calax sighed. "I think she said berserker, which is an apt description, I must admit."

Her golden brown eyes seemed to drill into him. "Then I will try to stay away from you in the next battle."

Calax smiled at her. She was nearly as tall as he was, with long raven hair knotted to the top of her head. Her clothing was bright red and so sheer he could make out her every feature.

She caught him staring. "It's a costume. Meant to delight the eyes of men."

Calax nodded. "It does have that effect."

She laughed. "We were just practicing our act. I would not ordinarily be wearing an outfit so, so revealing."

Calax tried his best not to look, but she was the closest thing to a goddess he had ever seen. "Forgive me for staring. I mean no offense."

She smiled. "None taken. Tell me, why are you here, on this ship?"

Calax welcomed the change of subject and started to speak, but Rhynt turned around and answered, "We are on a quest." The words made her gag once more, her vomit spraying the deck.

"I have a potion I think might help her," said Dimura. "I use it myself when the seas are rough."

"That would be kind of you," said Calax.

"But first, a quest? A quest for what?"

Calax puffed out his cheeks. "I mean to find the man—or men—who would see me dead."

She startled. "Dead? Wouldn't it be wiser, then, to flee?"

Calax shrugged. "For some, I guess, but not for me. A warrior always runs to battle, not away from it."

"Do you know who these people are?"

"Yes and no. I know there is one man behind it, but I do not know who he is."

"One man?"

"Yes, I found a note on the body of one of his men, requesting I be brought to the man."

"Brought? I thought you said they were trying to kill you."

Calax nodded. "Yes, the note said 'bring him to me,' but the actions of these men say otherwise. They have tried to kill me—kill us—several times in the past few days."

Dimura shook her head. "Aren't you afraid you're walking into a trap?"

"I'd rather face my fate then run away from it. I will not live in fear."

She shook her head. "It sounds more like stubbornness to me. Not a good quality."

"That may be, but it serves me well in battle."

Dimura looked over at Rhynt, who was bent over the rail again, heaving. "And what of her? Who is she? She cannot be older than fifteen or sixteen and yet she wears armor."

"She calls herself Rhynt, and she thinks herself a warrior. I met her but a few days ago. She was the pisspot to a monk."

Dimura's eyes grew wide. "A monk?"

"Yes, a man called d'Abo Pourcrey, the Red Monk."

Dimura began to tremble.

"Are you all right?"

"Yes, no," she began, and then disappeared.

65

Bookins smiled at his work and that of the mortuarian. The man, who smelled of death, had been more than eager to accept coin for his services and, most important, his silence and discretion.

The king looked dead but alive, which the mortuarian had said was the goal. Show the deceased in their best light, but not to the point that anyone thinks they're still alive. In the king's case, he only had to make him appear a little dead to carry off the illusion.

The mortuarian and his team, two strange, ghoulish men who seemed to be more of the grave than of life, had moved the king on a litter to Bookins' quarters, taking care not to be seen. Ordinarily, the body would be kept in the mortuarian's hall of the dead, waiting for the appropriate ceremony, nothing much for a commoner, but something grand for a king.

Bookins bent down over the body of the king, whose breath was so shallow it was nearly impossible to detect.

"Ah, moonflowers, you wicked, wicked things. Hold your spell for a spell."

He looked the king over one last time, then moved to the door, locking it behind him and shuffling down the hall. He had things to do in the council room, things best not seen by others, so he moved as silently and as stealthily as he could for an old man whose creaking bones alone could give him away in an instant. Still, he couldn't help smiling. *If all goes well, all goes well.*

66

The White Monk screamed, startling the king. "By the gods, what's wrong with you?"

The monk seethed. "The girl, that girl, the Red Monk is behind her."

"The Red Monk? I thought you said he was dead."

The monk seethed. "I thought he was."

"And how is this important?"

The monk rolled his eyes. "Don't you see? The skills she has, this far-seeing, it can only be the work of the Red Monk. He has trained her."

"Trained her? For what?"

The monk shook his head. "The Red Monk was—*is*—the most powerful monk in the known lands. He can even disappear at will."

The king scoffed at the idea. "Disappear? A trick, certainly. Why, I have seen minstrels disappear. I assure you, it's just an illusion."

The monk could not have rolled his eyes harder. He was dealing with an imbecile. "Majesty, I am talking about *real* magic, magic of a level that could defeat armies."

The king didn't like the sound of that. "You mean like our army?"

The monk nodded. "If he has trained the girl well, the Enturians would only need her to defeat us."

"Well, what about your magic? Can your gelas not protect us from her?"

The king was right. "Yes, Majesty, I shall send another. One thing she is not immune to is the sickness of the sea."

The king seemed to suddenly understand. "Ah, ah, yes!"

67

Whelan paced the deck. "A gela, you say?"

"Yes," said Calax. "In the form of a beautiful woman, perhaps the most beautiful woman I have ever seen."

Whelan smirked. "Beauty? *Beauty?* That is of no importance. What's important is that this wizard, whoever he or she is, can send gelas over water. Now *that* is power."

Calax shrugged. "Is it true that a gela must be the likeness of a real person?"

"Yes, and usually someone close by."

Calax brightened. "So the real Dimura could be aboard this ship? She mentioned being part of a carnival."

"Yes, yes, she and the carnival players and their animals are below decks even now, practicing for a performance they hope to give to the king of Enturia." He waggled his eyebrows. "And they've hired me to play lute."

"And this Dimura is there?"

"She is indeed."

Calax started to stride away, but Whelan grabbed him by the arm. "Two things. First, she doesn't know you, so don't assume the looks the gela gave you will be the same. And second, before you go chasing her, answer me this. What did the gela talk about?"

Calax sighed and brushed Whelan's arm away. "All right. At first she appeared to be concerned about Rhynt's condition." He looked over at Rhynt, who was still draped over the rail in a state of utter wretchedness. "She offered Rhynt a cloth and said she had a potion that would help ease her sickness."

Whelan's eyes went wide. "A potion?"

"Yes, why?"

Whelan looked over at Rhynt with alarm. "Did she give it to her, the potion?"

"No."

Whelan puffed out his cheeks. "Whew, that's good."

"What? I seem to be missing something."

"Don't you see, she wanted to *poison* Rhynt."

Calax's mouth dropped open. "Of course, of course."

"What else, Calax? Did she say anything else?"

"She asked about me and why I was heading to Enturia and then asked about Rhynt. When I mentioned she had been the pisspot to the Red Monk, she went white in the face and disappeared."

Whelan began stroking his chin. "It can only be one person, d'Porto Saleen, the White Monk. He is very powerful, but the person he fears most is the Red Monk. Just mentioning his name would have shocked the gela—and him—to the core."

"So?"

"So, we need to be very careful. Once he has recovered from the shock, he will no doubt be after us again."

"Another gela?"

"Yes, but certainly not your Dimura."

Calax smiled. "I would go see her now."

"Indeed," said Whelan, "but first let's deal with Rhynt here." He pulled a small stick out of his pocket. "I have some weir root. Just the thing."

He walked over to Rhynt and pulled her back from the rail. "Here, my dear girl, chew on this and the sickness will soon fade."

He lifted the root to her mouth, but Calax knocked it away and drew his dagger. "Stop, gela!"

Whelan laughed, recovered the root from the deck, and broke it in half, popping one half into his mouth. "I am Whelan, and this is weir root." He chewed on it and swallowed. "See?"

Calax put away his dagger. "All right, but I think we'll all have to be careful about what we eat or drink from now on."

Whelan nodded. "Indeed."

He turned to Rhynt, who stared back at him weakly. "What's going on, Whelan?"

Whelan smiled and shook his head. "You look a complete wreck. Here, take this and chew it down, and then we'll talk more about the gela."

She took the weir root and began chewing, her lips puckering.

"Yes," said Whelan, "it is a bit sour, but you know what they say, nothing fights sour better than sour."

She sighed, then gave him a strange look. "Wait, did you say gela?"

Whelan laughed. "The root already works. Yes, you were almost poisoned by a gela. Fortunately, you were too sick to notice."

She looked back and forth between Whelan and Calax. "Tell me what happened, now."

"We shall, my dear, but first we shall go below decks and watch the carnival players practice their arts."

Rhynt raised her eyebrows. "A gela *and* a carnival? What else have I missed?"

68

There was something about the council room that always made Bookins shiver. Perhaps it was because it was kept so neat. Everything was placed just so, and a staff of seven kept even the dust at bay. Or perhaps it was the size of the hearth. A man could stand in there, perhaps two, and although wood was neatly stacked in it, a fire was never lit, which only chilled the room further for Bookins.

One of the staff cleared his throat in an obvious attempt to get Bookins' attention.

Bookins turned to the man. "Yes?"

"Are we finished here?"

Bookins looked at the bier that they had brought in and placed at one end of the room. As was customary, they had draped it in royal green and set candelabras taller than a man at either end.

"Yes, this will do nicely."

"Will you be needing our help with the coffin?"

Not on your life, thought Bookins. "No, the mortuarian's men will handle that."

The man looked concerned.

"Don't worry, I'll see to it that they don't track in mud or let even a single dust mote enter."

"Yes, baron." The man bowed and with a quick jerk of his hand, motioned his staff out of the room.

Bookins waited until the door clicked behind them before setting about his real reason for supervising the placement of the bier. He only hoped he could remember. Was it the fourth bookcase from the hearth or the fifth?

He tried the fourth, pressing his hand at the corner, but nothing happened. He tried the fifth with the same result. Had the king been kidding Bookins when he told him about the secret passage? He tried the sixth bookcase. Nothing.

And then he had another idea. Perhaps he was counting from the wrong end of the room. He walked to the other end of the room and then walked back to the fourth bookcase from that end. The bookcase clicked open from floor to ceiling, enough for him to grab its edge and pull it the rest of the way open with a loud creak. *No one's been through this in ages*, he thought.

All he could see was darkness. He would need a candle. He walked over to one of the candelabras, took down its foot-long candle, and set it on the floor. He took out his flint and a little pinch of moss he kept with it, and set about lighting the candle, which resisted mightily.

Finally, though, the wick burst into flame, and Bookins was on his way into the tunnel. Once inside, he closed the bookcase behind him and began walking slowly, taking care not to slip on the wet stone floor. *At least there are no steps*, he thought. The slope was hard on his knees, but he continued onward a few steps, where he came upon a torch affixed to the wall. He lit the torch with his candle, set the candle aside, and took the torch down, holding it high to see his way.

The tunnel snaked downward, and he could see there were more torches spaced out every twenty yards or so, which he lit when he came upon them. The more he lit, the brighter the tunnel became. He could make out elaborate paintings depicting gods and warriors and strange animals he'd never seen before.

He walked on and on, the tunnel descending farther and farther, its slope becoming more of a challenge with each step until he came to a large wooden door. In its center was a circular block of wood on a pivot. *A peephole*, Bookins thought.

After some effort, he managed to open the peephole and peer through it. The sunlight was so bright, it startled him, forcing him to blink. But when he tried again, he could make out what lay outside. The door opened under a pier. He could see waves lapping fifty feet or so away.

"And it's the right pier," he said out loud.

He turned the knob of the door and opened it a crack to make sure that the door wasn't stuck from years of inactivity. The door opened easily.

He decided to take a chance and stuck his head out to see what he could see. To the right was another pier and another pier after that, fishing boats moored to each, bobbing in the low chop. To the left there was a small expanse of beach and then a view of the harbor.

A noise above him, someone walking down the pier, startled him. He pulled his head back in and carefully closed the door without a sound. *This will work*, he thought.

He left his flint and a bag of moss at the bottom of the door, and retreated back up the tunnel, extinguishing torch after torch as he went.

This will work. It must.

69

She had never been so sick, but now, thanks to Whelan's weir root, the dizziness and nausea had passed, though she remained weak.

Whelan had stayed by her side, helping her down the ladder to the second deck and finding a seat for her so she could rest and recover but still have a clear view of the carnival players as they practiced. They were an odd lot: tumblers, jugglers, clowns, and mean-looking bystanders who, Whelan explained, were behind-the-scenes movers, lifters, and builders.

"There's also a freak show, I'm told, but they keep them out of sight, along with their animals."

"Animals? What kind of animals?"

"Oh, the usual. Horses, drapples, and declawed lions."

"Will they let us see them, do you think?"

"No, I'm afraid not, but their leader—see him over there, the man in the tall black hat—did say that he'd cut the price of admission for us once we reached land."

Rhynt managed a chuckle. "How kind."

Whelan smiled down at her. "I see you're on the mend."

"Ha! My leg feels like mush, but yes, your root did the trick."

"Good, good." He pointed over at Calax, who was attempting a conversation with the real Dimura, who seemed unreceptive. "Speaking of tricks, take a look at that."

"Who is she?"

"A dancer in the show, but the very image of the gela who tried to poison you."

Rhynt nodded. "But she didn't."

"No, because she disappeared at the mere mention of the Red Monk. Very odd."

"Odd, yes, but maybe not so odd. Whoever is sending the gela must fear the Red Monk."

"And you."

Rhynt nodded. "Aye, but why? An old monk and a pisspot. Who would care?"

Whelan laughed. "I think you sell yourself short. Not many pisspots of my experience can start fires or far-see."

Rhynt shrugged. "I guess. Just tricks the monk taught me."

"But powers nonetheless." He caught sight of Calax returning from his attempted conversation, looking none too pleased. "Ah, here comes our heart-wounded warrior."

Calax walked up and slumped down next to Rhynt. "Heart-wounded is right. She will not deign to speak with me."

"Where the gela would."

"Yes, but this woman—this woman—is a shrew."

Rhynt squinted up at him. "Really? What did she say?"

Calax slapped his knee. "It was not what she said, but what she *refused* to say."

"Which was?"

"*Anything.* She may as well be a mute. I said hello and she turned away. I said hello again and mentioned her name, and she grew alarmed and fled."

Whelan laughed. "She doesn't know you, and yet you knew her name. Of course she was alarmed."

Calax sighed. "I do not understand women."

"Or girls," said Rhynt with a giggle.

Calax sighed again, more deeply. "It is true."

"I remember a girl once," said Whelan. "So beautiful my heart near burst in my chest. It was a fine summer's day when—"

"Stop," said Calax. "I cannot bear it. Not another song or tale from you, please."

Whelan turned away from Calax and gave Rhynt a sly smile. "Well, then, I guess we should change the subject. What would you like to talk about, Rhynt, that doesn't involve women and broken hearts?"

Rhynt knew immediately. "Food!"

"Aye," said Whelan. "The weir root does that to you. First it eases your pain and settles your stomach, and then comes a mighty hunger."

Rhynt nodded quickly. "I could eat an entire rabbit. No, two."

"You are in luck, then," said Whelan. "I had a chat with Marthe's cook, and they do indeed have rabbit on the menu. A hearty stew with rabbit and cruxleaf and bog potatoes."

Rhynt wiped her mouth. "You have right set me to drooling."

"Me as well," said Calax. "Perhaps a stew will stop my stewing."

Whelan laughed. "I foresee a change in the fair Dimura, one to your benefit, Calax."

"Oh, what change?"

"Not now," said Whelan. "You will see when we are at table."

"Which can't come soon enough," said Rhynt.

The Green Monk, d'Bedo Brendyl, cringed when he saw the bier, which made Chancellor d'Mander chuckle. "What, second thoughts?"

"No, not in the least. This whole business of coffins and burials just unsettles me."

The chancellor laughed. "But you would poison a king, one already dying from only the gods know how many sublime maladies?"

The monk smirked at him. "Have your fun. If death is sublime, than surely its aftermath is a dark carnival."

"Oh, and what would you change of its aftermath?"

"I don't know. It is just such a grizzly business."

"Take some solace in the fact that its aftermath in this case will place you upon the throne."

"Indeed, but for all the years I've worked for this, waited for this, it may come to an abrupt end at the hands of the Mystrosians."

The chancellor patted him on the back. "Take heart. I do believe that that fool Bookins has come up with a workable plan. All is not lost, my boy."

"I wish I had your faith in that old man's scheme. I would slit his throat for all the japes and jabs he has sent my way while under the protection of the king."

"Yes, I agree, a barony is far above his station. Don't worry, we shall deal with him right after the Gathering. Speaking of which, are you ready?"

The monk rolled his eyes. "I have been ready for ages."

"Do you foresee any problems with your siblings? Do you think them *amenable* to your elevation?"

The monk snorted. "Them? Those peasants and bastards, the human offal of the king's ill spent seed?"

The chancellor smiled. "I'll take that as a firm no."

"Indeed."

"Even so, I shall prepare them as proscribed to make them even more amenable."

The monk shrugged. "Whatever, I fear none of them."

"And just in case, and I do mean *just in case*, mind, I have provided a guarantee of sorts."

"What?"

"Something to assure the outcome should one of your siblings prove more than offal."

"What are you talking about?"

"Come, over here." He motioned d'Bedo Brendyl to the far wall and pressed the corner of a bookshelf, which dropped open, revealing a small chamber whose entire length was occupied by a gleaming green sword. "I had it made especially for you, a blade worthy of a new king."

The monk gasped and took the sword out of the chamber, whipping it through the air to get a feel for it. "It is a marvel."

The chancellor held the monk's hand from swinging farther, returned the sword to the chamber, and clicked the panel shut. "Remember, it is the seventh bookcase down from the hearth, and the fourth shelf from the floor."

The monk nodded, smiling. "I shall remember."

"Now," said the chancellor, walking to the empty bier, "we must find Bookins and see what is taking so long. A king so shriveled should not take so long in preparation."

"The mortuarian seemed most secretive when I confronted him about the preparations. Said that kings take longer, whatever that means."

The chancellor nodded. "That is true, but still."

"Still, five gold coins seemed to have urged him on to greater speed."

"Ha! You bribed him?"

"Yes. He said the coffin would be here on the morrow. We can have the required ceremony, make quick work of the Gathering, and then move on to my coronation long before we see ships on the horizon."

The chancellor nodded. "Although."

"What?" said the monk.

"I was just thinking about Bookins."

"Ah yes, I will gladly dispatch him after my rise."

"No," said the chancellor. "I was thinking we should wait to see how his plan unfolds, and then kill him."

The monk cocked his head and smiled. "Exquisite."

71

Dinner couldn't come fast enough for Rhynt. When the call was made, she was the first to the captain's long table, positioning herself halfway down its length, directly across from the steaming kettle of rabbit stew. The smell was so intoxicating, she thought she might faint.

She was not alone in her hunger, all the invited guests scrambling for seats. Calax sat down to her left and Whelan to her right, with the beautiful Dimura directly across from Calax. The others she did not know. Crewmen perhaps. But all of them, every pair of eyes, focused on the kettle.

Marthe was the last to arrive, sitting down with a grunt in the captain's chair. He smiled and nodded at each guest in turn and then turned to Dimura. "If you please, Dimura."

She smiled, pushed back from the table, and went to fetch the captain's bowl. "A full bowl, captain?"

He smiled at her. "Have I ever had less?"

"No." She took his bowl, moved to the kettle, and ladled a full serving, being careful to deliver it to Marthe without spilling a drop.

"Thank you, Dimura." He picked up his spoon and tasted the stew. "Ah, perfect. Dimura, see to the others."

She moved around the table, ladling bowlful after bowlful until everyone had a steaming bowl of stew in front of them.

Rhynt leaned over and whispered to Whelan. "Do you think it safe?"

Whelan nodded in the direction of the captain. "He seems to be enjoying it."

Rhynt didn't need coaxing. She picked up her spoon and began shoveling in the stew, which tasted even better than it smelled. Soon the only sound in the cabin was the clatter of spoons on bowls and the slurps and moans of appreciation from the guests.

Finally, the stew was gone and everyone sat back, satisfied if not completely sated. Rhynt caught the captain staring at her out of the corner of her eye. "Captain, do you stare at me?"

The captain seemed taken aback. "Oh, I did not mean to do so, young lady. It's just your hair. I have never seen quite that color of red. It is like a fire ablaze."

Rhynt ran a hand through her hair. "It's just hair."

"But delightful hair." He looked around the table. "Don't you agree?"

Dimura was the first to speak. "I wish I had such a color."

Calax shook his head and took a chance. "But your own hair is lovely."

Dimura rolled her eyes and looked away.

Calax leaned over to Whelan and whispered. "I thought you said—"

Whelan held up a hand and whispered back. "Not yet. Abide."

Calax sighed and stared at the ceiling.

"So, captain," said Whelan, "I wonder if you have an estimate of our arrival in Enturia."

The captain wiped his mouth and sucked at his teeth for the last morsel of stew. "The winds have smiled on us. We shall arrive shortly after you awake tomorrow."

Rhynt turned to Calax. "What then?"

Calax hadn't thought it through. He knew he wanted to find the man that had sent assassins to kill him, but he didn't know where to start. "Um."

The captain jumped in. "Oh, I know. We will be landing at a certain pier, beneath which is a secret door. The men who paid your passage said you are to open that door and follow the passage."

"Passage? To where," said Whelan.

The captain shrugged. "They did not tell me that."

"*Who* did not tell you that?" said Calax, as alarmed as he was intrigued.

The captain shrugged again. "Two men, one shorter than the other, both in cloaks. Couldn't make them out, and they didn't offer their names."

"And you didn't think to ask?" said Rhynt.

The captain was full of shrugs. "I did think to ask, but they paid such good coin, I thought better of it. Good coin is good coin."

"I don't like the smell of this," said Calax.

"Nor I," said Whelan.

Rhynt thought to add her misgivings as well, but the corners of her mouth suddenly went numb as the world faded to black.

72

In the dream, Rhynt is running with the hill tigers across the plain, headed for the chasm. Thrilled by her speed, she looks down to see that her mechanical foot is now a real foot, her toes digging into the loose soil, propelling her forward, far ahead of the hill tigers struggling to keep up with her. The precipice looms and she decides to leap to the other side. And then she is leaping, her speed slowing as she flies over the chasm, the far side not getting any closer as she begins to plummet. She hears the roar of the tigers behind her, but all she can do is scream.

A hand startled her awake. A boy, about her age, was pushing at her shoulder. "Wake up, wake up."

Rhynt sat up and looked around. There were others in the room, which appeared to be a dormitory of some kind with a row of beds on each side. Everyone was dressed in white tunics with green sashes around their waists.

She looked down at her clothes. She was wearing the same white tunic. "Where am I? Where is my armor? Who are you?"

The boy cocked his head. "You really don't know? I mean about where you are?"

"No, I don't."

He rolled his eyes. "Well, I am called Tribly. I have no idea where your armor is or even why a girl would have armor. And, of course, we are in the King's dormitory, awaiting the Gathering ceremony, which should begin soon."

Rhynt tried to take it all in, but could only shake her head.

The boy seemed exasperated. "We are the children of the king, as you must be. Otherwise, you wouldn't be here, would you?"

She laughed, drawing stares from everyone in the room. "Me? A daughter of the king? What nonsense. I am an orphan, left by my mother in the wilds to die."

"Die, why?"

Rhynt pointed at her mechanical foot, which she was relieved to see.

The boy gasped. "You're a spoilt? Truly?"

"A spoilt? What are you talking about?"

"That's what they call the likes of you, the incomplete ones, the disfigured ones, the wildlings cursed by witches." He gasped again. "But you didn't die. How is that possible, a babe in the woods?" And then it came to him. "You must have powers. Are you a witch?"

Rhynt shook her head. "I am no witch." She said this perhaps too loudly, all the other siblings turning and staring at her with wide eyes. "Truly, I'm not. But what is this Gathering?"

Tribly beamed at the chance to tell her. "The king, our father, has died, I'm afraid. May he rest in peace. So, now that he is dead, there must be a Gathering to decide who shall next be king or queen."

"One of us?"

"Yes, exactly."

"I don't understand. Wouldn't the oldest among us by rights be king or queen?"

"Ah," said Tribly, "that is not how it works in Enturia. Surely, you know that."

"No, I have only been here a day." She wondered how long she had been asleep and wondered where Calax and Whelan were. "Wait, what happened to my friends? A warrior named Calax and a minstrel named Whelan."

Tribly shrugged. "I have only seen you. You were carried in a few hours ago."

"Okay, about the succession."

"Yes, what happens is, after the King's memorial ceremony, we will all be escorted into the King's council chamber for the Gathering ceremony. There, a successor shall be chosen."

"Chosen how?"

Tribly looked around the room. "We all have theories, but no one is sure. Some say we will draw names out of a hat or draw straws. That seems a silly way to decide on the next monarch, at least to me. No, I think we will be judged on our skills. You know, the best orator, the comeliest, and such. I'm hoping they will be looking for the best singer. I sing like a bird, I do."

"But you don't know."

He shook his head. "No, but isn't it exciting. One of us will rise to king or queen."

Rhynt was about to say not really, when the door swung open with a bang and two men walked into the room.

"I am Chancellor d'Mander and this is d'Bedo Brendyl, the Green Monk. He, too, is a child of the king and will be joining you in the Gathering."

Tribly raised his hand. "Is it time?"

The chancellor smiled. "Yes, indeed it is." He scanned the room. "Ah, I see that Rhynt has arrived. How wonderful."

Rhynt had never seen these men before. "How do you know me?"

The monk smiled at her. "Dear sister, your name came to us by way of a gentleman of your acquaintance, known to you as Salibar."

Rhynt's eyes went wide, memories of his harsh training methods flooding in. "Salibar?"

He turned to the chancellor and smiled. "Yes, and your name came from him quite reluctantly, just before he died."

And now she understood. The hours of relentless training in that room. It was for this Gathering ceremony. Her first thought was to run, but she managed to calm herself just as Salibar had taught her. She could hear his voice even now.

You must be calm, and then you must act—quickly, decisively.

She looked up at them. "Well, then, I am pleased to meet you."

She watched the monk smile. *Oh, he is a sly one.*

73

In Calax's dream, Salibar hovered over him, screaming. "Again. The order of preference, again!"

Calax forced himself to look into the man's eyes with as much defiance as he could muster. "The order of preference of the hearth tools is poker, shovel, tongs, brush."

"Good, and what about the wood in the hearth?"

Calax nodded. "Only as a last resort."

"And why is that?"

"The wood is thick and bulky, exposing your fingers to strikes."

"Good, good, and what about the ash in the hearth?"

He had tricked Calax on this one before. "There will be no ash. There is never a fire in this hearth. A second looking for it is a second lost, along with your life."

"Excellent. I'm glad you remembered this time. Now, are there any other good weapons in the room?"

"Yes, the teardrop crystals in the chandelier, but these too are a last resort. A man with a poker can easily fend them off."

Salibar took a step back and crossed his arms. "So, do you think you are ready?"

Calax had been asked this question over and over, and hated to hear it. "Yes, I am ready," he screamed.

"Ready for what?" said Whelan, rousing Calax awake. "You've been dreaming."

Calax sat bolt upright. He was still sitting at the table, as was Whelan. The captain and the other guests were all still there, slumped over the table, their heads resting in their empty bowls, quietly snoring.

Calax looked at the empty chair between them. "Where's Rhynt?"

Whelan shook his head. "I don't know. I have just awakened myself."

Calax started to stand but noticed a small scroll of parchment sitting in Rhynt's bowl. He picked it up, uncurled it, and read the words out loud. "*You will know her by her red hair and crippled foot, and the name Rhynt. You must bring her to me.*"

Whelan knitted his brow. "What does that mean?"

Calax sighed. "It means she's been taken by the same people searching for me."

"But they've been trying to kill you. Why would they not kill her, and for that matter, kill you both right here at this table?"

"I don't know. Perhaps two groups are looking, and neither knows the mission of the other. The group that took Rhynt may not have known that I was a target as well."

"It is beyond curious," said Whelan, rising to his feet. "Shall we wake the others?"

Calax looked at them. "No, leave them be. Let's go up on deck and see where we are."

Calax stood. His legs felt weak, but he managed to follow Whelan up the stairs and out onto the deck. They looked at each other in amazement.

"We're here," said Whelan, "in Enturia."

Someone had docked the ship and lowered the plank. Whoever they were, they were gone now, as was the rest of the crew.

Calax pointed to a bluff above the docks. "Look, the carnival."

Brightly colored tents were being erected.

"Whatever happened to Rhynt," said Whelan, "no one else seems to have noticed. They're going about their business as if nothing has happened."

"And we should go about ours," said Calax. "Rhynt is here somewhere, and I mean to find her."

"I'll go talk to the carnival people. See if they saw anything."

"Right," said Calax. "And I'll take that secret passage under the pier—if we've even landed at the right pier—and see where or who it leads to."

"Okay," said Whelan.

They ran down the plank, Whelan heading for the bluff and Calax dropping himself down to the stretch of beach beneath the pier. It took him but a moment to find the wooden wall, press on the correct board, and open the secret door.

He peered into the darkness, then saw the flint and moss sitting on the ground. A torch was soon aflame and he was racing into the darkness.

74

Bookins wondered whether anyone noticed his heavy sigh of relief as the death ceremony for the king ended. The king's performance as a dead king continued on, the effect of the moonflowers persisting. Now all the king had to do was stay dead through the Gathering. Bookins hoped it would be mercifully quick. Then he could spirit away the king, using the tunnel to the docks. If all went well, they would be at sea, and free from the clutches of the men who had been poisoning him. Then the king could live out whatever days or hours he had left in him.

The sound of ceremonial horns interrupted his thoughts. The lords and ladies were filing out of the building, and the children of the king were walking in, followed by the chancellor and the Green Monk. Bookins shuffled to the door and moved by them, trying not to look into their faces. But one stood out, a young girl with red hair and a mechanical foot. A chill ran through him.

Rhynt!

He looked back at the children he had ignored. *Where is Calax? The bird said that they would be together!*

75

Rhynt moved slowly toward the door of the building, knowing what lay inside, a room identical to the room she had trained in. Now it was all real, and a tightness was gripping her chest, making it difficult to breathe.

And then an old man's face suddenly appeared in front of her. "Remember your training," he whispered and then was quickly gone.

She looked back at him as he shuffled away and then turned back to the door. The Green Monk nudged her through the doorway. "Move along, child, we don't have all day."

She followed the others to the far end of the room, where the dead king lay in state, a sword atop his chest. The sound of a door closing made her turn. The chancellor had shut the door and was making his way to the bier, shoving the king's children aside as he went.

He went to the far side of the coffin and looked down at the king. "Here is your king and father. This will be your first and last chance to look upon him. Pass by and view the man your mothers chose to take to bed."

He stepped back and motioned them to pass by the coffin. Children young and old complied, moving slowly and solemnly by the king. Some looked, some didn't.

As she waited her turn, Rhynt dropped into a trance, hoping to find Calax. She could see carnival tents. She could see their ship at the docks. Farther out to sea, she could see a many-tentacled monster swimming toward the harbor, churning up huge waves as it came. And then she saw them, Calax and Whelan racing down the plank of the ship. *Will they find me?*

She broke her trance and looked down at the king, her father. It was startling to see her own features reflected in him. He had her nose, surely, and perhaps the shape of her face. But what was he like? She would never know. A boy behind her pushed her along and soon she was standing with the others by the long council table, where glasses of wine awaited them.

The chancellor picked up a glass and held it high. "A toast to the king," he said.

Everyone picked up a glass of wine, the youngest giggling at the thought of their first glass.

The chancellor continued. "He was a noble king who had many adventures and did his best for his people." He started backing toward the door, glass still held high. "But now we must have a new king or a new queen to guide us onward. "Drink now to the king, and let us proceed with the Gathering."

The children raised their glasses to their lips. Rhynt did likewise, but when she noticed the Green Monk without a glass in his hand, she only pretended to sip at the wine before setting her glass back down on the table.

"Excellent," said the chancellor, lowering his own glass without drinking. "Now, as to the rules, there is only one. To be king or queen, you must fight to the death. Whoever survives shall be our king or queen."

He turned, walked through the door, and latched it behind him.

There was a moment of stunned silence, but then everyone seemed to move at once, some racing for the hearth, some hiding under the table, some cringing in corners. All seemed to be screaming except Rhynt and the Green Monk, who was laughing as he strode across the room, pressed on a panel, and pulled out a gleaming sword.

Rhynt's eyes went wide. How could she fight a grown man with a sword? She turned and ran to the hearth. All that was left were the tongs. She grabbed them and began fending off the blows from a teenage boy with the hearth's poker. Seconds later, he dropped to his knees, blood spraying from his head, the edge of the hearth's shovel buried in it by a teenage girl who was shrieking, her eyes wild.

The wine, thought Rhynt. *It is making them crazy.*

Rhynt ran away from the girl before she could remove her shovel from the boy's skull, and raced for the table. She jumped up on it and leaped for the chandelier, taking care not to let her legs dangle down within reach of the Green Monk's sword.

As she tugged at one of the largest crystals, she watched the Green Monk move around the room, striking blow after blow, heads and arms flying off the children. The girl with the shovel charged him but was cut down with one stroke, the blade splitting her skull down to the shoulders.

The monk spotted her clinging to the chandelier and laughed. "Come down, child, that won't help you." And then he screamed. Trilby was biting the monk's leg, growling like a dog and frothing from the mouth.

The monk raised his sword, pierced Trilby through the stomach, and then began slicing back and forth until Trilby's guts spilled on the floor. The monk looked around the room and then back up at Rhynt. "It seems you will be the last flower to be plucked."

As he said this, a bookshelf opened wide and Calax charged into the room, sword at the ready.

"You," shouted the monk.

Calax could not believe his eyes. He was in Salibar's room again, and the thought of it stunned him. He glanced briefly at the dead king, and then turned to the monk. "What is this?"

D'bedo Brendyl laughed. "Your end, I think." He swung his sword, which Calax fended off with his own.

Then Calax noticed Rhynt swinging on the chandelier. "Stay," he shouted as the monk was on him again, their swords ringing.

He is fast, thought Calax, *and skilled*. He fought back, swinging his sword again and again, each blow parried by the monk with ease, although Calax had the advantage. With each blow the monk retreated back toward the hearth.

"Come on," said the monk. "Is this truly the mighty Calax Halfhand?"

"It is," said Calax, swinging again. "And you shall know that with your last breath."

When the monk was backed up against the hearth, Rhynt saw an opportunity. She dropped into a trance and the hearth exploded with fire, forcing the monk to move quickly from the hearth and lunge at Calax, who wasn't expecting the sudden burst of flames. The monk's sword came from an unexpected angle, striking Calax's sword and flipping it into the air.

Calax watched the sword fly away and clatter on the floor.

The monk cocked his head and smiled. "You see? Even the great Calax Halfhand is no match for me." He laughed, then shouted, "Me, *King* Brendyl!"

Calax began moving back, his mind racing. Then he remembered the king's sword, and raced for it.

The monk raced after him, laughing. "No place to run, no place to hide, it seems, eh? Well, I'll make it quick, I promise."

Calax was under the chandelier now, the monk just behind him, raising his sword, preparing to strike. He wouldn't be able to make it to the coffin and the king's sword. Then Calax heard Salibar's voice once more. *Remember your weapon of last resort.*

The sword came down, and Calax spun around and grabbed the blade with his metal hand, twisting it out of the monk's grasp.

High above, on the chandelier, Rhynt saw her chance. As the monk passed beneath her, she leaped from the chandelier, grabbed him around the neck with her tongs, and let her body's weight twist his neck to the breaking point.

She hit the floor hard but rolled away from the monk, who lay lifeless beside her, his head looking in the wrong direction, his eyes open but elsewhere. She sprang to her feet and raced into Calax's arms.

"Are you all right?" he said.

"Yes, and you?"

He looked down at his metal hand, which still grasped the monk's sword. "I think so." He let the sword clatter to the floor. "Of course, I wasn't expecting the fire."

"Sorry."

A voice startled them. "Am I dead, then? Is this heaven?"

The king was sitting up in his coffin, staring at them.

"Ah," he said, finally noticing them, "We seem to have a new queen, or king. Wait, that's not right. We should have one or the other, not both."

Rhynt, still breathing hard, turned and faced him. She could barely get out the words. "I am no queen."

The king chuckled, then coughed and coughed again. "I said something very similar when I was fifteen. The Gathering is a nasty business, but it is our tradition."

"I would change it in a minute. What use has it?"

"Well, those who believe in the tradition say that the job of king or queen should fall to the strongest."

"But the strongest could be weak of mind," said Calax.

"True, that is always a possibility, but not in your case, sir." He turned to Rhynt. "But even so, the way this little girl outwitted the monk showed cunning and intelligence. We will need that if we are to defeat the Mystrosians."

Rhynt smiled at him. "Thank you, but I don't know about that. Fear makes us do things betimes."

The king nodded. "Yes, and sometimes we call that fear courage."

Rhynt shook her head. "Or luck."

The king cocked his head. "You are also wise. Now girl, come closer."

Rhynt moved to the side of the coffin. "Would you like me to help you out of that?"

The king looked down at the coffin and laughed. "It's a coffin befitting a king, don't you think? But no, I think my fool has put me here, and I'll not move from it until I hear otherwise from him. The man always has a plan."

"Okay, so . . ."

"So, it is as I thought. You are the daughter of the demigod Gratznoor."

Rhynt's eyes went wide. "A demigod? Named *Gratznoor?*"

"Yes, and don't let that ugly name fool you. She was the most beautiful creature I had ever seen. Like you in so many ways. Your hair, your eyes, the way you move." He looked down at her metal foot. "And of course, like her, you have a withered leg."

"But a demigod?"

"Yes, and I suspect you may have some of her skills. Or perhaps you may be even stronger. Can you far-see?"

Rhynt nodded. "Yes, and I can start fires."

"She could do both, and more. Perhaps we can spend time together, and I can test you. I remember some of her incantations."

"Does she live?"

The king frowned. "I do not know. When you were born with the shriveled leg, I was forced to spirit you away. She never forgave me for that, and left, to the gods only know where."

"You abandoned me?"

"No, no, I had Bookins send you to a friend of the court, a man named Salibar. Otherwise, as is our custom, you would have been put to death. Children with infirmities are considered bad luck, even the children of demigods."

Rhynt glared at him. "Forgive me, but it sounds like a vast cruelty. And just so you know, I hated that man."

"Then you should hate me as well. I knew one day they would gather you for the ceremony. I just wanted to give you a fighting chance. And it seems to have worked."

Rhynt started to say something, but she heard the door latch squeaking. "Quick, be dead."

The king lay back down, and Rhynt and Calax turned to face what was to come.

76

The screams and shouts and sounds of fighting coming from the building made Bookins cringe, but Chancellor d'Mander seemed to be enjoying himself, laughing heartily at each new scream. *Poor Rhynt*, thought Bookins. *May her end be mercifully quick.*

The chancellor turned to the crowd, which had grown to hundreds, and shouted. "We shall have a winner soon. And a new king!"

The crowd did as crowds do, cheering wildly. Some were just learning for the first time that their king was dead and that a new king or queen would soon rule them. Would he be a good king? A bad queen? They gave that no thought, as crowds do not by nature think. They just respond.

And then everyone heard the clear voice of the Green Monk, shouting at the top of his lungs. "Me, *King* Brendyl!"

The chancellor raised a fist in the air. "Yes, it is d'Bedo Brendyl, our new king!"

The crowd cheered.

"He shall be coming out that door to greet us as king. Show him how you feel."

The crowd cheered again, and then they all waited for the door to open. After some minutes of silence, the chancellor turned to the crowd once more. "Stay where you are. I shall see what is delaying our new monk-king."

The chancellor strode to the door, Bookins shuffling along behind him but staying back. If the new king was the Green Monk, he wanted to give him wide berth. When he came out, Bookins would sneak in and tend to the king.

The chancellor lifted the latch and pushed the door open a crack. He could hear hushed voices. "What's this?"

He flung the door open and charged in, his eyes going wide when he saw Rhynt and Calax standing beside the coffin and the Green Monk lying at their feet, dead.

Bookins tried to enter, but the chancellor pushed him back out. Bookins could only watch now through the open door. Something had upset the chancellor, but what?

The chancellor sneered at Bookins and then turned back to face Rhynt and Calax. "How can this be?"

"Believe it," said Rhynt, her voice steadier and stronger than she could ever have imagined. She sounded like someone else. She sounded like a queen.

"Well, that is no matter, for I shall put an end to both of you."

Calax cocked his head, making his neck bone crack. "Come on, then."

The chancellor drew a dagger from beneath his cloak and moved toward them. Calax looked around for the monk's sword, but it was now closer to the chancellor.

The chancellor laughed. "No weapon? What a pity." He took a step closer. "Oh, but the dagger is just the beginning. I seem to have access to a sword as well."

He took another step forward, bent down, and lifted the sword. "This shall be your end."

Calax steadied himself, waiting for the charge.

The monk smiled at him. "Prepare to die." He took another step forward, but then his eyes went wide. The king was sitting up in his coffin, glaring at him.

"Here, Calax," said the king, handing Calax his sword. He turned to the chancellor. "Now let's see who's prepared to die."

The chancellor took one step toward Calax, then his eyes went wide once more and he fell face down on the floor, a yellow arrow embedded in his back.

"Tch, tch, tch," said the king. "I was so looking forward to a fight."

77

It had all happened so quickly. The chancellor had walked in, there had been shouts, and then an arrow had whizzed by Bookin's ear so close he could hear its shrill whistle before it disappeared through the doorway. He could tell by the heavy thud that the arrow had hit its mark. But which mark?

He shuffled for the door, his knees screaming from the effort, and peered in. He couldn't believe his eyes. The chancellor and the monk were dead upon the floor, the king was sitting upright in his coffin, laughing, and Rhynt was in animated conversation with a warrior that could be none other than Calax Halfhand himself. "By the gods."

"By the gods, indeed," said the king. "Come, Bookins, and meet our new queen."

Bookins walked in, a look of total confusion on his face. "Queen? Why not king? Who won? Why do two still live?"

"Bookins, stop your blathering and let me explain," said the king.

But having heard the king's explanation of what had just transpired, he was still left shaking his head. "But we still have a quandary. If you're king, how can she be queen? And if she lives, Calax, by tradition, must die."

"Oh, Bookins," said the king, "you really are a king's fool. Firstly, I abdicate my thrown, making Rhynt queen. She has won her title and deserves it."

"And as queen," said Rhynt, "I herewith pardon Calax Halfhand and appoint him Supreme Commander of my army."

She turned to the king. "I do have an army, right?"

The king shrugged. "Well, seven hundred men who march around in bright uniforms, anyway."

She rolled her eyes at Calax. "Looks like you have work to do."

Calax was about to answer, but with a strum of a lute, Whelan the Wanderer walked in. "What's going on here?"

The king sighed. "Do we have to explain this again?"

"Aye," said Whelan, "but bide your time a moment. Rhynt, Calax, some people you know and other friends are on their way."

"Who?" said Calax.

The roar of hill tigers and the screams of the crowd gave him part of the answer he was seeking. A moment later he had the rest as the hill tigers ran in, followed by the Red Monk and Zyrx.

Rhynt squealed with delight. "Mela, Mila, Spook!"

The tigers came to her, curling their bodies around her, purring loudly, the king and Bookins wide-eyed by the spectacle.

Finally, the king found his voice. "Your mother had a familiar, a white crow, but you—three hill tigers—your powers must be great."

"Familiars?" said Calax. "Only witches and demigods have familiars."

Rhynt smiled at him and waggled her eyebrows. "At your service."

"A witch queen?" said Bookins. "I have never heard of such a thing."

"No," said the king. "A demigod." He thought for a moment. "Or rather, a *semi*demigod to be precise."

"But still," said Bookins. "There is no precedent."

"Well," said the king, "would you have preferred the Green Monk?"

Bookins looked down at the monk's body and shook his head. "No, I'll take a semidemigod over a monk any day." He noticed the Red Monk frowning. "Red Monks excepted, of course."

The Red Monk laughed.

"Wait," said Rhynt. "How is it you're here? Zyrx, you said you were going on a long journey."

Zyrx shrugged sheepishly. "A little lie, but true in a way."

"Let me explain," said the Red Monk. "I knew the Mystrosians were on their way, and I also knew the Enturians had sent troops to find you and Calax."

"You mean kill us," said Calax.

"You yes, her no."

"What?"

"The chancellor did not think the Green Monk—or anyone—would be a match for you, so he secretly changed the orders issued by the king to find and bring you to the Gathering. He's the one who wanted you dead."

Calax gave the king a harsh look.

The king shrugged. "It is just tradition."

Calax turned back to the Red Monk. "I don't understand. Why are you here with Zyrx? You disappeared at the tavern. Then what?"

The Red Monk did his best to explain. He knew that both Calax and Rhynt were being sought for the Gathering. He also knew that they would be stronger if they traveled together. The Mystrosians would be herding everyone east, so it would have been natural for Calax to stop at Zyrx's hearth on the hill. And there Zyrx could provide them with formidable weapons and armor.

"But stopping there was my decision," said Calax.

"Yes, yes," said the monk, but had you chosen another direction, I would have sent a gela to dissuade you."

"A gela?" said Rhynt. "You can send gelas, too?"

"Yes," said the monk, annoyed by her interruption. "I can, *you* can, the White Monk can. But that is another matter. Please let me continue."

The Red Monk also knew that Enturia was no match for the Mystrosians, so he set about a plan to bolster their defenses. First he would do his best to get Calax and Rhynt to Enturia safely, or as safely as he could manage. Her skills and Calax's strength as a warrior would see them through, and they would be assets for Enturia. Then he would go to Zyrx, who he knew had some sway with trolls.

"I make their armor," said Zyrx, interrupting. "And they like my jokes."

The Red Monk gave him an admonishing look and continued. With the protection of the hill tigers, he and Zyrx went from bridge to bridge, asking the trolls to delay the Mystrosians any way they could and then make their way to Enturia.

"They even agreed to destroy their bridges," said Zyrx, interrupting yet again.

"Wait," said Calax. "Where are these trolls?"

The Red Monk gave him a dismissive look and wave of the hand. "Please, I need to finish my story. Anyway, then we came upon the carnival troop. I did a few tricks and, well, Zyrx being a dwarf, they signed us up on the spot."

"Wait," said Rhynt. "You were on the ship with us?"

"Yes."

"Then why didn't you show yourselves?"

The Red Monk shrugged. "We thought to, but when we decided to do so, you were all asleep at the captain's table, and the carnival manager was insistent that we help set up the tents."

Calax was shaking his head. "I still don't understand why you'd encourage us to go to Enturia and certain death for at least one of us."

"Ah," said the Red Monk, holding up a finger. "Things didn't go as planned." He turned to Bookins. "Did they?"

"No," said Bookins.

Everyone looked at Bookins with surprise.

Bookins threw up his hands. "I thought you would arrive well before the king's death, and that's what I said in the messages I sent to our friend here, the Red Monk."

"Messages?" said Rhynt.

Bookins nodded. "We exchanged birds, pigeons. Anyway, the plan was for you to arrive well before the Gathering. I would have then persuaded the king to accept your aid, cancel the Gathering, and make Calax king."

The king chuckled. "And what gave you the idea that I would go along with that plan?"

Bookins sighed. "I know you well, Majesty. You know the likely outcome would have placed the Green Monk on the throne, and I know that thought was abhorrent to you."

The king sighed. "It is true. Go on."

"So," said Bookins, "when I discovered that the king was slowly being poisoned by his son and the chancellor, my only thought was saving the king." He pointed at the doorway to the secret tunnel. "I gave him moonflowers to feign death and would have spirited him away down the tunnel to the harbor."

The king shook his head. "A fine plan for me, and I thank you for it, Bookins. But your plan had one serious flaw."

"Yes, I know. It accelerated the Gathering. Even so, I had no doubt that Calax would be victorious and that he would spare you, Queen Rhynt."

Rhynt shook her head. "You have obviously never seen what this man becomes in a fight. His eyes go red and he kills anything within the reach of his sword."

"Oh," said Bookins. "Well, it all worked out in the end."

"So far," said the king. "There is the matter of the Mystrosians."

"And a sea monster," said Rhynt.

Calax was mystified. "What?"

"A true monster. I see it coming, and it grows closer by the second." She turned to the king. "How many archers do we have?"

The king shrugged. "I don't know."

"Seventy, your Majesty," said Bookins.

Rhynt nodded. "We shall need every last one. Come, to the docks."

She turned and ran for the tunnel, everyone else running after her, save for Bookins, the king, and Whelan, who began strumming on his lute. "I must set this tale down in a song, one worthy of the events."

"Well, you do that," said the king. "And make me young and handsome while you're at it."

Whelan gave the king a quick bow, then turned and walked into the tunnel, strumming on his lute.

The king looked about the room. "Bookins, I don't suppose my roller chair is handy."

"Yes, Majesty, just within the tunnel. Here, let me help you out of that coffin."

The king smiled at him. "Good. You know, these things are quite comfortable."

"Yes, Majesty."

"Oh, and stop calling me Majesty. You have a queen now."

"Yes, Majesty."

He helped the king down and into his roller chair, then wheeled him toward the tunnel, two old men off to fight a sea monster.

78

News doesn't travel fast when you are a dying king assisted by a decrepit old fool. When the king and Bookins emerged from the secret passage, all was chaos. No one was following the orders of Queen Rhynt or Calax, who was in a heated debate with a general about who outranked whom.

"Oh, dear," said the king to Bookins. "Can you shout them to silence for me."

Bookins, out of breath from the long descent, nodded grudgingly and cupped his hands to his mouth. The word he had chosen to shout was *stop*, but what came out was more like the scream of a cat that's been stepped on. And although the word failed to emerge, the screech had the desired effect: everyone stopped and turned to the king.

The king attempted to stand but plopped back down in his roller chair. Bookins rushed up and helped him to his feet. The king did his best to look regal. "Let it be known that on this day, by right of battle, a new queen rises as an old king moves on to his dotage. You now take your orders from Queen Rhynt and Supreme Commander Calax Halfhand. Now, kneel before your queen."

Everyone kneeled. The king gave Queen Rhynt a bow and with Bookins' help, lowered himself to his knees. "May your rule be long and bountiful."

"Rise, good king," said Rhynt, "but stay. I will have need of your counsel for however long you grant me."

The king struggled to get up, but Bookins was soon there again, helping him back to his feet and the comfort of his roller chair.

"I do not know whether I have hours or months, but they are all yours, good queen," he said.

One of the generals stepped forward. "But what of Bookins' harbor defense plan?"

The queen turned to Bookins, who quickly filled her in on his planned ruse.

"That is excellent," said Queen Rhynt, "but first we must deal with the sea monster." She turned to Calax. "Have the general array our archers around the harbor and wait for my signal."

"Aye," said Calax, turning to the general. "Come on, we have work to do."

Soon all seventy archers were spread out around the harbor. When the monster came in, it would have no means of escape. Queen Rhynt moved to the end of the pier, followed by her hill tigers, and fell into a far-seeing trance. She could see it moving closer, churning up waves as it came. She raised an arm and shouted, "Ready!"

The archers nocked arrows.

The monster moved ever closer.

"Draw," she shouted.

The archers drew back their bowstrings, waiting for her command to loose arrows.

"Steady, steady," she shouted. The monster was now coming into clearer view, and what she saw shocked her. She dropped out of her trance and shouted, "Hold, hold!"

The archers relaxed their drawstrings and looked back and forth at one another, clearly confused.

The queen ran down the pier, her hill tigers striding alongside her, and jumped down to the beach, motioning everyone to follow.

"It is not a monster," she shouted. "It is friends."

The waves reached the beach first, followed by more than fifty trolls. There were bridge trolls, mountain trolls, plains trolls, and even a woodland troll thirty feet tall.

Queen Rhynt welcomed each one as they came ashore, but she was searching for one in particular, who came out last.

"Bebo," she shouted as he walked out of the water. "Over here."

Bebo nodded, laughed, and strode over to the queen. "We come, we fight, we win," he said, "but first we have joke, yes?"

The queen laughed and beckoned him to bend over so she could whisper in his ear. His laugh was almost a roar.

"Good one," he said. "Me tell others now." He strode away and began telling the joke to the others. Soon, everyone on the beach, trolls and humans alike, were laughing, the humans not knowing why but laughing all the same.

And then the trolls suddenly stopped laughing and began tugging on a thick rope that went from the beach to what looked like a barge just outside the harbor. As they tugged, the barge came closer and closer, until finally Queen Rhynt realized it was no barge at all. *It's the tower!*

When it reached the beach, the trolls continued tugging at the rope until the tower was upright. As the water drained away from it, a small door in its side opened and Blusk and Phendour, each no taller than a thumb, rushed out, immediately growing to their normal size.

"By the gods," shouted Calax, rushing to them, hugging them each in turn. Queen Rhynt followed with hugs all around.

"We thought you dead," she said.

"We thought *you* dead," said Phendour. "We have thought of nothing else these past five years."

Queen Rhynt looked puzzled. "Five years? It has been but days."

"Time moves at a different pace within the tower," said Blusk. "And that may be good for all of us."

"What do you mean?" said the queen.

"We have spent the past five years raising and training an army," said Blusk. "Five thousand warriors wait within. None have seen battle, but I would stake my life on them."

Zyrx, who had been listening intently, rushed up to the queen, motioned her to bend down, and whispered in her ear.

Her eyes grew wide. "That is excellent. Go quickly."

Phendour looked puzzled. "What was that about?"

"Zyrx is a master blacksmith and armorer. A few hours in your tower world and he will have armor enough for our trolls and our army. Armor such as you have never seen."

Phendour laughed, then looked in awe at the trolls. "Yes, by the gods, we have trolls on our side."

Queen Rhynt smiled at them. "Perhaps my reign as queen will be longer than a day, then."

Now it was time for Blusk and Phendour to look puzzled. "Queen?" said Phendour, "but how?"

The queen chuckled. "That is a tale I will save for another day. For now, know that I am happy to have you and your army with us in this fight."

She turned to Calax. "Supreme Commander, take charge of your new army and array them for battle."

Calax shook his head. "Perhaps you have forgotten, Majesty."

"What?"

"The witch's curse. They cannot leave the tower."

The Red Monk was quickly beside her. "That is no longer a concern, Calax." He turned to the queen. "You need only touch the tower and the curse will be lifted."

"Truly?"

The Red Monk nodded. "Indeed."

She turned to Calax. "Follow me and we will set things right."

Calax nodded and followed her to the side of the tower. When she touched it, it seemed to shimmer for a moment, and then a doorway opened. Elves began pouring out, each growing tall and looking around in wonder as they entered a new world.

Rhynt turned to Calax. "Now, sir, attend to your new army."

Calax nodded and strode away with Phendour and Blusk, who teased him mercilessly. "Oh, *supreme commander*, what shall we do now?" said Blusk. "Please, *please*, let us partake of your battle wisdom," said Phendour.

The queen watched them go with a smile, then turned back to the pier, racing down its length with her hill tigers, and falling into a trance.

Ships with black sails filled the horizon. Hundreds of ships in a broad line. In front of them, racing for the harbor, was the ship Bookins had said would tempt the Mystrosians into the harbor. But that wasn't happening. The Mystrosians were not taking the bait. The battle would have to be fought along the entire coast. She dropped out of her trance and turned to look at her army. Warriors on foot and horseback were emerging from the tower. But would they be up to the task?

She looked down at her blood-stained white tunic, and smiled. Whatever was to come, first she had to find her armor and her sword.

"Come, Mela. Come, Mila. Come, Spook. Let us gather our armor and swords."

She turned and looked back at the horizon. "And our courage."

End Part

"Yes, of course there was a battle. Men, women, and trolls died. There were heroes and cowards and mischievous gelas. There were battle stratagems and battle blunders and a harbor red with blood. Who won, you ask? Why is that always the question when I tell this tale? Kingdoms come and go, some silently, some in blood. What does it matter? Time moves on, only the tale remains. Calax and Rhynt died hundreds of years ago. You should know that, but apparently Enturia no longer remembers. How many reigns have come and gone between then and now, I wonder, that you would think my tale a myth?

"You ask the wrong questions, soldier. Indeed, you do. What you should have asked about was the yellow arrow. Ah, I see you realize that now. The arrow, the arrow, who's behind the arrow? What started this tale and raised a pisspot to queen? A yellow arrow.

"Here, look at this golden yellow arrow. It can be fired with a bow or without a bow or as I am doing now, by nocking it to a string on my lute. Do you see now how it works?

"So, you see, I know this tale is true. Not a single fact has been lost by faulty repetition over the centuries. I know this, because I am Whelan the Wanderer, the Yellow God, the Seventh God, Randall himself, the God of All Gods."

Whelan set down his lute, grabbed a stick, and began poking at the fire. When he turned to continue his story, the soldier was running away.

"Come back, I will tell you of the battle and the Fool's gambit. How it unfolded in all its splendor and horror."

The soldier continued running. "Why do they always run when I tell them my name?" He shook his head and rolled his eyes. "Mortals."

And then he began to laugh. "But what would I do without them?"

Other Books by Len Boswell

Fantasies:
Barnum's Angel

Simon Grave Mysteries:
A Grave Misunderstanding
Simon Grave and the Curious Incident of the Cat in the Daytime
Simon Grave and the Drone of the Basque Orvilles
Simon Grave and the Sons of Irony

Other Mysteries:
Flicker: A Paranormal Mystery
Skeleton: A Bare Bones Mystery

Memoirs:
Santa Takes a Tumble

Nonfiction:
The Leadership Secrets of Squirrels
Stick Figures: The Life and Art of Len Boswell

About the Author

Len Boswell is the author of ten additional books, including the award-winning *Simon Grave Mysteries*. He lives in the mountains of West Virginia with his wife, Ruth, and their two dogs, Shadow and Cinder.

Note from the Author

Word-of-mouth is crucial for any author to succeed. If you enjoyed *The Cave of the Six Arrows*, please leave a review online—anywhere you are able. Even if it's just a sentence or two. It would make all the difference and would be very much appreciated.

Thanks!
Len Boswell

Thank you so much for checking out one of **Les Boswell's** novels.

If you enjoy our book, please check out our
recommended title for your next great read!

A Grave Misunderstanding

"The Bottom Line: A truly hilarious mystery in the tradition of Janet Evanovich,
Thomas Davidson and Rich Leder."

–BEST THRILLERS

View other Black Rose Writing titles at
www.blackrosewriting.com/books and use promo code
PRINT to receive a **20% discount** when purchasing.

www.ingramcontent.com/pod-product-compliance
Lightning Source LLC
Chambersburg PA
CBHW010729100726
47899CB00009B/2994